Prai se for *A Love S*

"*A Love Such as Hec*
love story that history lovers are sure to appreciate. I enjoyed the
first two books in the *Heaven Intended* series, so it was fun
diving into the third book. We even get a glimpse at characters
from the previous two books.
   Fans of historic fiction are going to love this!"
Theresa Linden,
award-winning author,

"Thoroughly enjoyable! This book abounds with the virtues of
faith, hope and love. Lauer shows us that even during times of
war, love wins."
Virginia Lieto,
Author, Editor and Public Speaker

"*A Love Such as Heaven Intended* is a sweeping love story that
is nearly impossible to put down. With equal parts intriguing
adventure, fascinating history lesson, and blossoming romance,
Amanda Lauer has another hit on her hands."
Leslea Wahl
Author of *The Perfect Blindside,* 2018 Catholic Press
Association winner

"The third installment in Amanda Lauer's Civil War romance
series matches beautiful and determined Josephine with Michael,
a West Point Military Academy graduate who seems to be on the
wrong side of the conflict. Filled with historical and military
detail and a unique setting for a Civil War novel, *A Love Such as
Heaven Intended* will please both fans of history and of
romance."
Carolyn Astfalk,
Author, *Stay With Me* and *Rightfully Ours*

A Love Such as Heaven Intended

(Heaven Intended #3)

A Novel

By Amanda Lauer

Full Quiver Publishing
Pakenham, ON Canada

A Love Such as Heaven Intended
copyright 2019
by Amanda Lauer

Published by Full Quiver Publishing
PO Box 244
Pakenham, Ontario K0A 2X0

ISBN Number: 978-1-987970-11-1

Printed and bound in the USA

Background cover photo courtesy: Fred A. Collins, Jr.
Back cover photo: Anna Coltran of Belle Gente Photography
Cover design: James Hrkach

NATIONAL LIBRARY OF CANADA
CATALOGUING IN PUBLICATION
ALL RIGHTS RESERVED

To Joseph, Katherine, Declan, Evelyn and Benjamin —
my cup runneth over with love

"I WANT something to do."

This remark being addressed to the world in general, no one in particular felt it their duty to reply; so I repeated it to the smaller world about me, received the following suggestions, and settled the matter by answering my own inquiry, as people are apt to do when very much in earnest.

"Write a book," quoth the author of my being.

"Don't know enough, sir. First live, then write."

"Try teaching again," suggested my mother.

"No thank you, ma'am, ten years of that is enough."

"Take a husband like my Darby, and fulfill your mission," said sister Joan, home on a visit.

"Can't afford expensive luxuries, Mrs. Coobiddy."

"Turn actress, and immortalize your name," said sister Vashti, striking an attitude.

"I won't."

"Go nurse the soldier," said my young brother, Tom, panting for "the tented field."

"I will!"

Louisa May Alcott – *Hospital Sketches,*

Published 1863

Chapter I
Friday, May 20, 1864
Washington, D.C.

Josephine tugged at her starched white collar. *If I have to listen to one more speech, I think I shall scream.* She surreptitiously glanced around to see if the other young ladies seated near her were as uncomfortable as she was. They sat straight backed, hands folded demurely in their laps with only a drop of sweat rolling down a temple here or there testifying to the stifling late-afternoon heat in the auditorium.

How they appeared so nonplussed was a wonder. All the graduates wore similar white muslin day dresses which, in and of themselves, were not overly warm, but the hoops and layers of undergarments made them unbearable.

Miss Amelia White, the director of Georgetown Academy for Young Ladies, walked onto the stage, picked up a sheet of paper from the podium and began her introduction of the ceremony's keynote speaker.

"It is my pleasure to introduce to you Miss Louisa May Alcott," said Miss White, looking first at the young ladies in the front rows and then at their parents seated behind them. An uncharacteristic smile came to her lips. She extended the paper to arm's length to read her notes. "Miss Alcott is a distinguished novelist, raised in New England, who took up writing at an early age to help support her family when they suffered financial distress."

Miss Alcott had made a prudent choice, Josephine observed. The woman, who was standing on the far side of the stage, was dressed to the nines from the top of her feathered bonnet to the tip of her black satin and leather lace-up Balmoral boots. Layers of matching ruffles adorned her exquisitely tailored peach silk dress and day bodice. The gossamer sleeves capped the ensemble nicely and were undoubtedly cooler than what the girls wore.

"Miss Alcott is an avowed abolitionist and considers herself a" — Miss White scrunched her eyes — "feminist."

Josephine's ears perked up. She and her classmates knew of the abolitionist movement. It was quite trendy in the city to show concern about the plight of the Negro. The word feminist was unfamiliar but sounded intriguing to Josephine. The warmth of the room faded as she focused more closely on Miss White's words.

The older woman's brows furrowed briefly before she continued. "In 1860, Miss Alcott began writing for the *Atlantic Monthly*. Two years later, she served as a nurse in the Union Hospital here in Georgetown for six weeks. Her letters home were published in *Commonwealth*, Boston's anti-slavery newspaper. In 1863, the letters were compiled into a book titled *Hospital Sketches*. In the tome, Miss Alcott describes the mismanagement of hospitals and the indifference and callousness of some of the surgeons she encountered. She received critical acclaim for her observations and humor. Currently, Miss Alcott is writing a book, with the working title *Moods*, about a 'true-hearted abolitionist spinster.'" Miss White's eyebrows raised. She glanced out and concluded. "May I introduce to you, Miss Louisa May Alcott."

The crowd politely clapped as the writer stepped to the podium. After thanking Miss White and Georgetown Academy for Young Ladies for their gracious invitation to address the class of 1864, she paused and scanned the group of young ladies before her and then articulated her first statement. "We all have our own life to pursue, our own kind of dream to be weaving, and we all have the power to make wishes come true, as long as we keep believing." She allowed a moment to pass for her words to sink in.

Josephine's breath caught in her throat. She gripped the wooden seat of her chair and leaned slightly forward. *Do women have dreams other than marriage and children?*

The writer left that to be considered and began the tale of her childhood and early years, including her education at the feet of naturalist Henry David Thoreau and instruction from educators and writers Ralph Waldo Emerson, Nathaniel Hawthorne, Margaret Fuller and Julia Ward Howe.

The eloquent and engaging presentation kept Josephine spellbound. She listened as Miss Alcott described how, in 1847, she and her family served as station masters on the Underground Railroad, housing a fugitive slave. Through that she met Frederick Douglass, the escaped slave who was now one of the leaders of the abolitionist movement and the author of *Narrative of the Life of Frederick Douglass, an American Slave.*

"He who believes is strong; he who doubts is weak," said Miss Alcott with authority. "Strong convictions precede great actions."

Josephine sucked in her breath and clasped her hands in front of her in excitement. She turned to scan the faces of the three dozen girls in her class to see their reactions. Some gave a slight nod in agreement but most seemed ambivalent. *Aren't they listening?*

Josephine faced forward again. A seed was planted in her brain. *I, Josephine Katherine Bigelow, will make an impact on this world!* She would not fade away into anonymity, living the life of a lowly homemaker and socialite.

The term "women's suffrage" penetrated her thoughts. Josephine brought her attention back to Miss Alcott.

"When it becomes legal for women to vote, I intend to be

the first female in my province to register," she said. "Let my name stand among those who are willing to bear ridicule and reproach for the truth's sake, and so earn some right to rejoice when the victory is won." Gasps were heard throughout the auditorium.

As the speech went on, Josephine's excitement grew. Miss Alcott delivered her concluding line with gusto. "Far away, there in the sunshine, are my highest aspirations. I may not reach them, but I can look up and see their beauty, believe in them, and try to follow where they lead."

Josephine was first on her feet when the ovation began. She had never felt so inspired in her life. Miss Alcott ascribed to the philosophy of political, economic and social equality between the sexes. Having the boldness to campaign for equal rights for women, of *any* race, was simply scandalous — but utterly intriguing.

I shall henceforth be known as a feminist! It was quite outrageous and she knew that her stodgy father, Brigadier General Matthias Bigelow, would disapprove. If he'd said it once, he'd said it a hundred times: "Just as they say about children in the company of adults, women should be seen and not heard when it comes to matters of the state."

As for her mother, Jacqueline Johnson Bigelow, she, likely had no clue what a feminist was but, regardless, would support her only daughter in her endeavors, as she always did. Josephine could do no wrong in her eyes.

After acknowledging the applause, Miss Alcott took her leave and Miss White stepped back to the podium and welcomed Archbishop Martin John Spalding to the stage. Dispensing the diplomas to the graduates of Georgetown Academy for Ladies was one of his first duties as archbishop, having been promoted from coadjutor bishop of Louisville to the seventh Archbishop of Baltimore just three weeks earlier.

Eventually the ceremony came to a conclusion. The girls

congratulated one another, hugged, grabbed their friends' hands and shed a few tears as the realization hit them that, after four years, this was the last time they would be together as a group.

Gradually, the graduates and their families filed from the building toward the tables set up under the shade of the massive oak trees on the lawn. Plates of ham and chicken, bowls of beans, carrots and potato salad, mounds of biscuits, and pitchers of lemonade awaited their arrival.

Josephine was assigned to sit with her father, mother and older brother, Hubert, for the meal. Before they took their seats, her mother gathered the four of them together and pulled a wrapped gift from her reticule. "Josephine, your father and I have something for you. Congratulations on your graduation, dear." She handed the box to her daughter.

Delight overwhelmed Josephine. For weeks she had dropped hints about a particular item that she hoped to own one day. The box seemed to be the appropriate size to hold such a gift.

"Congratulations, Josephine," echoed her father and brother as she carefully untied the ribbon and unwrapped the paper from the box. She lifted the lid and spotted a cameo brooch. Carved from copper-colored agate, it depicted the profile of a Greek goddess. The woman wore a miniature necklace with a tiny diamond set into the center of the pendant. It was so beautiful, it rivaled the brooch that Miss Alcott wore.

"Oh, Mother, Father. It's stunning! Thank you so much!" Josephine scooped the trinket from the silk lining of the wooden box and inspected it closer. "I will always treasure this."

"As we will you, my love," said her mother. Josephine hugged each member of her family and then pinned the brooch onto the linen bodice of her dress. She beamed while she chatted and laughed with her friends and their families as they enjoyed their repast.

When everyone had their fill, the servants stepped forward to clear the tables and the families started to take their leave. Another round of weeping ensued as the girls made their final goodbyes.

In actuality, their separation would be brief as friends were already making plans to get together over the weekend. Josephine was the organizer in her group and invited her five dearest friends to a picnic lunch Saturday at the Georgetown waterfront park situated on the Potomac River.

Even with all the commotion going on and the plans running through her head for the next day, Josephine's mind kept returning to Miss Alcott's speech. She intended to give the writer's words more serious consideration later, when she could finally hear herself think.

Chapter II

The horses' hooves clicked against the cobblestones as the carriage rolled along, giving cadence to Josephine's thoughts. She sat uncharacteristically quiet on the ride back to the house, mulling over Miss Alcott's words.

One particular line was burned into her memory. "We all have the power to make wishes come true." As the youngest child and only girl in her family, Josephine was used to having her wishes granted, not granting wishes for other people, but the idea intrigued her.

Miss Alcott spoke of political, economic and social equality with men but what was the point of obtaining such things if a person didn't use their newfound status to make a mark on the world?

That was precisely what Miss Alcott achieved through her writing. Her exposé caused hospitals to examine their procedures and policies and implement changes to create a more hospitable environment for their staff and patients.

Inspiration struck Josephine like a bolt of lightning. *I will follow the footsteps of Miss Alcott and not only be a feminist but a writer as well!*

Since Miss Alcott had already exposed hospitals, Josephine needed to disclose the conditions in another institution. After thinking through several options, she came up with a grand idea.

She wanted to hash out her plans with someone more experienced than herself. Glancing from her father to her brother, she chose the less-intimidating option. She would seek out Hubert for a private conversation after they returned to their house.

Being seven years her senior, Hubert was the one to whom

Josephine most often presented her inspirations before approaching their parents. Lately though, he was so distracted that she worried he would not be in the proper state of mind to offer any advice. He had his hands full juggling his military duties and a fiancée impatient to set a wedding date.

When the carriage finally pulled to a stop, Josephine jumped out unassisted and headed directly to her bed chamber on the second floor of the house, calling for Cecilia as she went. The day dress stuck to her skin and would be next to impossible to remove without her handmaid's help.

Once she was divested of her dress, stockings, hoop and crinoline, Josephine slipped on a light frock and walked across the hall to Hubert's room. The sound of her knocking on the six-paneled oak door echoed through the hallway.

As she waited for him to open the door, she considered his situation. He had proposed to Miss Francine Causten the day after he graduated from West Point three years ago. War had just been declared and no one imagined that it would drag on this long. Francine was of *the* Causten family, and Hubert was determined to give her the wedding and honeymoon that she deserved — a Herculean task at any time but even more daunting in the middle of a war.

To further complicate his life, Hubert was running out of tasks to fabricate that could keep him tied to his desk outside their father's office in the capitol. Hubert's commanding officers were dropping hints that it was time he proved himself on the battlefield. As a West Point graduate, he had a commitment to five years of active duty.

However, the young man had no desire to take up arms. Hubert claimed that he was not the war-mongering type. He didn't even like arguing with Francine. *It was somewhat pointless anyhow because he seldom won,* Josephine thought. If he did, she wouldn't admit it anyway.

The bedroom door swung open and Hubert, barefoot and

dressed in trousers and shirt sleeves, peered down at Josephine. "What is it?"

"I need to talk to you for a minute privately," said Josephine.

"Come on in." He swept his uniform jacket, trousers, shirt and a pair of socks off the velvet-upholstered armchair near the paned-glass window. "Have a seat."

"Thank you."

Hubert walked to the marble-topped washstand and opened the side door to reveal several bottles and glasses. "Now that you're a secondary school graduate, I can offer you a drink. A glass of sherry, perhaps," he said, holding up a decanter.

"No, thank you!" Josephine scrunched up her face. The memory was still fresh in her mind of last summer when she and her friends snuck her mother's sherry decanter from the sideboard buffet in the dining room. The girls hid behind an outbuilding and downed the amber liquor to the point of inebriation. She felt on the brink of death the entire next day. Now, just the thought of sherry gave her the dry heaves. Hubert knew it darned well.

He grinned at her. "You don't mind if *I* have a drink, do you?"

She shook her head. "Be my guest."

"So,"— Hubert stuffed the cut glass stopper back into the whiskey decanter — "what can I help you with?"

"After hearing Miss Alcott speak this afternoon, I have decided that I want to become a writer."

"A writer, say you?" He nodded in approval. "Fantastic. Now you can declare yourself an English major when you enter university this fall."

Josephine glanced down at the Oriental carpet under her bare toes for a moment then pulled her shoulders back, tilted her chin up and looked him squarely in the eye. "Let me clarify. I want to *be* a writer. I don't want to *study* to be a writer. I've decided to rescind my application to the university."

The glass nearly slipped from Hubert's hand. He mouthed the word, "Oh," but no sound came from his lips.

"Hubert, can you help me break the news to Father?" Josephine asked entreatingly.

"And have Father think that I'm part of this harebrained scheme? No, thank you. I need to stay on his good side so I can keep my position at the White House."

Pushing out of the chair, Josephine stamped her foot on the carpet and scowled at her brother. "You're a coward!"

"You can call me what you want, sis, but I'm not putting my neck on the line for you."

"Fine. I'll tell him myself. But just see if I put your name in the foreword of my novel. You'll wish you had gone to bat for me then."

"It's a chance I'll have to take," said Hubert, laughing.

Josephine stomped out of the room and shut the door soundly behind her. In the hallway, she took a few seconds to compose herself and listened for her parents' voices. Hearing them conversing in their bed chamber, she crept down the hallway, the polished hardwood floor cool beneath her feet, and stopped in front of the portal. She took a deep breath and knocked on the door.

"Who is it?" her mother said.

"It's me, Josephine."

"Come in, dear."

Josephine turned the oval carved-brass handle and pushed open the door. Her mother sat on a stool in front of her carved mahogany vanity dresser and pulled pins from her hair while her father unhooked the suspenders from his trousers.

"Father and Mother, I just wanted to thank you again for the brooch. It's more beautiful than anything I could have imagined."

Her father snorted. "Surprising, since you described what you had in mind so precisely to your mother these past few weeks," he said.

"Matthias," scolded Mrs. Bigelow. "'You're welcome,' would have sufficed."

"All right. You're welcome, darling daughter. Anything else?"

"There is one other tiny thing that I thought I'd bring up with you. Wasn't Miss Alcott inspiring today?"

"She certainly was," said Mrs. Bigelow. "I'm sure her parents are proud of her."

"That's exactly what I was thinking, Mother. Wouldn't you and Father be proud of me if I did something equally extraordinary?"

The general stopped unbuttoning his shirt and lowered his eyes to stare at his daughter. "I don't like the sound of this."

Steeling herself, Josephine opted to plunge ahead. "Following the lead of Miss Alcott, I am going to become an author." Her father raised his eyebrows, but she kept going. "I will forsake university to work on my first book, an exposé on life in a Union encampment. You're a brigadier general, so it should be easy enough to introduce me to the commander at a nearby camp."

The first word out of her father's mouth was, "Hrmpf." Then the lecture began. "Disenroll from the university to pursue another one of your grandiose ideas? Do you remember when you wanted to join Mr. Daniel Rice's circus as an acrobat? Your mother would've fainted to see you in that skin-tight costume."

"I agree that was absurd, but I was just a child of thirteen when I came up with that."

"What about last year when you wanted to use your singing talents to join the theater?"

"I remember that," her mother said. "John T. Ford posted audition notices for a musical at Ford's Athenaeum."

"But, Father, in my defense, the play featured the estimable John Wilkes Booth, so it would have been an outstanding opportunity. And I had three years of thespian experience from Georgetown Academy for Young Ladies, so my chances of getting cast were favorable."

His stare was unflinching. "As I said before, and I'll say again, no daughter of mine…"

When her father got on his high horse, Josephine stopped listening. She knew exactly where the conversation would lead. When his rant subsided, she decided to try another tactic. Using her aforementioned acting skills, she pretended to acquiesce.

When he narrowed his eyes at her, she knew she was skating on thin ice. *Of all the jobs in the White House, why must my father be the brigadier general heading the intelligence department?* she bemoaned. The man had the uncanny ability to sniff out a lie as it was still being formulated.

However, luck was on her side. Or, perhaps it was his preoccupation with the battle between Lieutenant General Ulysses S. Grant and General Robert E. Lee in Fredericksburg, but her father took her word that she would no longer pursue the subject and dismissed her from the room.

If he thinks I'm giving up that easy, he has another thing coming, Josephine fumed as she trudged back down the hall. *I will follow my calling, Father's blessing or not.* By the end of the year she would legally be an adult and there would be little he could do to stop her.

But, in the meantime, how could she begin her endeavor without the wily general knowing about it? Lying was out of the question. That would warrant a trip to Confession. She had enough to do over the next few days and scant time as it was. Rather, she would tell him the truth, albeit a limited version.

The next morning, Josephine approached her father at the breakfast table. He sipped coffee from his bone china cup as he skimmed over the newspaper headlines.

"Good morning, Father," she said cheerily.

"Good morning, Josephine," he replied before turning back to his paper.

"Father, I've been thinking. Since there are three months until school starts, I would like to use my free time this summer to volunteer."

That statement was enough to get the man to set his newspaper down. "Go on, I'm listening."

"I heard they're in need of female volunteers at the soup kitchens, orphanages and hospitals. And the prison too," she added in what she hoped was a nonchalant tone. "There's a prison close to the house. Maybe I could volunteer in some capacity there." Josephine cast her eyes down and held her breath, waiting for his answer.

She had no idea what a volunteer did in a prison, or anywhere for that matter, but that would get her foot in the door to start her detective work. Writing about life behind the doors of a prison would be exponentially more exciting than writing about life in a Union camp.

"That is an admirable thought, Josephine. With all the captives being shipped to Washington from the Atlanta campaign, they are short-handed at the prison. I will see if I can make arrangements for you to spend time there on the weekdays."

Josephine did a double take. Her father approved so quickly that she thought he may have misheard her. "This will be a fine opportunity for you to perform the Corporal Works of Mercy," he noted.

Corporal Works of Mercy? They studied that in theology

class last year. Let's see... feed the hungry, give drink to the thirsty, clothe the naked, shelter the homeless, visit the sick... visit the imprisoned and bury the dead.

"I hadn't thought of that, but you're right, Father."

"And, with any luck, it will keep you out of trouble until you leave for university."

She bit her tongue rather than give the saucy retort that first came to mind. She didn't want to ruin her golden opportunity. Instead, she demurely said, "Thank you, Father."

"You are so very welcome, dear."

Something about how he responded didn't sit well with her, but she put that thought aside. With her father's pull in the military, she was sure that he would instruct the prison staff to find some duties that would not be too taxing for a young lady. She could knit, she could fold laundry and she knew how to clean. *God forbid it came to that.* In the long run, the duties that she would be assigned were irrelevant, it only mattered that she was now in a position to witness the abominable circumstances prisoners endured.

Thus, five days later, she found herself standing in view of the foreboding gate to Old Capitol Prison with God alone to protect her — make that God and the carriage driver that her father insisted accompany her. *That man knew how to ruin everything.*

Chapter III

Palms sweating, Josephine fidgeted with her new cameo pin as she stepped into the shade of the Old Brick Capitol building. In her youth, she had passed by the structure more times than she could remember but, up until this very moment, seldom had given it a second glance.

Old Brick Capitol was a landmark in Washington, D.C. The rectangular structure had housed the members of Congress and the Supreme Court after British forces invaded the city and set fire to the original capitol building. But that was decades ago. Most recently it had been used as an upscale boarding house. Vice President John C. Calhoun lived in that building after his term until his death fourteen years ago.

Josephine stood towards the edge of the walkway as several civilians and soldiers walked past her to enter the building. She recalled what she knew of the establishment. Barracks and several outbuildings had been added to the property when the estate was converted into a federal prison in 1861. Considering that it housed political prisoners, spies, Union officers convicted of insubordination, captured enemy soldiers, and — if the rumors she heard were true — prostitutes, the building was relatively nondescript. Only the handful of soldiers marking paces along the border of the property gave any indication as to its true purpose.

Taking another two steps forward, Josephine paused again to look around. It appeared that she was the only woman in the vicinity, thankfully. Under any other circumstances, she wouldn't be caught dead traipsing anywhere near such a place, but on this bright, sunny morning she was on a mission. She was now ready to make something of her life.

Her father didn't know it yet, but Josephine's days of formal education were behind her. *Good riddance!* While she certainly had the brains to excel in school, she found the whole prospect of going to class day in and day out, plus attending Mass *every... single... morning,* quite tedious. Her grades were acceptable but, as her favorite brigadier general noted on more than one occasion, she didn't live up to her academic abilities.

That was neither here nor there as she had her diploma attesting to the fact that she had completed the prescribed coursework. Josephine never wanted to attend university anyhow. What good were degrees in such things as romance languages, musical pedagogy or even English, for that matter? That crusty parchment was merely bait to lure eligible bachelors into webs woven by pedigreed young ladies.

She couldn't really fault her peers. Before the encounter with Miss Alcott, finding an outstanding match had been her top priority as well.

Circumstances certainly had changed in the last week. But, if they hadn't and she would have been commencing the search for a husband, the pickings were less than desirable at this moment. Every last man of good stock was off playing soldier in the hostilities that had ravaged their country for more than three years. It was to the point where Josephine was of the mindset to walk into Mr. Abraham Lincoln's office herself and demand that he put a halt to this foolishness. The war put a terrible damper on not only *her* social life but her friends' social lives as well.

But, for now, the hunt was off. When she was ready to settle down, Josephine couldn't imagine it would be that difficult to find a desirable mate. There was no rush. At seventeen, she still had a good five years before the word *spinster* would be whispered in reference to her behind the socialites' silk fans. No one would dare say such a thing to her face, but those old biddies thrived on gossip.

Her mother could certainly attest to that. The woman claimed to be above such sordid behavior, but Josephine and Hubert knew differently. They often joked that Mrs. Bigelow never repeated gossip so it would behoove her friends to listen closely the first time.

At this moment, Josephine had more important things to pursue. With the plan she formulated, fame and fortune would come her way long before her classmates even finished their university studies.

She turned and motioned for her driver. Charles hustled to get ahead of her to open the rusted metal gate.

Josephine strode into the compound, the heels of her kid leather boots tapping on the brick pavement as she went. She came to a sudden stop and a gasp escaped her lips. The place was not what she expected find at all.

Over the weekend she had read *Hospital Sketches* with the hope of preparing herself for this day. After just one chapter of Miss Alcott's novel, Josephine was overcome with gratitude that she wasn't volunteering in a medical facility. That position was best left to a person with a stronger disposition than herself. She could put up with filth and perhaps a rat or two, but she could not tolerate the sight of blood.

Standing in the foyer of the prison, she could hardly believe her eyes. Where was the rubbish? Where were the vermin? Other than the armed men milling about, she could have been standing in the lobby of the Morrison-Clark Inn. *How in the world will I write an exposé about something that has nothing to be exposed?*

A woman approached Josephine. "Pardon me. I'm Mrs. Clark, the prison matron. Would you be Miss Bigelow?"

"I am," Josephine said, giving a small curtsey.

"It is such a pleasure to meet you, Miss Bigelow," the lady

said sincerely. "Brigadier General Bigelow was here yesterday and told us of his benevolent daughter and her willingness to be of service to the prison. You appear to be just as sweet and innocent as he described you!"

Sweet and innocent? *Ha!* "That father of mine, he is just so gracious," exclaimed Josephine, doing her best to keep a smile plastered on her face. *Perhaps he had forgotten about the sherry incident.*

"He said you'd be with us all summer. That is so generous of you, Miss Bigelow."

"What can I say?" said Josephine. "It is my calling to be of service to humanity."

Mrs. Clark reached out and squeezed Josephine's hands in her own. "Aren't you just precious!"

Josephine shrugged her shoulders.

"I'll show you around the grounds, Miss Bigelow. As the prison matron, I'm in charge of the female inmates, the care and cleaning of the buildings, training volunteers, and the laundry area, so I know every square inch of this compound," said Mrs. Clark proudly. "If you'd like to dismiss your driver, miss, he can come back at four o'clock to pick you up."

"Of course." Josephine nodded to Charles and, with her head turned away from Mrs. Clark, mouthed the words "Two o'clock." He tipped his hat in acknowledgement, then turned and walked out the main door.

With that taken care of, Mrs. Clark commenced the tour. The entrance from First Street opened to a broad hallway that was used as a guard room. Next to that was the office for the superintendent, captain of the guard and the clerk.

"Interviews with the prisoners are held here. They are questioned, searched and admitted. For some, eventually discharged here as well," noted Mrs. Clark.

Higher-ranking prisoners were kept in the adjoining room, Josephine learned. A mess hall rounded out the first floor. The second floor had five rooms that opened onto a hallway, the biggest of which held twenty-one cots. On the third floor was another large room littered with cots. The U.S. Capitol dome was visible from two sides of the building.

After perusing that floor, the women walked the three flights downstairs and went out the back entrance. According to Mrs. Clark, the brick-paved enclosure was one hundred yards square. On the right side stood a one-story stone building with the guard house, cook house and wash house. Beyond that was a wooden building that had another mess hall, the hospital and a sutler shop, where a merchant sold provisions to the soldiers.

Inmates out for morning exercise filled the yard. Josephine spotted trenches along the edge of the property. She assumed the prisoners used them as latrines. Fortunately, no one was near that area. She had no desire to see a man relieving himself.

An adjoining row of buildings called Duff Green's Row occupied the left side of the property. It was also used as space to hold prisoners. The female prisoners were kept in a segregated area toward the back of the yard. Josephine spied a few scantily clothed women in their yard. A couple were quite well-endowed and, judging by their exposed décolletage, proud of it. *So, the rumors of women of the night imprisoned at Old Capitol were true.*

Most of the ladies had bright red rouge on their cheeks and lips and eyes lined with soot. Josephine couldn't help but stare. They weren't called painted ladies for no reason.

Maybe all was not lost, she thought. Instead of focusing on the conditions of the prison, which would be unacceptable for herself but were certainly adequate for a ne'er-do-well law-breaker or enemy soldier, perhaps she could write a story on the plight of the women prisoners and what caused them to be in such wretched circumstances.

If only Belle Boyd hadn't been released in December, Josephine could have written an exclusive story about the infamous Southern female spy. Belle was formally introduced to the Washington, D.C., society shortly before the war began. When the hostilities erupted, it was said that she sided with the Confederacy and ran a spying operation from her father's hotel in Virginia.

On the Fourth of July in 1861, Belle shot and killed a drunken Union soldier who accosted her and her mother. The girl could have been tried for murder before a military tribunal, but General Robert Patterson ruled that the young lady was only protecting her mother. Belle kept up her deceitful life and, according to reliable sources, was betrayed by her lover. That led to her arrest and incarceration at Old Capitol Prison.

Not more than two weeks ago, Josephine heard that Belle boarded a Confederate blockade runner called *The Greyhound* to sail to England, but it was halted by the *USS Connecticut* and she was arrested again. Her whereabouts at this moment were unknown to the general public. Perhaps Mrs. Bigelow and her cohorts knew something. They seemed to be in on everything.

As they walked back toward the main building, Josephine wanted to ask the matron about the female prisoners, particularly if any of them were long-term residents. It was said that prostitutes were only held for a day or so before being released back to the red-light district, commonly known as Hooker's Division, named in honor, or perhaps dishonor, of General "Fighting Joe" Hooker.

General Joseph Hooker commanded the Army of the Potomac and had quite the sordid reputation in the Washington, D.C., area. His headquarters were described as a combination bar and brothel and, between the lavish parties, the wayward women, and the gambling, was known to be a bed of iniquity for his undisciplined soldiers.

Looking over her shoulder, Josephine took a last glimpse of the women. They appeared to be soliciting new customers. Some called out to the men, a few saucily exposed their ankles by lifting their skirts, and one was cozied up to the guard on watch. It was quite the scene.

When Josephine finished her shift, she intended to record her observations from the day in her journal. If she did that faithfully every evening, by the end of the summer she'd have enough fodder for a novel. Miss Alcott had written her bestseller after only six weeks of volunteer work in the hospital. Given twelve weeks, Josephine was confident that she'd come up with something equally compelling.

As the tour concluded, men were being led back inside the building for lunch. Mrs. Clark directed Josephine toward the stone wall. "Please step aside so the prisoners can pass, Miss Bigelow."

Josephine obediently did as she was told and took two steps back. She quietly watched the queue of men shuffle past her. Most of them glanced her way. Some had curious expressions and others appeared interested for what Josephine sensed were less than pure intentions. A chill went down her spine.

As the last man approached, he turned his head and peered directly at her. Josephine's eyes widened, and her right hand flew up to cover her gaping mouth.

Breaking his stare, she sized the man up. He was gaunt and the facial hair was a new addition, but she would recognize that tall, muscular frame anywhere.

"Michael?" she asked out loud in amazement. "What in heaven's name are you doing here?

Chapter IV

Not allowed to break rank, Michael followed the young lady with his eyes until he was too far into the building to see her anymore. Their interaction caught the attention of the other men as well. When the group was out of earshot of the girl, a few men jostled Michael. He shrugged his shoulders.

She'd distinctly said his name, they could all attest to that. None of the other fellows in line bore the name Michael, so she was obviously addressing him. He'd be darned if he could recall who she was.

How could any man forget a creature as comely as her? He shook his head in wonder. Marching on, he followed the other men into the mess hall. Conversations echoing through the rafters made it hard to hear his thoughts.

Michael had tucked half of the small loaf of bread from breakfast into his Richmond Depot jacket pocket. If only he could have saved some coffee. It seemed inhumane that they were only served the brew in the morning. Of course, he really couldn't complain. While it might have been rationed, the coffee in a Union prison was much better than anything available to the Confederate troops — or to the Southern civilians, for that matter.

He joined the line that ran past two female kitchen workers. They ladled scoops of vegetables into the tin mugs proffered by each man as he walked by. The fare was rutabagas and carrots. Nothing was peeled but at least they were boiled, so they were palatable.

No matter what they were served, though, it was never enough. What he wouldn't give for one of his stepmother's meals at this moment. She was a fine cook.

His father began courting the young widow at the beginning of Michael's fourth year at West Point. They were married several months later — the day after the mandatory mourning period for Michael's deceased mother concluded.

Michael took his seat and continued to reminisce. He was informed about the nuptials through letters sent to him from his kid sister, Amara. She and his younger brother James were convinced that the woman had coerced their father into marrying her.

When Michael finally met the lady over Christmas break that year, he could surmise why his father was in such a hurry to speak vows with her. The new Mrs. McKirnan was young. She was closer in age to himself than to his father and, with her petite frame, platinum blond hair and fetching visage, she was very attractive. His father, on the other hand, was past his prime. He had been quite the looker back in the day, but he had put on weight through the years. It seemed the more prosperous his dry goods business got, the more rotund he became.

That striking lady, by chance, had a daughter who was Amara's age. Miss Theresa was the spitting image of her mother. She didn't seem to have the guile her mother had, or the common sense, for that matter, but Michael imagined young men were drawn to her, especially now that she was of courting age.

Michael made the Sign of the Cross and said his meal prayer before plucking a carrot from the mug. After more thought, he could see what brought his father and stepmother together. The man may have been a dozen years older than Mrs. McKirnan, but he could offer her something that wasn't easy to come by in the middle of a war — security.

Even in the leanest of times, people still needed to purchase essential goods. That's what kept his father's shop going the last three years. His handsomeness may have diminished, but his business remained steady, for the most part, and kept their family afloat.

If the companionship makes the two of them content, who am I to judge? Michael would leave that up to his siblings. Besides, he hardly saw the pair anyhow and, when he was in Atlanta, Mrs. McKirnan did her best to win him over with her culinary skills. Even now, all these months later, he could picture her fried chicken, sweet potatoes, collard greens and pecan pie fresh out of the cook stove. If his father hadn't already been on the portly side, he certainly would have been after being married to that woman for any length of time.

Picking up a chunk of rutabaga, Michael tried to visualize a piece of nice, juicy chicken. He couldn't stretch his imagination that far so he decided to count his blessings for what he did have. A lot of soldiers were worse off than him right now. He savored what little bit of food he had.

"A penny for your thoughts?"

Michael broke from his trance and pivoted his head to look at the stranger sitting beside him. "Just thinking about home," he said.

"Can't blame you," the soldier replied. "Got a missus you're hankering over?"

"Nope. Just kin that's wondering if I'm dead or alive."

"Same here."

The men sighed nearly in unison and went back to eating. Michael returned to his musing.

The last letter he sent to the house was this past November, the week before he was apprehended. Amara was probably worried sick about him. Despite the six-and-a-half-year age difference, the two of them had always been close. She had faithfully corresponded with him, but they hadn't actually laid eyes on each other since he left Georgia the December after he graduated. Amara had been almost fifteen at the time. Now she was just a few months shy of eighteen. He couldn't believe his little sister was almost grown up. Amara had always been a cute girl. Michael would put money on it that the little imp had grown into a gorgeous young lady. She was probably giving the local boys a run for their money. Assuming, that was, there were any young men in Atlanta at this point.

"Got a brother in the service too. What about you?" Michael asked his lunchmate.

"I'm the only boy. That's all Mama could handle," he said with a laugh.

"My kid brother James, he's a hothead. When the war broke out, he couldn't wait to enlist. Father insisted he graduate high school first and join up when he turned eighteen."

James had the aptitude to attend university and applied to West Point. However, once hostilities were formally declared, their father refused to send him to "enemy territory" where he'd be coerced to pledge allegiance to the United States of America and the Union Army.

That directive suited James fine. His birthday was the last week of November, so he was one of the youngest boys in his class. All his friends had already thrown their hats into the ring with the Confederate Army.

Skipping the superfluous details, Michael finished the story. "The day after his birthday, James enlisted as a private in the 42nd Regiment, Georgia Infantry, which was based out of Camp McDonald." He paused to get his facts straight.

"His regiment moved to Tennessee, then on to Mississippi, where it was attached to General Barton's Brigade in the Department of Mississippi and East Louisiana. They fought at Chickasaw Bayou and Champion's Hill. Last July 4, they were captured at Vicksburg. However, James wasn't there to witness that day, as he was wounded during their previous engagement. The ball that he took to his right thigh caused him to lose his leg."

The man winced.

Retelling this story, Michael recalled the devastation he felt when he'd heard the news. He just couldn't picture his brother as a cripple. Every time he thought about how things had turned out for him, it was like taking a blow to the gut.

James was sent back to Atlanta after he was discharged from the hospital and, ultimately, military service. Amara kept Michael abreast of the situation and was grieved to relay that James was no longer the same exceptional young man that he once was. He had lost his drive, his determination, his keen sense of humor, and most unfortunately, his joie de vivre. She wrote that he now spent his nights prowling about the underbelly of Atlanta and took to sleeping all day. On top of that, he had developed a fondness for the elixir that the doctor prescribed to ease his pain. Taking that altered his personality in a less-than-agreeable way.

The conversation between the two men dwindled to a halt. Michael didn't want to talk about the epiphany he'd experienced after learning of his brother's devastating injury, the moment he'd felt called to do something to bring an end to the conflict quicker. Back then, he didn't know what that something was, but in time, the answer was presented to him.

Michael convinced himself that the actions he took since then were accelerating the conclusion of the hostilities. That being the case, he was making plans for his post-war life. He intended to make his way to Atlanta, find James, and get him back on track. He was also going to sit down with his father and discuss plans for the dry goods store. The business adjoined their house and, as the oldest son and heir, he had spent a good portion of his childhood working there.

A bell rang to dismiss the men from lunch. Getting up from the bench, Michael walked to the rough-hewn wooden table at the entrance to the mess hall and stacked his mug on top of the pile before exiting the room.

McKirnan Dry Goods… Michael could just picture the hand-painted wood sign that hung over the front porch of his father's business. Two creaky ladder-back chairs flanked an oversized whiskey barrel set in front of the dusty picture window. A checkerboard had been painted on the cover of the barrel, and a bag of checkers was always at the ready for any old fellows wishing to play a game.

That business consumed his father's life. Michael always swore that he would never make a career for himself as a merchant. Being at the beck and call of the local citizens and their house slaves made for a mundane existence.

He'd planned to use his training from West Point and live the soldier's life. Make a name for himself as he crisscrossed the nation on horseback preserving law and order amongst its citizenry. He could see himself working at outposts in the Indian territories and moving further west as more states came into the Union.

But, after three years as a soldier, Michael had experienced enough military life. It wasn't nearly as glamorous as the professors at West Point made it out to be. The brass ring that he strove to grab had lost its luster. Now, he just wanted to return to Atlanta, find himself a nice young lady and settle down. He spent many a night dreaming of how he would expand his father's business by venturing into new markets to build a legacy for his future children.

Michael stifled a yawn as he trudged behind the other men back to the bunk area. He thought about James again. There must be something to occupy him now that his military career was over. Maybe it would be worth the effort to train him to take the reins of their father's business.

If that were to happen, then I could go out West and make my mark in the business world out there. They were giving away land for a song in Texas and the more families that settled there, the more people who'd need goods and services. It was definitely something to consider.

He would have more time to ponder that later, he thought as he settled himself on his cot. The room was filled to capacity. During their time indoors, most of the men whiled away the hours playing cards, conversing or sleeping. Others positioned themselves in front of the double-hung windows, hoping to garner the attention of passersby to catch up on the news of the war, or, if they could convince someone to step up to the window, get a note back home to their loved ones.

Citizens were forbidden from interacting with the men, but, surprisingly enough, several times a day someone would approach the window and engage in conversation with one of the inmates.

Michael wasn't sure what motivated folks to stop. The men would try to catch the attention of young ladies as they passed by the facility. After enough trial and error, they determined how to achieve the best results... in the quickest amount of time... with the fewest words. They found that the plainer a woman was, the higher the chance that she would take the bait. After all, it wasn't every day that such females drew the undivided attention of young men. Apparently, even if the motive for the attention was suspect, it was better than no consideration at all.

Some romances had even begun that way. Whether they would stand the test of time, it would be hard to say, but it helped keep the men occupied. Side bets were placed as to who would, and who would not, be successful in gaining attention from an outsider.

For Michael, he preferred to make use of his time lying on his cot thinking. Some days he'd go over things in his past, other days he'd look to the future when his prison days were behind him.

On this particular day, he stared at the cracks in the plastered wall, using his hands for a pillow, and walked through memories of the last few years. He hoped that if he combed through as many details as he could recall, he'd remember how he knew the stunning girl who had called out to him earlier.

Chapter V

Mrs. Clark started walking again, but Josephine stood still several seconds before scurrying to catch up with her guide. Never in her wildest dreams did she imagine that she would run into anyone she knew at Old Capitol Prison. Other than her parents and Hubert, she had told no one of her plans to spend time here over the summer. Her friends would have been appalled to learn that she would expose herself to such a vile situation.

In addition, it would be ill-advised to make her whereabouts known publicly. If word got out that the daughter of Brigadier General Matthias Bigelow was serving at the facility, she could put herself in jeopardy. Perhaps a desperate prisoner would kidnap her and use her to barter for his release or, she shuddered to think of it, he might commit some dastardly deed upon her person as revenge for being held captive by her father's men.

While the likelihood of something such as that happening was slim, seeing as how armed guards stood in every corner of the facility, it could occur. Actually… such a scenario *might* have its advantages for Josephine. If she decided to become an author instead of an investigative journalist, she could use that situation as the storyline for her debut novel.

That thought made her stop dead in her tracks. How intriguing would that be? Say the man was a Rebel soldier, and thus her sworn enemy, and he stole her away from the grounds using her as a human shield to make his getaway. Obviously, the guards wouldn't fire their weapons for fear of injuring the damsel in distress.

The soldier could drag her through the streets until he found an unattended horse and buggy. He'd trundle her onto the conveyance, jump onto the seat beside her, snap the horsewhip, and send the team of horses barreling out of town at a frenetic pace. They would travel west for days, taking side roads to avoid detection. At first, she'd hate him, as would be expected, but in time she would see that there was more to the man than his wicked façade revealed. She would have the ability to change him and in due course would grow to love him and, whether he expressed it or not, he would grow to love her as well. *Given enough time, what man wouldn't?*

Through her guidance, the soldier would turn from his evil ways and become a man of solid character. She envisioned the title of her book. *The Captive Diary of Josephine Katherine Bigelow, A True Story of Abduction by a Despicable Prisoner of Old Capitol Prison.*

Mrs. Clark turned down another hall. Josephine resumed walking. The tempo of her thoughts matched the tempo of her pace as she scurried to catch up to the woman.

She could be the American version of Victor Hugo, or more precisely, the *female* and *feminist* American version of Monsieur Hugo. *Wouldn't that be something?* His book *Les Misérables* captivated Josephine when it came out the year before last. It told the story of Jean Valjean and his nineteen-year struggle to lead a placid life after serving a prison sentence for stealing bread to feed his sister's children during a time of economic depression in France. Jean Valjean escaped from his imprisonment, just as her protagonist would.

Josephine imagined holding book signings at the local bookseller. Would she sign the books *Josephine Bigelow or Josephine Katherine Bigelow?* When she had time, she would put pen to paper and practice her autograph.

Meanwhile, she needed to focus on her duties at the prison, whatever those turned out to be. If she were to write this tale someday, she'd have to be able to offer her readers the humdrum details of life as a female volunteer in a correctional facility.

Mrs. Clark led Josephine to a dining area. After a light lunch with other staff members, she was escorted to the wash house, which was situated on the far corner of the property.

"Here you are," said the lady brightly.

The building was nothing worth noting. White paint peeled off the weathered exterior. Three wood plank steps led up to the door centered between two unshuttered windows.

"Wonderful. It was so kind of you to show me the inner workings of the prison, Mrs. Clark. You are indeed a fine hostess," said Josephine, making mental notes of her surroundings so that she could work the details into her manuscript. "I'm sure it could be interesting to witness the process of laundering in an operation this size. What's next on the list?"

"This is the last stop for you today, Miss Bigelow."

"Pardon me?"

"This is where you'll be spending your days this summer."

"I'm not sure I heard you correctly."

"This is the area where we are in most need of help," replied the older woman, loudly enunciating each word as if talking to an elderly person.

I'm dumbfounded, not deaf! Josephine pressed her lips together to keep those words from spouting out of her mouth. She chose instead to give her host a charming smile. "There may be a tiny mistake here. I was under the impression that my help would be needed for tasks such as light housekeeping or maybe helping in the office with correspondence. I did receive the highest marks for penmanship when I was a student at Georgetown Academy for Young Ladies." She glanced down at her fingertips to avoid giving the impression that she was boasting.

"I'm sure your penmanship is admirable, Miss Bigelow, but your father was quite specific about which chores he wished to see assigned to you. He knows what a heart you have for service, so he requested that you either work in the wash building or in the infirmary."

Josephine felt the color drain from her face.

"He did, did he?" *Father knows darn well there is no way on God's green earth that I would volunteer in any medical capacity.* Evidently, he was setting her up for failure. That crafty soldier knew that she wouldn't dare risk soiling her reputation by working alongside the women on staff there. Everyone knew that only plain females were allowed to be nurses!

Her reputation wasn't the only thing at risk of being soiled if she worked in the infirmary. The colorful frock she wore would be as well. One glance at anything bloody or gruesome and she would heave. It had happened before, like the time her brother split his head open on the corner of their brick house. He'd been backpedaling as he attempted to catch a ball thrown by the neighbor boy and didn't realize how close he was to the building until he ran into it.

Father thinks he can get the best of me, but I will stick it out in this facility all summer, come hell or high water. The situation had turned into a dare, and Josephine never backed down from a challenge. Her friends could attest to that. Actually, the faculty at Georgetown Academy for Young Ladies could too. She had gotten into her share of fixes through the years at school. Nothing terrible, but enough to account for a fair number of the gray hairs on her father's head.

I will do whatever chore they ask of me. For the next twelve weeks, I will devote myself to this place if it kills me. He'll see what I'm made of.

With that, she turned her attention to Agatha, the middle-aged woman in charge of the laundry department, who was awaiting her arrival. The laundress politely introduced herself and expressed her gratitude for the assistance. As she did so, Josephine surveyed the area. She was familiar with wash houses, as she had walked past the one on their property plenty of times. To be honest though, she had never stepped foot inside because she had no reason to do so. The servants took care of all the laundry and just about everything else needed to make their house run smoothly.

Following Agatha inside, a blast of heat from the wash tubs sent Josephine back a step. A person might appreciate the warmth in the middle of a Washington, D.C., winter, but on an overly humid day in May, it was overpowering. She tugged at the collar of her dress as sweat ran from her temples to her cheekbones to her chin and then made its way down her neck.

"Over there," said Agatha, pointing to a tub of steaming water in the corner of the room, "is where the laundry is stirred. And here we have the washboard." A factory-made board with a ribbed-glass scrubbing surface leaned against the tub, and a bar of soap sat on the floor nearby.

"This tub has cold water and over here we have the washing bench," she added. Something akin to a baseball bat lay upon it. Through the open doorway on the opposite wall, Josephine could see rope lines strung up for hanging laundry and an open fire straddled by a metal tripod.

Agatha grabbed a faded gingham full-length apron and handed it to Josephine. "Here, Miss Bigelow. Put this on so you don't dirty your pretty dress."

The last thing that Josephine wanted was to add one more layer to her attire, but the woman was correct, she didn't want to splash soap on her frock. Before she tied the apron behind her, she pulled a dainty timepiece out of her pocket and glanced at the hands. She was relieved to see that it was already going on one o'clock. Charles would be coming for her at two o'clock. She would only have to roast for an hour.

Josephine glanced around the room with the hope of finding a mirror so she could check on the state of her hair. Cecilia had spent thirty minutes putting it up this morning. Five minutes in the overbearing heat would probably be all it took to ruin the girl's artwork. With no looking glass in sight, she ran her fingers over her locks. As she had suspected, she felt damp spirals hanging down her back rather than the perfect ringlets that had been there earlier in the day.

Phooey! Regardless of her state of disarray, Josephine was determined to soldier on. She listened attentively as Agatha went through the process of doing the wash.

"First thing we do is get a fire going. Then we fill this kettle with water." She pointed out the window, indicating the pump in the sunny yard. "Then we hook it over that tripod there. While that's heating, we gather the bags of laundry from throughout the buildings. Once the water's boiling, the kettle is brought back inside. Then the hard work begins."

"Oh." Josephine flinched. She was under the impression that what Agatha pointed out already *was* the hard work. *It gets more laborious?*

"We dunk the soiled clothes in the hot water to delouse them."

Delouse? Josephine shuddered and tried to focus on the rest of the instructions.

"Next, we move the laundry to the cool water and soap up one item at a time and then scrub it over the ribs of the washboard. The clothes with stubborn stains go to the washing bench to be batted.

Other than beating the dirt into submission, what is the point of doing such an onerous thing? Josephine wondered.

"After the final rinse, we carry the full baskets outside and pin the clothes to the lines." Agatha looked at Josephine expectantly. "What part of the wash process would you like to be assigned to?"

That question took some deliberation. The thought of touching lousy clothing was anything but appealing, but she could use a stick to grab each item so at least everything would be kept at arm's length.

She had no interest in the scrubbing job, the lye soap would be incredibly hard on her hands. It was difficult enough to get beauty products during wartime as it was. It would be a waste to squander her rose-scented hand cream because of such an endeavor.

Thumping pairs of pants seemed to be a wearisome chore, and she wasn't sure she had the strength to bat more than a few items. In the end, Josephine chose to take charge of the first step and the last step in the laundry process: putting the dirty clothes into the boiling water and hanging the clean clothes outside to dry. At least she'd be outdoors for part of the day to get a reprieve from the suffocating heat.

So the process began. The two of them washed and scrubbed and rinsed and hung. What Josephine thought would be an hour-long activity turned into three hours. With no sign of Charles coming to fetch her, she tried to think of a reason to excuse herself, but nothing plausible came to mind.

When they'd finally emptied the room of wash, dumped the tubs, extinguished the fire, and all the laundry was hung on the lines, Agatha closed up shop for the evening. She walked Josephine back through the compound to the front entrance where the day had begun.

Charles lounged in the doorway, shooting the breeze with one of the guards when Josephine approached. Seeing his mistress, he immediately straightened and took off his cap. Staring at her, he seemed a bit taken aback by her appearance. He tried to hide the smile that crept to his lips.

"Not one word out of you, Charles," Josephine said with a crabby voice. "Not one."

"No, ma'am. You won't hear one word from me," he replied, choking back his laughter.

If looks could kill, the prison staff would have been tasked with fetching another driver to bring their newest volunteer home that day.

Chapter VI

Michael lounged on his cot the entire afternoon and went through various scenes from his life, trying to recall where he had seen that young lady before. His first days in the Army seemed as good enough place to start as any.

He went into active service with military after graduating from West Point Military Academy. Double the number of men graduated from there in 1861 compared to 1860. Originally Michael and the other cadets in his class were scheduled to graduate in June of 1862. However, by their fourth year of school, scores of cadets had left the academy to return to their home states as each region withdrew from the Union. His home state of Georgia had seceded on the nineteenth of January, 1861.

The commandant of the institution at that time was General P.G.T. Beauregard. The U.S. War Department was in a fix, as it needed a thousand new officers. However, students were leaving West Point faster than they could be replaced. Beauregard insisted that he would stay loyal to the academy and encourage his cadets to stay loyal as well, as long as his home state of Louisiana remained in the Union. The members of the board did not find that reassurance good enough and, days later, asked him to step down from his position.

Two weeks after his exit, Louisiana did secede. Because of the turmoil at the academy and the departure of so many students, the War Department determined that the class of 1862 should graduate after four years of study rather than five. Thus, the classes of 1861 and 1862 graduated on the same day, June 24, 1861.

Michael rolled onto his side as his memories marched on.

He and the rest of the graduates were commissioned second lieutenants upon graduation. Students with outstanding academic records were offered high commissions in the militias of their home states, both North and South. Michael was in the top ten percent of his class so he assumed that he would receive a commission from a regiment in northern Georgia. Maybe even Macon County from whence he hailed.

As expected, an offer was extended to him. However, the timing was not right for him to accept. The structure was laid out to create regiments in his state, but the commanding officers were still securing uniforms, guns and ammunition, so they wouldn't be able to bring in recruits until later that summer.

Being a native Georgian, Michael swore allegiance to the Southern cause and chomped at the bit to put his four years of schooling to use. He intended to show the Union soldiers that the Confederacy was a force to be reckoned with. The wait was killing him. When he was offered an alternate commission with the 18th Arkansas Infantry Regiment, 3rd Confederate Infantry, Company B, he readily accepted it.

The sound of catcalls broke Michael's reverie for a moment. *Must be females in the vicinity.* Men swarmed to the windows. It wasn't worth the time or energy for him to get up, so he remained where he was.

During the first five months with Company B, he and his fellow recruits and volunteers never had a taste of battle. Their days consisted of drilling, drilling and more drilling. Men grumbled about the never-ending marching, but it was no hardship for Michael. After years of being on the bottom of the pecking order, he was happy to finally be near the top, issuing commands rather than being barked at day in and day out.

That didn't make time go any faster, but at least it was more bearable. What made life in camp interesting for

Michael was being privy to the strategizing that went on in the commanding officers' headquarters. He had no say in how the company maneuvered, but he got to sit in on the planning sessions and learn from his superiors how to gain the upper hand when boots hit the ground.

In all those months, the only females that Michael laid eyes on were the officers' wives and daughters, who were settled on the far edge of the encampment, and the women who did the laundry and served food in the mess tent. The young lady who called his name in the yard earlier was neither a camp follower nor one of the female workers. He would surely have recognized her.

Elevated voices across the room caused Michael to sit up. Two men were at the point of fisticuffs, arguing over a woman who briefly stopped by the window to engage in conversation.

It was ridiculous that people would come to blows in the prison. Hadn't they seen enough violence on the battlefield? Michael certainly had.

His company was deployed to Kentucky in December of 1861, where they had their first engagement at the Battle of Rowlett's Station. He was part of the contingent that blew up the Louisville and Nashville Railroad Bridge spanning the Green River near Munfordville.

In the course of a week, the Union forces repaired the bridge to the point where they could send troops across the span. His regiment attacked the Federal companies as they crossed the river.

It was baptism by fire for Michael. In his mind, he had conjured a picture of battle where marksmen shot across a field toward the enemy line. If your aim was true, a soldier would fall, but you wouldn't see the aftermath of your actions. His first taste of war proved that image false.

He could still remember vividly every detail of that day,

starting with the sound of the Union Army crashing through the underbrush towards his position. Michael carried the .32 caliber Smith & Wesson Model N. 2 Army revolver issued by the 18th Arkansas, but many of the other men were armed with rifles. The acrid smell of the gunpowder from the long guns stung his nostrils.

Upon seeing the wave of men coming toward his position, Michael assumed a defensive stance and took on the first soldier zeroed in on him. At West Point they had trained endlessly in hand-to-hand fighting, but standing across from a classmate with a dummy bayonet attached to his rifle was far different than being attacked by a man with a lethal weapon in his hands.

It was either kill or be killed. The combat skills he learned at West Point instinctively kicked in. One thing he hadn't learned at the military academy, he realized soon enough, was how war affects a man's spirit. When he issued the fatal blow to that first attacker, he felt as if his own heart had been pierced.

There was no time to consider his actions or even murmur a prayer over the corpse as another soldier with blood in his eyes ran screaming toward him. Mechanically, he braced himself for impact. The scrimmage this time was more intense, but Michael came out on top again.

He wanted to survive, but it pained him to realize that his life could only be spared at the expense of another man's. Bile rose in his throat as he surveyed the carnage. Turning in a circle, he saw men engaged in mortal combat all around him. Screams issued from dying lips, blood spouted from fresh wounds, and the heat of men battling to the death engulfed him.

Michael shook his head to clear that nightmare from his mind. He leaned against the plank wall behind his cot, gaining some relief from the warmth of the room.

What he wouldn't have given for some of that warmth the

first part of 1862 when their division made its way up to Tennessee. They literally and figuratively cooled their heels there until The Battle of Shiloh in April.

His sharpshooting skills were put to the test in that skirmish. Numerous Union soldiers were felled by his revolver over the course of two days. It was a different scenario than his first battle because there was no hand-to-hand fighting, but it didn't make it any easier seeing the death pall come over a man who died at his hand.

The Siege of Corinth followed and went into June. From there they were ordered to join the Kentucky Campaign, a three-month endeavor that was capped off by the Battle of Perryville on October 8.

Then it was back to Tennessee. From December 31 until January 3, 1863, they fought the Battle of Murfreesboro. Their regiment was encamped in Tennessee until June of 1863 when they were next pitted against Union forces at the Battle of Liberty Gap.

By this point, the war had moved to Michael's home state, and he and his men followed suit. The Chickamauga Campaign spanned the months of August and September in 1863 and came to a head at the Battle of Chickamauga on September 19 and 20.

Michael had an uncanny memory and kept meticulous notes of all Company B's engagements in his head. The Battle of Perryville was particularly harrowing, but it did add another bar to the insignia on his shoulder. He was promoted to First Lieutenant when the smoke died down. It would be another tale to share with his sons and grandsons someday.

His dream of traveling across the country came true, albeit in a smaller sphere, trekking back and forth between four states. The regiment trudged to Tennessee for the Chattanooga Campaign. They were at the Battle of

Missionary Ridge on November 25, 1863 and crossed back into Georgia two days later for the Battle of Ringgold Gap.

By that time, it had been almost two years since he was last home. As his regiment was given a twenty-four-hour reprieve, Michael asked if he could slip into Atlanta to see his family.

He was concerned about his father. At forty-seven, the man was getting on in years. The pressure of running a dry goods store in the midst of a war, protecting his family, and keeping his young wife happy would be enough to kill anyone.

Permission granted, Michael made the five-mile trek to Atlanta. He knew the roads into the city like the back of his hand and, if he left before the rooster crowed, he could get to his father's store before the sun rose.

Apparently, the Union soldiers had become familiar with those roads themselves. In his eagerness to get into Atlanta, Michael made one misstep and landed smack dab in a hornet's nest. He was surrounded by Union soldiers, unceremoniously disarmed and then sent to the stockade.

That explained how he came to be in a Federal prison. But it didn't explain how that young lady, who obviously knew him, showed up there.

Chapter VII

Josephine swished the carved-ivory fan back and forth near her face and gazed out the front of the brougham. She couldn't wait to get back to the house and divest herself of her dress, hoop and corset. She would direct her handmaid to strip her down to her undergarments and then redo her hair to get it off her neck. There were no engagements on the calendar that evening, so Cecilia could do something simple with her locks. It could be a ponytail for all that Josephine cared; she just wanted to cool down.

After they pulled in front of the Bigelow house on Capitol Hill, Charles disembarked and reached up to assist Josephine from the vehicle. She gingerly accepted his hand. The muscles in her shoulders and biceps were throbbing. She wasn't sure what hurt worse, the aching sensation or the thought of how her upper arms would appear after slaving over a laundry tub for the entire summer. The last thing she wanted was to ruin her perfectly slim appendages with lumpy boyish muscles and not be able to wear her pretty sleeveless gowns.

Josephine trudged up the front steps and went through the door Charles held for her. Perhaps she would have to rethink her strategy. If she was going to be stuck in the wash house for three months, the only dirt that she would find was the grime on the trousers that she was forced to wash. There would be precious little time to do any undercover work and see what really went on behind the gates of a federal prison. Somehow, she'd have to find a way to converse with the inmates to see what life in detention was really like.

Dare I speak with any of the female prisoners? Not too

many people intimidated her, but those loose women made her skittish. What drew a person into such a lifestyle was beyond her. Obviously, they didn't have the advantages that she had been afforded in life, but their appearances were acceptable, and none were long in the tooth, so why would they engage in such a sordid business?

Any one of them should have been able to lasso a husband. Perhaps not at this moment with the dearth of males in the city. But, when the hostilities finally subsided, there would be laborers and factory workers and perhaps even some businessmen open to marriage contracts with women from a lower social class.

The wooden stairs creaked below her kid leather boots as Josephine climbed the staircase to the second floor. *If I am to be kept busy every moment that I'm on the prison grounds, I won't be conversing with anyone other than Agatha.* After one brief conversation, she already knew everything of consequence about the woman. At the age of sixteen, she married her husband, Matthew, a prison guard. They had no children, both were in their mid-thirties and the two had lived in Washington, D.C., their entire lives.

Agatha's one claim to fame was that she and her husband belonged to St. John's Episcopal Church on Lafayette Square. It was across the way from the White House and was known as The Church of the Presidents. The first service was held there nearly fifty years ago, and every sitting president since then had attended church there at some point in his term. Pew 54, known as the President's Pew, was reserved for their use.

Or something like that. Josephine had tuned Agatha out halfway through her spiel. Just because their church was favored by presidents, Episcopalians were so full of themselves. Considering the fact that every president since George Washington had been a Protestant, where else would they go to church? If a Catholic ever became president, obviously he would attend Holy Trinity Church. All the respectable families in the District of Columbia went there.

Josephine walked through the doorway into her bed chamber, perched on the edge of the bed, and then sank back into the feather mattress. The fluffy pillows decked in starched white eyelet cases muffled her voice. "Cecilia!"

The younger girl scampered into the room a few seconds later. "Yes, miss."

"Can you take off my boots and stockings? I'm too tired to bend over."

"Of course, miss. Did you have a rough day?"

"You could say that." Josephine let out a sigh as Cecilia used the button hook to unbutton her kid boots. She let her mind wander as the girl worked.

With the Nativist movement, which had gained prominence some twenty years ago, the chances of a Catholic ever getting elected president were slim. American History class was a blur to her, but she did recall learning about nativism. It was a political policy promoting the interests of a country's native inhabitants over those of immigrants.

That movement caused a wave of anti-Catholicism to sweep the country, which led to mob violence, the burning of Church property, and the killing of Catholics. Roman Catholics were accused of destroying the culture of the United States, and Catholics of Irish heritage were blamed for spreading violence and drunkenness.

The Bigelow family, although Catholic, was not Irish, thank goodness. Josephine would abhor being of that tainted stock. Her family was of British descent. Their ancestors fled England after King Henry VIII declared himself the head of the Church of England.

Josephine could almost hear her old teacher lecturing in

her monotone voice. "King Henry VIII issued The Act of Supremacy in 1534 that declared His Royal Majesty to be the only supreme head on earth of the Church of England, thus exempting himself from the pope's rule. Any act of allegiance to the latter was considered treason because the papacy claimed both spiritual and political power over its followers." How that tidbit stuck in her memory banks was beyond her; she didn't even recall being awake for that whole lecture.

With the boots and stockings off, Josephine pushed herself up to sitting, slid her bare feet to the floor and presented her back to Cecilia. The girl started undoing the row of buttons that ran from the neck of the dress to the waistline.

"Did you know that my grandfather was a founding member of Holy Trinity Church?"

"No, miss, I didn't," said Cecilia.

"His name is inscribed on the plaque hung inside the front entrance."

"Is that so? I'll be sure to read it when we go to church Sunday."

Josephine leaned her weight on one foot as the unbuttoning process continued. "Our parish has quite the history. It was established by the first Catholic bishop in America, Archbishop John Carroll. He was cousin to Charles Carroll, one of the signers of the Declaration of Independence."

Noting their reflection in the vanity mirror, Josephine could see that the girl seemed duly impressed. Maybe Agatha would be as well. She'd have to mention that fact to her tomorrow. The Episcopalians weren't the only ones with renowned history.

After the Second Battle of Bull Run two years ago, Holy Trinity Church was appropriated by the government and commissioned a hospital to lend care to the two hundred men injured in the fight. For a year, the Bigelow family attended Mass at St. Patrick's Catholic Church, but they were back at Holy Trinity now.

Hubert had gone to the boys' school there before enrolling in Gonzaga College for his secondary education. Josephine was educated by a governess until she was old enough to attend Georgetown Academy for Young Ladies.

"It will be strange not going back to Georgetown this fall, don't you think, Cecilia?"

"That's true, miss," said Cecilia. She tugged the sleeve of Josephine's dress to pull it off her arm. "We've spent more time there these past four years than we have here."

"Uh-huh." Josephine wasn't sure if she'd miss that place or not.

The academy was housed in a long, white three-story building that had nineteen bedrooms, a library, several parlors, and porches in the wings. Having roommates didn't appeal to Josephine, but living in an establishment with hot running water made it more bearable.

Miss Lydia Scutter English was the founder and principal of the school. She was a stern headmistress but, as she always said, she "stood for what was fine." Miss English and nine other teachers oversaw the one hundred and forty young ladies who resided there.

The patrons of the school were some of the most famous men in the United States. Even Vice President Andrew Johnson sent his daughter there. Since many of Washington's elite had their offspring enrolled in the academy, it was Brigadier General Bigelow's first choice for secondary education for his little girl.

Josephine remembered laughing when he showed her the brochure for the seminary. It declared, "The girls would be provided with that amount of mental and moral culture necessary to render them amiable, intelligent and useful members of society."

The young ladies turned out to be amiable and intelligent enough — particularly when it came to entertaining members of the opposite sex. Miss Abigail was assigned to sit behind the parlor door when any of the girls had a gentleman caller. The students found her to be the ideal chaperone because she snored so loudly that couples could get away with just about anything once she fell asleep, which was usually moments after she situated herself in her rocking chair.

The young bloods of Georgetown used to gather on the far corner of the grounds with the pretense of fetching water from the large pump located there. In actuality, they were serenading the fairer sex. The girls who were bold enough would put together baskets of billet-doux and sweetmeats for the fellows.

It was widely known that the way to a man's heart was through his stomach. Josephine would have been daring enough to gather up delicacies for a sweetheart or even write a love letter to a young man — had she given a whit about any of them. None of those boys caught her eye. She was interested in older men, like Hubert's classmates. Something about a fellow in uniform made her heart flutter.

The soldiers she saw at the prison came to mind, specifically, Michael. She could have sworn her eyes were playing tricks on her when she spotted Master McKirnan. Even in the insufferable gray Confederate uniform, he was still the most handsome thing that she'd ever laid eyes on.

She sighed, disappointed that he had taken up with the enemy. Josephine thought for sure that Hubert and their other roommate would have talked some sense into him before they parted ways.

Or maybe they did?

Perhaps that's how Mr. McKirnan came to be in a Federal prison. Maybe he wasn't actually a Rebel. Maybe he was a

Union soldier posing as a Confederate to engage in espionage for President Lincoln. *Now that would be a story worth writing about!*

Chapter VIII

After supper, the men were sent outside for a couple hours. Michael skirted around a group of inmates animatedly discussing the root cause of the war. Any other day, he would have eagerly joined in. Politics and war history were topics of great interest to him.

But tonight, he was intent on knocking his brain to jiggle the memory loose of how he knew that young lady. Or, how she might know him. He took a seat on the rough wooden steps of the infirmary.

At no time in his military career did he recall running across any female that matched her looks. With a face and figure like hers, there would have been no way in heck he would have forgotten her. He must have met her before he entered the service.

As a youth, Michael attended Immaculate Conception School in Atlanta. He obviously didn't meet her there, since it was an all-boys' school. The McKirnan family had been members of Immaculate Conception Church since his father emigrated from Ireland. The young lady wasn't a fellow parishioner, he knew that. In their brief interaction, he noted that she didn't have the Georgian drawl but had what sounded like a Northeastern accent like the girls who occasionally came to West Point for an event.

Every so often, the academy hosted balls and other get-togethers and female guests were invited. She hadn't been one of them though, he would have remembered her.

Michael leaned back against the door of the infirmary and watched as the sun began its descent to the western horizon. Interesting how the setting sun appeared the same no matter where you saw it. The view he had now reminded him of dusk settling over West Point.

It had been three years since he last was on the campus. Memories of graduation day flooded back to him.

It was quite the occasion. He and his fellow classmates, dressed in their woolen full-dress grays, assembled on the training field and broiled in the mid-afternoon sun as they stood throughout the entire ceremony. Their families sat behind them in wooden chairs, the women holding lace parasols over their heads to protect their skin from the harsh sun.

After Lieutenant Colonel Alexander Hamilton Bowman gave his closing comments, the men were officially graduated and the newly minted officers tossed their caps in the air. It didn't matter where they landed, since the cadet caps were no longer part of their uniforms. Hours earlier, almost every graduate had tucked a slip of paper with his name written on it into the lining of the cap and added a token or coin as well. The graduates' siblings were allowed to run onto the field and take a cap home as a souvenir.

Michael was positioned between his two roommates for the ceremony. He was the only one from a Southern state. Regardless of their different political ideologies, the three of them had been fast friends since their days as Plebes back in '57. The two Northerners liked to rib him for his drawl, especially when he let down his guard and threw a "y'all" into the conversation.

George Armstrong Custer was the eldest of the roommates. He taught school in Ohio before enrolling at West Point. The young man was quite the interesting character. He was named after a pastor, George Armstrong, because his devout mother had hoped he would join the clergy when he grew up. Michael couldn't possibly imagine him in that occupation. Custer was a born prankster and was always testing the boundaries, and the patience, of their professors.

In the four years that they had been there, Custer amassed a record seven hundred and twenty-six demerits. He had the honor, or perhaps dishonor, of holding one of the worst conduct records in the history of West Point. He came close to getting expelled every year because of his excessive demerits, most of which he earned for pulling pranks on fellow cadets, including his roommates. Michael would join in George's mischief if it was harmless enough and the chances of getting caught were low.

Under normal circumstances, a cadet with such a poor class ranking would have been destined to an obscure post after graduation, but Custer had the fortuitous luck of being commissioned a second lieutenant in Company G, 2nd U.S. Cavalry. Having been raised in the country, the young man was an excellent horseman. He could outride his roommates any day, especially Michael, as his family had never owned horses.

George fought in the First Battle of Bull Run just a month after graduation. He may not have shown much discipline when they were in school, but he turned out to be an excellent cavalry officer. When Michael read the reports about the Battle of Gettysburg the following summer, he couldn't believe his eyes. George had been promoted to the rank of brigadier general for the Union Army. He had never heard of anyone advancing so rapidly through the ranks of the military.

As for their other roommate, he was far from the adventurous type. Born and raised in Washington, D.C., he was obligated to serve the Union Army after graduation, but he wasn't keen on sticking his neck out and potentially having his head disengaged from it. But luck was on his side as well. His father held a prominent position on President Lincoln's staff and was able to secure an administrative position at the White House for him. It had been some time since Michael had given the fellow any thought. Even though they were as thick as thieves in school, after graduation they went their separate ways.

On April 12, 1861, Confederate artillery fired on the Union garrison at Fort Sumter and the War Between the States began. It pained Michael to be at odds with his two roommates, but allegiance to The Confederate States of America superseded his loyalty to his companions. He prayed to God that he would never stand across the battlefield from either one of them.

Unless the Confederate Army made its way to the lawn of the White House, the chances of seeing Hubert in that scenario were rather slim. He could shoot just as well as the other fellows, but reading was more appealing to him than soldiering. The man had a good head for numbers, so he was probably doing more for Uncle Sam by working at a desk job than he ever would on a field of battle.

Hubert had an air of seriousness about him but possessed a keen sense of humor as well. He actually made a fine sidekick and had a hand in a few of George's escapades.

Michael was curious to meet his friend's family after the graduation ceremony. Hubert's father, a brigadier general, was as stodgy as Michael had anticipated he'd be. Hubert's mother was a typical socialite. North or South, they all sang the same tune. The biggest surprise that day was meeting his little sister. She was thirteen going on thirty. A young lady with a mind of her own, who wasn't shy about sharing it, rattling off a mile a minute in her distinct Northeastern accent.

She may have only been a teenager then, but no one could deny that she was a beauty. Her hair was a rich brown and her matching lashes framed her saucy eyes. He had never seen such an unusual shade of green before and the devil was in them, no doubt. For a girl her age, she had a nice figure already and was fashionably dressed. S*omeday that* *girl is going to keep some poor man on his toes.*

She must've been all grown up by now, Michael thought. *I wonder where life has taken her?*

Then the revelation hit him. He knew exactly where life had taken her — to the grounds of Old Capitol Prison.

Chapter IX

"Miss Josephine, time to get up."

Josephine cracked one eye open. "Five more minutes, Cecilia."

"Miss, that's what you said five minutes ago and five minutes before that, too."

"It's so early," Josephine complained, before pulling her pillow from under her head and plopping it over her face. *Who in their right mind schedules anything before ten o'clock in the morning?* she grumbled to herself. Was it actually plausible that the wash house was busy every day of the week? How could there possibly be that much clothing to launder?

"Miss, the cook is frying up side pork," said Cecilia in a conspiratorial tone. Josephine slid the pillow down and sniffed the air. "And I told her to save the crispiest piece for you."

"Fine," said Josephine begrudgingly. She tossed the pillow aside and rolled out of bed. Was there perhaps a chance that she could volunteer only two days a week instead of five? Would Father be willing to renegotiate? She let out a sigh. It wasn't even worth the breath to ask him. The man was infamously stubborn and once he made his mind up about something, he seldom changed it. If she so much as broached the subject with him, she would probably never hear the end of it.

Letting out another sigh, she resigned herself to her fate and turned to Cecilia. "Will you please fetch a light frock? The one with the bell sleeves that fall just to my elbows."

"The sage-colored one?"

"Precisely. But leave the corset in the armoire."

Cecilia's eyebrows raised in question.

"Appropriate or not, I'm not wearing one today." Who would know? No one was up at this ungodly hour. Besides, with her trim waist, the undergarment was unnecessary anyhow. No point torturing herself in the heat by wearing extra layers of clothing.

Dressed in clean pantaloons and a fresh shift, Josephine lifted her arms so Cecilia could slip the dress over her head.

"It's going to be another hot day today, miss. I can fashion your hair in a way that will withstand the heat."

Josephine took a seat on the velvet tufted chair next to her vanity. She pouted at her reflection in the oval mirror.

"We'll just plait your hair into two braids, Miss Josephine," said Cecilia cheerily.

Josephine stared at her with mistrust. It wasn't even seven o'clock in the morning. Who could possibly be that chipper so early in the day?

Of course, it was easy enough for her to be high-spirited. *With me gone all day, she can pass the time doing whatever she very well pleases.* She wouldn't doubt it if the girl went back to bed after she left. *If the roles were reversed, that's what I'd do.*

Watching the girl's reflection as she worked, Josephine couldn't help but scowl. It didn't seem to bother the little songbird one bit. Cecilia kept to her task, whistling some frivolous tune as she went along. "Ta-da," she announced, stepping back from the vanity to admire her handiwork.

"Oh my goodness, I look like a dairymaid!" exclaimed Josephine, tossing the two French braids with a shake of her head. "I'm volunteering at a prison, not a farm!"

"This will keep the hair off your neck," said Cecilia.

"People will think I'm a schoolgirl, not a sophisticated young woman working for the war effort."

"How about I pin them on top of your head? Would that be acceptable?"

"I suppose."

When that task was finished, Josephine stomped down the stairs to the dining room and asked the cook to bring her a cup of coffee.

Her mother gathered her brows in curiosity. "Since when did you start drinking coffee, young lady?"

"Since I started my new volunteer position, Mother. How do you expect me to be alert this time of day without something to awaken me?" She sat down and grabbed an apple from the porcelain fruit bowl in the center of the table.

"Josephine, you're only seventeen. You're too young to start such a habit," chided her mother. "A cup of tea would be more fitting." She nodded toward the delicate porcelain tea cup set before her.

"Mother, by the time you were my age, you and Father were already married. And you were expecting Hubert."

"Josephine, you know it's bad-mannered to speak about a woman in that condition." She paused for a moment. "However, you do have a point, dear." Mrs. Bigelow turned in her seat and called out to the cook. "Magdalene, make that a *small* cup of coffee for Miss Josephine."

The woman stepped into the dining room, bobbed her head and went back through the swinging door to the kitchen. Not a minute later, she returned with a cup two-thirds full of steaming coffee. Josephine thanked her and proceeded to fill the mug nearly to the brim with milk from a cut-glass pitcher. She then topped the concoction off with two heaping teaspoons of sugar. Her mother's eyes widened as she watched the procedure.

"What?" asked Josephine defensively. "You don't expect me to jump right in and drink it black, do you?"

"It is an acquired taste, I'll give you that," said her mother with a laugh. "I, for one, never did acquire it. Apparently, you get that from your father."

"Speaking of Father, where is he?"

"He's already at the capitol building. He mentioned some business about a raid or something along that line."

Raid, schmaid. It was of no consequence to her. Josephine had no interest in war talk. Her father assured her that the Union Army would prevail and things would return to normal before long. *Any time now would be lovely.*

Josephine stabbed a piece of side pork. The smell of the seared fat made her mouth water. She sliced off a bite-sized portion. Unless, by some chance, the war came to a sudden conclusion, she would honor her word to her father and go to the prison on the weekdays.

At least he wasn't making her go there seven days a week, she thought as she bit into the piece of pork. As it was, her summer schedule would only allow her only one day each week to socialize with her friends. Personally, she would be amenable to spending the entire weekend with them, but Sundays were reserved for quiet introspection, according to her father.

She couldn't wait to see her friends this Saturday. Like every week, they would talk, they would laugh, and they may even indulge in a bit of gossip. But at least it wasn't on the Lord's Day. Now that she had run into Michael, undoubtedly that story would be the highlight of their conversation. She'd relish sharing it with her confidants.

After Josephine ate her fill of the side pork and took a final sip of coffee, she ran upstairs to polish her teeth before taking her leave.

Charles waited for her in the brougham. "Miss Josephine," he said, as he looked over his shoulder to pull the vehicle onto the street, "what time would you like me to fetch you today?"

"I'd like you to fetch me after lunch, but God forbid I leave the laundry area before every last trouser is washed, so come back for me at four o'clock."

The man was suddenly overtaken by a coughing attack.

Josephine glared at his back. *Hrmph!*

Chapter X

After breakfast, Michael strolled into the yard and found the same group of men who had been discussing the war yesterday. This time he joined them, interested to hear how their theories aligned with his.

Michael had extensive knowledge of the current situation and war in general, having sat through more lectures on government, civics, war and history than he could count.

West Point had graduated a good number of men who went on to have stellar military careers. When the war broke out, celebrated generals fought on both sides of the conflict. Those sympathizing with the Southern cause included General Robert E. Lee and General Thomas Jonathon Jackson, or Stonewall Jackson, as he was now known. The most famous generals aligned with the Union were General Ulysses S. Grant and General William Tecumseh Sherman, who was currently besieging Georgia.

As Michael listened to the men talk, he realized they only superficial knowledge of the war but a plethora of theories. Arms crossed in front of him, he half listened as his mind retreated to the military leadership class that he took his last year of school. They had a secession-leaning professor who enumerated his list of ten factors that led to the declaration of war.

With his sharp memory, Michael could still picture the notes as he had meticulously written them three years earlier.

The bulk of the money to run the federal government came from Southern states via a tariff on goods they produced. They were treated as an agricultural colony of the North.

The United States was founded as a constitutional federal republic. President Lincoln's war of aggression changed the union to a democracy with socialist leanings. Confederates sought to preserve a limited federal government.

The South believed in Christianity as presented in the Holy Bible. The North had human secularists who believed there was no God and all problems could be solved by man, science and government.

Southerners and Northerners were of different genetic lineage. British, Scottish and Irish vs. Anglo-Saxon and Danish. The cultures had clashed for more than a thousand years.

The North wanted control of the Western territories. Northern industrialists wanted the South's resources. Newspapers printed in the North slandered the South to indoctrinate the common people of the North.

New Englanders attempted to instigate massive slave rebellions in the South. Most Southerners did not own slaves and would not have fought for the protection of slavery. The majority of educated Southerners favored a gradual emancipation of slaves that would allow the economy to adjust to a paid labor system without economic collapse.

Lincoln provoked South Carolina into firing on Fort Sumter so he could claim the Confederacy started the war. He had refused to meet with a Confederate peace delegation.

Dusk approached and the bell rang to signal the men to return to the bunk areas. The men near Michael kept up their conversation about the war as they were marched back into the building. They had varying opinions on the topic.

All in all, Michael felt that he had been shown a fair picture of the cause for the war since his professors at West Point were both Southerners and Northerners. But, honestly, he had a hard time determining which side was right and which side was wrong.

Of course, he never mentioned that to his father, who was staunchly in favor of states' rights. Mr. McKirnan left Ireland to escape the oppression of the British government. He always said that he didn't escape one form of tyranny to be subjected to another. If he had to, he'd fight the Yankees himself. But at his age, he had no business fighting a young man's war. Even if Mrs. McKirnan would grant him permission to do such a thing.

Not that Michael advocated war, but war history fascinated him. It was one of the things that drew him to the military academy. He particularly enjoyed reading biographies of famous war figures such as General George Washington or the notorious General Benedict Arnold, who fought for the American Continental Army and later defected to the British Army.

It was nearly dark by the time they returned to the bunk area. Michael stripped down to his skivvies, folded his clothes, placed them at the head of his cot for a pillow, and then pulled back the rough wool blanket. A cool breeze blew in through the windows. The lightweight covering would keep him comfortable, even if it was itchy as all get-out.

After saying his prayers, the story of General Arnold came back to him. The man was born in Connecticut, joined the Army outside Boston and distinguished himself through acts of intelligence and bravery. Despite his successes, he was passed over for promotions by the Continental Congress as other officers claimed credit for some of his accomplishments.

Because of that and other nefarious goings on by his adversaries in military and political circles, Arnold became bitter. He was also frustrated with the alliance between the colonies and France and the failure of Congress to accept

Britain's 1778 proposal to grant full self-governance to the colonies. He decided to change allegiances and opened secret negotiations with the British.

Michael rolled onto his side and recalled more details of the general's life. In July of 1780, Arnold was awarded command of the military fort at, interestingly enough, West Point. His scheme was to surrender the fort to the British, but it was exposed when American forces captured Adjutant General of the British Army, Major John André, carrying papers that revealed the plot. Upon learning of André's capture, Arnold fled down the Hudson River to the British sloop-of-war *Vulture*, narrowly avoiding capture by the forces of George Washington, who had been alerted to the plot. After officially switching his allegiance, Arnold received a commission as a brigadier general in the British Army.

Restlessly, Michael flipped to his other side. He recalled a newspaper article about West Point that he read last year in *The Soldiers' Journal*. It said that nine hundred and seventy-seven graduates from the classes of 1833 through 1861 were alive when the war began and of those men, twenty-six percent joined the Confederacy and sixty-five percent fought for the Union. Thirty-nine graduates from Southern states fought for the Union, and thirty-two from Northern states fought for the Confederacy.

The side with which a man aligned wasn't a given, as was evidenced by those statistics. People followed their convictions. Before his first taste of war, Michael was so sure of himself and had no reason to question the righteousness of the Southern cause. But so many things had changed since then.

Some six months back, he was given the opportunity to reconsider his alliances. After analyzing the offer, Michael felt led to alter his course. He prayed that he had selected the path of the greater good, one that would bring him fame rather than infamy, but only time would tell.

Chapter XI

Josephine thought about the day ahead as the Brougham approached the prison. She thanked her lucky stars that men didn't wear undergarments. Being subjected to touching such items would have sent her over the edge. It was bad enough washing the ladies' drawers. A shiver of revulsion snaked down her spine. *Lord only knows how many men had their hands on that lingerie before it made its way to me. Ewww.*

Charles pulled up to the curb in front of the building and jumped from his perch to help Josephine down from the vehicle. Once she reached the front door safely, he gave her a nod and climbed back up to his seat.

Stepping into the front hallway once again, Josephine swept her eyes over the area to see if any prisoners were being escorted through. Her primary mission for the day was to get a word with Michael to find out what circumstances brought him to Old Capitol Prison. She was dying of curiosity to hear what had transpired in his life since his graduation from West Point.

Unfortunately, the only occupants of the space were the armed guards, one of whom, the highest-ranking officer, offered to escort Josephine to the laundry facility.

The inmates were in the mess hall, so she only saw guards and prison employees as she made the trip to the courtyard. When she got to the wash house, she discovered that Agatha already had a fire going out back and water in the large kettle.

It was time for Josephine to begin the routine of dropping clothing into the hot water piece by piece. She swirled each item in the hot water, the steam enveloping her and making her appreciate the braids that Cecilia had fashioned today. Meanwhile, Agatha pounded away on the soiled items. After each piece was dunked a second time, the two of them lugged the heavy basket outside and pinned the clothes up.

Josephine clipped a dripping shirt to the line and glanced at the empty basket, their third load done. Her back ached as she stooped to pick it up, but it was refreshing to be outdoors. A moment later, she stepped inside the sweltering laundry building, where Agatha dipped yet another piece of clothing.

"If you don't mind, I'll do the rounds this morning to pick up the soiled clothing," said Josephine. It really didn't matter to her if the woman minded or not, that chore would give her a break from the wash house, and maybe she could discover where Michael was quartered.

"There's still plenty here," replied Agatha, motioning to the pile of clothes stacked in the corner of the room.

"That's true, and they'll still be there when I get back."

Agatha's eyes widened slightly but she offered no dissent. "You'll need an escort."

"I will go search one out directly."

With that settled, Josephine removed her gingham apron, hung it on the hook by the door, and strode off towards the main building.

What will I do if I spy Michael? Was it permissible to talk to inmates? With all the other men around, she doubted they'd be able to have a private conversation, but at least she could ask how he ended up in Washington, D.C. She would love to hear some daring tale, but chances were he had been captured during the Atlanta campaign that her father had been rambling on about as of late.

She found an escort easily enough because guards were posted at every turn. The first man she approached, a sergeant, was more than happy to assist her. She decided to start at the farthest end of the prison, and when her soldier's arms got full, they would head back to the laundry building to drop the load off. It made sense to do the longest runs first while she had the most stamina.

At each stop, she checked inside the bags, as instructed, and then handed them to her helper. An officer probably wouldn't normally lower himself to the status of laundry boy, but the man seemed amenable to be of service to her.

It worked ideally for Josephine since a strapping male could carry more bags than she could, lessening the number of trips back to the wash building. She strode from room to room with the man trailing several steps behind her. At each doorway, she bent down, opened the bag and poked around for *contraband*, as Agatha called it. Josephine wasn't exactly sure what any man would try to smuggle out of the sleeping quarters. God knew how few things they had in their possession as it was. Perhaps notes were passed that way, but it seemed somewhat futile. Who would read them anyway?

Regardless, Josephine did as she was instructed. It was to her advantage anyway. While she poked through the clothes, she had a moment to glance up and survey the rooms to see if she could spot Michael. With his height, he would certainly stand out in a crowd.

Searching the second floor proved to be fruitless. While the men seemed to enjoy having a female eye them up, or more precisely, having a female for *them* to eye up, she didn't recognize anyone. There was only one room to collect laundry from on the first floor. If Michael wasn't there, she'd have no clue where to find him.

Thankfully, when Josephine approached the last open door, she spied Michael lounging against a wall on the nearside of the room. He turned his head slightly and looked her right in the eye. Josephine stood locked in his gaze, frozen to the spot.

In her mind, she was transported back three years to that sunny day at West Point Military Academy. As she sat with her parents, she scanned the crowd of graduates for her brother. She spied Hubert in the last row, second spot from the right. Her mother indicated that the fellows on either side of him were his roommates. At one point in the ceremony, all the men were instructed to face their friends and family and give them a round of applause for supporting them through their years in school. Hubert, Cadet Custer and Cadet McKirnan turned around in unison.

Josephine's jaw dropped when Michael McKirnan came into full view. She had been admiring his profile from her vantage point during the ceremony but, now having a full view of the man, she found herself breathless. Every girl admired a fellow in a uniform but with Michael's height, ramrod straight posture, wide shoulders and narrow waist, Josephine couldn't imagine a more strikingly handsome man. The pièce de résistance was his face. He had a solid jaw and chiseled cheekbones and an infectious smile, which framed perfectly aligned teeth.

When the last pronouncement was made, the young men received their commissions and tossed their caps in the air. Josephine kept her eye on Michael's cap. The second it hit its apex, she sprang from her chair and sprinted towards the soldiers to gain her prize. This was no time to be ladylike. She hitched her skirts up and made a beeline toward the cadets.

At thirteen, she was probably one of the oldest children in the mix, and that gave her the distinct advantage of speed and dexterity. She didn't care how many children she had to jostle out of the way, she would do whatever it took to get that cap.

Josephine got her coveted memento that day. She had found a piece of paper tucked in the band, with two things written on it in precise cursive: Michael's name and a quote from the Bible. "I can do all things through Christ who strengthens me" Philippians 4:13. Three pressed flowers and a fifty-cent piece were concealed in the band as well.

She could still remember the smell of the cap, a distinctly masculine scent, the essence of outdoors and fresh air with a hint of musk. The treasured item was still stored in her armoire. Occasionally, she would put it on her head and think back to when she met that handsome soldier.

After that day, Josephine truly thought that she'd never see Michael again. Yet here he was in the flesh, standing just eight feet away, his eyes drilling right through her.

He lifted a brow as if to garner her attention, which she gladly gave to him. Then he slightly inclined his head towards the window. The motion was barely perceptible, but she had a guess of what he indicated.

Chapter XII

Michael pushed off the wall he'd been leaning against and sucked in his breath as he watched her retreating figure. It really *was* Hubert Bigelow's little sister; there was no doubt about it. Of all the people he'd known in his lifetime, she was the last person he expected to see inside these prison grounds. Or any prison grounds, for that matter.

Thinking back, the moment that he saw her standing by the female staff member yesterday, he immediately sensed that Josephine wasn't an inmate. As the daughter of a brigadier general, the idea would have been rather preposterous. Even if she had committed some ghastly crime, her father had the clout to keep her out of the hands of the authorities. But what could compel a young lady from her social rank to step foot inside such a facility?

Regardless of what brought her here, Michael couldn't imagine that she would stay long. It was a wonder that she was here again today. He followed her with his eyes as she moved further down the hall with the officer, who was shaking his head in disbelief.

Josephine had certainly surprised him.

The surprise was actually twofold. First, that she'd returned to the prison building, and second, that she'd come to the men's quarters. Or, more precisely, that she'd come to the very space in which he was quartered. Was she looking for him?

Had he left an impression on her during their brief encounter three years ago? She'd certainly left one on him. But, other than a few fleeting thoughts, he really hadn't had the time or the reason to give his old roommate's younger sister much thought since.

Until yesterday. Josephine may have been a fetching schoolgirl, but she was beyond lovely as a young lady. She was stunning. It wasn't just her physical attributes that made her stand out either. He could sense a spirit of determination and strength in her. *There's more to this little lady than just her pretty packaging.*

Of course, he wasn't the only one to take notice of the girl. She drew the attention of most every man in the room, and not in a pious way, as far as he could tell. Thank goodness she had an escort with her. He guessed a good number of the men would like to get to know her — in the biblical sense, that was.

His hands curled into fists. A protective instinct overcame him. Josephine was, after all, Hubert's sister, so he felt duty bound to safeguard her. He had to admit, though, there was more to it than that. For some reason their paths had crossed once again. It was not happenstance. God surely had a hand in this. Had He brought the woman of his dreams to the door of this prison? It was said that the Lord works in mysterious ways.

Michael cracked each of his knuckles one at a time. It wasn't like him to waste time daydreaming. Of course, considering his present circumstances, time was the one thing he had in abundance. If something was to occupy his thoughts, it may as well be Josephine. He had little else to ponder as he waited for his next exchange and next assignment.

With Josephine out of sight, Michael turned away from the door and stared up at the wooden joists in the ceiling as his mind wandered back in time.

In the first year of the war, prisoner exchanges were conducted primarily between field generals on an informal basis. Not wanting to legitimize the Confederate government, the Union was reluctant to enter formal agreements. With the war escalating in 1862, General John

Dix and Confederate General Daniel H. Hill reached an agreement where every imprisoned soldier was assigned a value according to rank. One private was worth another private; corporals and sergeants were worth two privates; lieutenants were worth three privates; and a commanding general was worth sixty privates. Under this agreement, thousands of soldiers were exchanged, freeing up space in the overcrowded prisons.

This gentlemen's agreement relied on trust from each side, but it broke down when the Confederates refused to exchange Negro Union soldiers for the release of their captured soldiers. The pace of the official exchange dropped dramatically, but local commanders were still allowed to make informal exchanges.

From what Michael had heard, something was in the works for him. However, since it didn't appear to be imminent, he was determined to find a way to communicate with Josephine. He was curious to hear what had transpired in her life since the war began. Actually, he was curious to hear everything about her life. The few tidbits that he knew of her came from Hubert, and he wasn't particularly verbose on that topic. Or any other, for that matter.

To be fair, when Michael attended the academy, he had little interest in his roommate's sibling, even if she was "the prettiest girl in Washington, D.C.," as Hubert once boasted of his sister. Josephine had been a child then, but she was all grown up now. Or at least she appeared to be grown up. She must be close to the age of majority.

When he'd nodded to Josephine, he hoped that she correctly interpreted his signal. He wanted her to meet him by the window. Who knew when her daily tasks at the prison would be completed? His plan was to position himself next to the portal the rest of the day if there was even one chance of talking with her privately.

Michael got up and — thanks to his height and build — muscled his way through the group of gawkers to get a prime spot in front of the window on the left side of the room. The men enjoyed watching the big city scenes: couples walking by arm in arm, horses pulling buggies in the street, newsboys hawking papers on the corner, and painted women selling their own wares across the way.

While no one relished being held prisoner, at least the men were out of the line of fire, they had cots to lay their heads on, simple provisions three times a day, a break from the endless drilling, and, most importantly, the hope of surviving the war.

The inmates at Old Capitol Prison were actually some of the more fortunate ones. Compared to life in the prison camps, they lived high on the hog. The most notorious prison was Camp Sumter, or Andersonville, as people called it. It was the largest Confederate military prison and was built several months ago, after Confederate officials decided to move the large number of federal prisoners in Richmond to a place with more security and access to more food.

It was said that four hundred new prisoners arrived there every day. Between disease, poor sanitation, malnutrition, exposure to the elements and overcrowding, men were dropping like flies. The place was built for ten thousand prisoners but already had double that number. Michael thanked God that he'd never be imprisoned there.

Fortunately, fate had something, or should he say *someone*, else in mind for him. After staking out his position for a good two hours, Josephine emerged from a door just east of where he stood. He watched her saunter down the walk toward the road as though she hadn't a care in the world.

She popped open a parasol and, when she got to the street, took a sharp right turn and strolled towards the corner, keeping the parasol tilted to block her face from the view of passersby. Josephine scanned the windows of Michael's cell. Spying him, she casually turned towards the building and walked through the grass to a spot directly in front of the barred window.

"How do you do, Mr. McKirnan?"

Chapter XIII

"Considering the circumstances, I'm doing well, Miss Bigelow," said Michael.

Josephine's heart gave a jolt. *Oh, my goodness.* She distinctly remembered that voice. It was perfect, just like the rest of him.

When she had first been introduced to Michael at West Point Military Academy, the top of her head barely reached his chest. Now, positioned outside the prison window, Josephine was happy to note that her eyes were level with his shoulders. Her present height, taller than most of her peers, made her a suitable match for a man of his stature.

She could just imagine the two of them sashaying down the U Street Corridor in Washington, D.C. — after he was released from his imprisonment, of course. He would place himself on the side of the walk closest to the road, as would any gentleman who cared about the safety of his fair companion. If they managed to elude their chaperone, she might be amenable to a chivalrous kiss. She pictured him leaning down to brush his lips against hers. The thought made her cheeks warm.

Josephine blinked to bring herself back to the present moment. "How good to hear, Mr. McKirnan, or make that..." She stood on her tiptoes to get a closer view of the two bars on his sleeve. "Pardon me for asking, but what is your rank? I'm not familiar with the Confederate insignias."

"I'm presently a first lieutenant, Miss Bigelow. But, seeing as we're already acquainted, no need to use my formal title. You may call me Michael, if that is acceptable to you."

"It most certainly would be, *Michael.*" Josephine shifted her eyes up to the left and imagined writing First Lieutenant

Michael & Mrs. McKirnan in her neat script, then Josephine & Michael McKirnan, and then finally Josephine Bigelow McKirnan. That was it! She had found her pen name! Well, technically a pen name was supposed to be a name other than the author's name, but Josephine Bigelow McKirnan had such a nice ring to it.

She flashed him a smile. "And, of course, you may address me as Josephine."

"*Of course.*"

Josephine kept smiling at him. She wasn't often struck dumb but, goodness gracious, she was entranced by the man's devilish good looks. The sound of another man clearing his throat caused her to disengage from her perusal of the man's uncommonly handsome face.

Several feet behind her stood one of the prison guards who, just moments before, had been positioned on the corner of the prison lot.

"May I help you, sir?" asked Josephine in a businesslike tone.

The soldier brushed down the front of his jacket and adjusted his sleeves. It wasn't the first time that a man became tongue-tied in her presence. Clearing his throat again, he spoke up. "Your pardon, miss, but civilians are not allowed to fraternize with the prisoners."

"Why should that be any concern of mine?"

"Um, I know for a fact that the man standing there is a prisoner, and, unless I'm mistaken, you're a civilian, miss. Therefore, it's my job to ask you to step away from the window," said the guard.

"You are certainly correct that this man is a prisoner and I am a civilian, albeit the daughter of a brigadier general, but a citizen nonetheless. However, that rule doesn't apply to me," she said haughtily.

"It doesn't? How's that, miss?"

"I'm a citizen volunteer here. It just so happens that I'm

conducting official prison duties at this moment, if you don't mind."

"Miss, I wasn't informed of any such thing going on here today," he replied.

"Consider yourself informed now, soldier."

He pulled his head back and his mouth fell open slightly. Regaining his composure, he nodded to her. "Of course, miss."

Waving her hand in dismissal, she turned away from him. "If it makes you feel any better, you may stand watch over us from the corner," said Josephine over her shoulder.

"Yes, miss."

She heard the soldier's boots striking the walkway as he retreated to his post. With that affair taken care of, Josephine brought her attention back to Michael, who grinned at her in amusement. "Where were we?" she asked.

He chuckled and then shook his head. "I believe I was just giving you a short lesson on the military insignia of the Confederate Army."

"Oh, that," said Josephine. She peered at him closer. "How is it that such an outstanding young man such as yourself, who built a stellar reputation at the United States Military Academy, would take up arms with the Rebel Army?"

"You do recall that I hail from Georgia, do you not, Miss Josephine?"

How could I forget? That voice of his is as smooth as silk. As intoxicating as nectar to a bee. I could listen to him read the Bible cover to cover and never tire of hearing him speak.

"Atlanta, wasn't it? And you may call me just plain Josephine."

"There isn't anything plain about you, Josephine," he said, giving her a wink. "And you have a fine memory for details."

She smiled at the compliment. *Isn't he the charmer!*

"I'm not sure how much you follow the political goings on in the country," continued Michael, "but you know Georgia seceded from the Union just months before the war started, correct?"

"I'd heard something of it. My father speaks of politics incessantly, to the point where I let things slip in one ear and out the other. And when Hubert joins in, I make my escape through the nearest exit," she confessed.

He gave her a smile.

Those teeth! Could the man be any more perfect?

"I understand that politics may be a bit dull for a woman of your sensibilities," said Michael.

Did he just call me a woman? It was nice to be considered a grownup and not the little girl that he once knew. She was practically an adult anyhow. It was only six months and four days until her eighteenth birthday. With any hope, the war would be over by then and her coming out party could go on as planned. It would be horrid to be a debutante with no beaus to which she could be presented.

She and her friends had been planning their cotillion since freshman year at Georgetown Academy for Young Ladies. The women's society in Washington, D.C., hosted the event to introduce girls from prominent families to polite society. It always took place at the finest hotel in the city and it included young ladies from the District of Columbia whose fathers were ambassadors, diplomats, governors, business owners or even cabinet members at the White House, like her father. In addition, the finest young ladies from Europe were invited, including princesses, countesses and baronesses.

Josephine heard Michael saying something about the war but darted back to her own thoughts. The cotillion was by invitation only. Debutantes were recommended by previous debutantes or their parents, with the final selection made by the hostess. Preceding the ball were a number of events, such as dinners and parties for the debutantes, not the least of which was the bachelors' brunch. When the day finally came for the ball, each debutante would be escorted by two men: a cadet from West Point and a civilian.

Wouldn't that be something if Michael could be my escort? To heck with having some lowly cadet escort her. She could walk in on the arm of an Army first lieutenant. The fact that he was an officer in the *Confederate* Army could be an issue, but she would find some way to work around that. Or her father would. The man never said no to his little girl when she was *gravely* serious about something.

Oh, my goodness, Michael must think I'm a dolt. Josephine willed herself to stop staring at his visage and focus on his words.

He stopped speaking, as if waiting for an answer.

Josephine scrambled to come up with something to reengage in the conversation. "Uh, speaking of politics, I know you're from the South, but surely after spending as much time as you did with Hubert and George Armstrong Custer, and having tutelage from the fine Union officers at West Point, you must have given some thought to defending the Union. How was it that you chose not to fight on the right side?"

"Who's to say that I'm not fighting on the right side?" asked Michael in a mocking tone. "It's somewhat subjective, is it not?"

"Perhaps from your perspective, Michael," answered Josephine. "Anyhow, I would imagine after graduation you left New York to join a Georgian regiment. How did you happen to find yourself a prisoner so far from where you started? My understanding is that the warfront has shifted back to your state."

"That's a very good question, Josephine. But the tale is somewhat long and probably would take up more time than you have to spare this day. Perhaps *you'd* like to share the story of how you came to be in this very spot in which I happen to be incarcerated."

She was more than happy to relay the story of how she landed on his doorstep. There was plenty of time. After dropping off the last bag in the wash building, she had told Agatha that she was going to go into the main building to get a little relief from the heat and have something to slake her thirst. Keeping Michael engaged in conversation would serve both purposes — she could drink in more of his handsome visage and she could escape the heat of the god-forsaken wash house.

Chapter XIV

Michael wished that he could slow time down. Listening to Josephine describe the years leading up to their first encounter was music to his ears. He could just imagine what a cute little thing she must have been as a child. From what Hubert said, she could get away with murder. Her classic pouty face was all it took for her parents to cave in to her demands.

Considering that her father was a brigadier general, that tidbit of information surprised him. More than likely, though, he never faced someone on the battlefield as determined as his daughter once she set her mind on something.

From a distance, Michael heard the dinner bell ring. Just hearing that made his stomach rumble. The activity around him ceased, conversations turned to mumbling, and the men shuffled to the door, forming a line.

Josephine looked at him questioningly. "Do you need to go?"

"I've got a few minutes. Where were you again?"

"And then there was the time when my friends and I decided to play a trick on our neighbors."

Michael could've stood next to this portal for hours, listening to her sweet voice. A face-to-face conversation with a woman who was not only attractive, but highly amusing as well, was more than he could've ever wished for in his situation.

"The folks who lived in the opulent houses on our street had fancy double front doors, so we'd sneak up to the porch after dark and tie the handles of the two doors together with string, then we'd knock and run to hide behind the nearest bushes. The man of the house or one of the male servants would attempt to open the doors and when they couldn't, it inevitably led to frustration."

She paused. "That was one way to expand a young girl's knowledge of the English vocabulary," said Josephine with a laugh. "Who knew that such fine, upstanding men could out-swear sailors? It was all in good fun until one day. We were up to our usual shenanigans, and the gentleman who was attempting to open the doors got mad. The more he cussed, the louder our giggles got. That fellow got the last laugh, though. Before we knew what was happening, he burst out the back door of his house and raced toward the foliage in which we were hiding. We took off like scared jackrabbits. Thank goodness hoop skirts weren't in style yet, or we would have gotten the whipping we deserved. After that experience, we changed our ways."

Michael noticed the line of men snaking out of the room and put his hand over his midsection to quiet his stomach. "Oh, you decided to forsake the life of a hoodlum?"

Josephine tilted her head and looked up at him with sparkling eyes, which he noted were the same green as the Atlantic Ocean on a stormy day. And a perfect match to the dress adorning her trim figure.

"No. When I said, 'Changed our ways,' I literally meant, 'Changed our ways.' We came up with other pranks that had less risk of bodily harm. Have you ever heard of the pouch trick?"

This girl could have given me a run for the money back in the day. Of course he had heard of the pouch trick. As a matter of fact, he and his younger brother and their friends thought they'd invented it. But he didn't want her to stop speaking so he acted as though this was all new to him.

"The pouch trick, you say? What was that all about?"

"I know you need to leave, so I'll make this quick," said

Josephine. "It was simple enough. We had a small coin pouch and we tied a piece of sewing thread to the handle. When there was a lull in traffic on our street, we would place the purse along the edge of the road. Inevitably a person would come by and bend over to pick it up. Meanwhile, we'd hide behind the shrubs on the other side of the street. When the person put their hand out to grab the pouch, we would jerk the line and the pouch would fly out of their reach."

She sighed, obviously relishing the memory. "I can still see their astonished visages. Thank goodness none of our neighbors had weak hearts."

"That is fortunate," said Michael. "But if someone would have had a heart attack, would that not have made you feel guilty?"

"'Survival of the fittest,' as they say," she responded matter-of-factly.

He doubted that she would have really been so callous, but he enjoyed her impish spirit. Not only that, he was impressed that she was versed in the works of Charles Darwin and his book *On the Origin of Species*. Or perhaps the adage was in vogue now since Herbert Spencer coined the phrase in his tome *Principles of Biology*.

Either way, he immensely enjoyed spending time in her presence. She had such an infectious energy about her. But, when the last man shuffled out the door of the bunk area, he had to make his goodbyes. He reached his hand out to hers. She hesitated but then placed her hand in his and gave him a firm handshake.

"Thank you, miss," he said, his fingers lingering over hers. "It's been a pleasure."

"The pleasure has been all mine, Michael."

She paused, her eyes downcast. "I must apologize for monopolizing our conversation."

"Nothing to apologize for, Josephine. Your stories were entrancing."

"I'm sure that you have tales to relay as well, Michael. Perhaps we can arrange to meet again at this same spot tomorrow?"

He cringed inside. There was no guarantee that he'd be here tomorrow. His mission was accomplished. Any day now, he'd be moved to a different prison.

Realizing that he was still holding onto Josephine's hand, Michael reluctantly let go, relishing the smooth, fair skin and perfectly manicured nails. His hands were rough compared to hers. She didn't seem to mind though.

Doing his best to come up with something noncommittal, Michael replied to her request. "That's an outstanding idea, Josephine. I can't make any promises, but if I can be here, I will. Hopefully you'll be able to break free from your duties."

"Oh, I can guarantee that I'll be here," said Josephine with a note of surety. "What can they do if I leave my post? Fire me? Demote me? Dock my pay? I think not." She shrugged her shoulders. "Such is the life of a humble volunteer."

Michael did his best to hold back a guffaw by pretending to suppress a cough. *If she wasn't already committed to her volunteer duties, this little lady could have a fine career as a stage actress. There was no stopping that firecracker.*

She'd be a tough one to corral, but he'd love to give it a shot. Life would never be dull with a spirited gal like her by his side.

However, some things were not meant to be and Michael didn't want to give Josephine any ideas and have her develop feelings towards him. The chance of them setting eyes on each other again was slim to none.

He politely bade her good evening. After she was out of sight, he hustled out the door to catch up with the tail end of the line heading to the mess hall.

During the meal, the other soldiers were as boisterous as usual, but Michael was lost in thought. Why would God show him a glimpse of heaven with that angel Josephine if there was no chance of pursuing a relationship with her?

Was this some sort of purgatory he had to live through in atonement for his sins? He'd always tried to keep to the straight and narrow path, but Lord knew, over the course of his life, he'd missed the mark more times than he could count. And then there were all those men who died on the battlefield at his hand...

It pained him to consider, but maybe he and Josephine weren't meant to be together. His shoulders drooped and he let out a sigh. Perhaps God was sending them separate ways so they could travel the paths that He chose for them — whether it was to their liking or not.

Chapter XV

Josephine would have skipped back to the wash house if she could've done it without looking childish. She had been infatuated with Michael since the moment she first laid eyes on him at West Point. To have an adult conversation with him for nearly an hour was more than she could have wished for. He was so attentive and seemed fascinated to learn more about her. She would have stayed there all day if he hadn't been forced to go to the mess hall.

When she stepped into the room, Agatha glanced up from the kettle of laundry she was stirring and gazed at her quizzically. Josephine brushed it off, crossed the room with her head held high, grabbed her reticule from the peg on the wall and turned to face the older woman.

"I'm off," Josephine said breezily.

Agatha's eyes widened in surprise. "But you just got back. I was ready to send the guard after you, seeing as I haven't seen you since early afternoon."

"No need to worry about me; I can take care of myself."

"I'm sure you can, miss," Agatha nodded towards a pile of laundry, "but the laundry can't. Were you intending to finish the job before you left?"

"No," said Josephine bluntly. "Those clothes aren't going anywhere. I'll be back in the morning. Meanwhile, I don't want to keep my driver waiting." She turned and walked out the door.

Josephine swore that she heard Agatha mumbling under breath, "But you had no problem keeping me waiting." Choosing to ignore the rude remark, she headed towards the main building so she could meet Charles in the front entryway.

As she expected, he was awaiting her arrival. At least the man never complained. Either he was so accustomed to what the Bigelow family referred to as "Josephine Time" or Brigadier General Bigelow paid him enough that he didn't mind biding his time watching for the young lady who, as it was widely known, took forever and a day to get going, regardless of where she needed to be.

After Charles perched her upon the buggy seat, Josephine laid her head back against the horsehair cushion and relived every moment of the previous hour. She wasn't born yesterday — she knew when a man was showing interest in her. Michael displayed all the signs, such as asking sincere questions about her youth and keeping his alluring deep blue eyes locked on hers.

She hadn't had time to expand on her reasons for being at Old Capitol Prison, but after she shared her story with him tomorrow, it would be the perfect segue to ask how he came to be there. Would it make sense for a person doing a secret exposé to let one of the subjects know her true objective? She would have to decide if Michael could be trusted or not. *For goodness sakes, the man was named after an archangel. How could he be anything less than trustworthy?*

Tomorrow being Friday, it was the last day of the work week for Josephine. Over the weekend, she certainly wouldn't miss the drudgery of laundry work, but she would miss the chance to see Michael. That thought made her determined to make the most of her time with him when they had their next *tête-à-tête*. If she could find an excuse to stop by the prison on Saturday, she would, but that would be difficult to pull off since her father was generally home that day.

Josephine spent her evening lounging on the fainting sofa in her bedroom. She wrote notes in her journal with the new fountain pen that she had talked her mother into buying for her. Transcription took a while since she had two days' worth of memories to record. She had been too exhausted after her first day of volunteering to pen anything.

Of course, she mostly wrote about the dashing Michael, whom God had thought fit to bring back into her life. If she had the artistic skills that her mother and brother possessed, she would draw a sketch of him. But she could do no justice to the man with the muscular build, lean hips, long legs, the shock of dark brown hair that graced his head with its hints of auburn highlighted by the sun, the dazzling blue eyes, the stubble of a beard that gave him a roguish demeanor, and the wickedly handsome smile.

But no likeness, regardless of how skilled the artist, would rival seeing Michael in the flesh. After even such a fleeting amount of time together, Josephine found herself head over heels for the man. His only flaw was the gray uniform he wore.

"Oh, bother," she said out loud before a sigh escaped her lips. *Why did he have to go and join the Rebel Army?* In actuality, Josephine couldn't care less what color uniform he wore. She was sure he would be as handsome in blue as he was in gray. However, she had a feeling that her father would not be so forgiving.

What if the feelings she sensed from him were true? The platonic relationship that they shared had blossomed into friendship quickly enough and had soon after evolved into infatuation — at least for Josephine. If she played her cards right, she was convinced she could use her womanly wiles to get him to fall in love with her.

Someday they could say that their romance began at that lowly prison window. *La fenêtre d'amour*, the window of love. She needed to include that in her book, so she wrote down the words and doodled small hearts around them.

She was certain of one thing. For her plot to unfold

properly, she had to keep him in her sight. Or more like sights, if one were to use the analogy of a hunter bagging one's prey. *Ooh, that would be clever phrasing should I choose to write a romance novel!*

At that moment, that notion appealed to her. After two days of volunteering in the prison, she was bored of the whole thing. But she would never tire of thinking about that specimen of a man, the first lieutenant. The gears started spinning in her head. The whole exposé didn't appear to be panning out, so she would start a romance novel and use a character based on Michael for her protagonist. *Now that is research I will relish doing.*

Pursing her lips and furrowing her brow, Josephine couldn't help but consider the biggest impediment to her and Michael beginning a real courtship. Why had he committed himself to President Jefferson Davis, the man who fancied himself commander in chief of the Confederate States of America?

She had a variety of tricks up her sleeve, but even she couldn't think of anything that would convince her father to bless such a union. Her mother would be amenable to anything that made Josephine happy but, for some reason, her father thought he knew what was best for her.

Various scenarios played through her head of introducing her father to Michael or, rather, re-introducing her father to Michael. After all, they had met at Hubert's graduation. Of course, at the time, all the young men wore identical full-dress gray jackets and cross belts, so their allegiances were not on display. Her father spoke highly of Michael that day with his class rank and having his pick of assignments to start his military career.

Brigadier General Bigelow made it no secret that he wanted Michael to do the right thing and join the side of preserving the Union. The young man, as polite as he was, listened respectfully to his superior officer yet remained noncommittal.

At least that gave Josephine an angle with which to start. She was relatively sure that her father would remember Michael, as the two had conversed for several minutes that day: first as part of a group of several graduates and their families and then privately apart from the crowd.

As busy as her father was, she doubted he had any idea what path the young man chose to follow once he left the academy. Assuming that Michael survived his stint at Old Capitol Prison — and Josephine saw no reason he wouldn't, and assuming that he fell for her — and again, she saw no reason that he wouldn't, they just needed to bide their time until the war came to a conclusion. After that, Josephine would strongly encourage Michael to pay her a formal visit at their house and start off their courtship on the proper foot with her father.

Mrs. Bigelow would be thrilled that Josephine had finally settled on one beau and could cut ties with all the other fellows who had pursued her. With the thought of planning one of the grandest weddings the city of Washington, D.C., had ever seen, the woman would welcome Michael with open arms.

Thinking of arms, considering that her father kept firearms in open view at their house, Josephine thought it best that this meeting be conducted with the young man dressed in civilian clothing.

She had a feeling that Michael would be just as dashing, maybe even more so, wearing the latest in fashionable men's attire. The thought of him dressed in checked trousers with a matching vest adorned with a pocket watch, a fitted jacket, a narrow silk tie, and a jaunty top hat as the finishing touch, nearly made her swoon.

Chapter XVI

As he stood in line waiting to get stew ladled into his tin mug, Michael mused about his encounter with Josephine. He finally broke out of his reverie when he sensed that someone was staring at him.

In the far corner of the room, a soldier leaning against the wall looked his way. Michael acknowledged the man with a slight nod. The solider then glanced toward the bench situated next to the rough-hewn wooden table in front of him.

After thanking the woman who dished up his meal, Michael crossed the room. He reached under the bench, with the premise of pulling it away from the table. His hand grazed something wedged between the wood slats. He pulled out a slip of paper and discreetly slid it into the pocket of his coat.

With that done, he sat down, took a sip of the stew and watched as more prisoners stepped into the room. The tables were filling up and an unfamiliar man took a seat on the bench near him.

"First Lieutenant Michael McKirnan," Michael said, holding his hand out to the soldier. "Don't think we've had the pleasure of meeting yet."

The man shook his proffered hand. "Second Lieutenant Joshua Brown, First Corps, Army of Northern Virginia, sir."

"Longstreet's Corps," said Michael knowingly. "Were you involved in the Battle of the Wilderness?"

"Involved is one way to say it. More like fighting for my life for three solid days," he replied.

"Sounds like your men went through hell and back. I'm

surprised anyone survived."

"You and me both, sir." The man gave a nod and tilted his mug back to swig down some of the stew.

"I've heard bits and pieces about the battle. You were engaged with Lieutenant General Ulysses S. Grant, isn't that so?"

"Yes, sir. I know this story through and through as I was tasked with recording the details for my commanding officer. He wasn't much for writing. From what I was told, Grant was attempting to move his men through the underbrush near Spotsylvania but Robert E. Lee outsmarted him and sent two of his corps on parallel roads to intercept him. May 5, Major General Couverneur K. Warren's Union V Corps attacked our Second Corps, commanded by Lieutenant General Richard Ewell, on the Orange Turnpike."

He paused a moment to wipe his mouth with his sleeve. "That same afternoon, Lieutenant General A.P. Hill ran headfirst into Brigadier General George W. Getty's VI Corps and Major General Winfield S. Hancock II's Corps on Orange Plank Road. The fighting was something fierce, especially as both sides were trying to maneuver in the dense woods. It was a draw that day."

"Is that so?" said Michael.

"The next morning at dawn, Hancock attacked along Plank Road, surprising the heck out of Hill's Corps. But, Gen. James Longstreet's First Corps arrived in time to prevent the collapse of the Confederate right flank. Longstreet followed up with a surprise flanking attack from an unfinished railroad bed that drove Hancock's men back to the Brock Road. Unfortunately, we lost momentum when Longstreet was wounded by his own men."

"Just tell me that you weren't the one that winged him," said Michael.

"I'd say not or my keister would be parked in a

Confederate brig, not in this here Union boarding house."

"That would have made you quite the celebrity around here." Michael laughed.

"I'd prefer to make a name for myself shooting Union generals, not my commanding officers," Joshua answered.

"You have a point there. What happened next?" Michael leaned forward, intent on hearing every tidbit.

"That evening Brigadier General John B. Gordon attacked the Union right flank, which caused quite the fuss at Union headquarters. But the lines stabilized and fighting ceased. On May 7, Grant disengaged and moved to the southeast. From what I heard, he intended to leave Wilderness to put his army between Lee and Richmond. Of course, that led to the bloody Battle of Spotsylvania Court House."

"Isn't that something?" Michael shook his head. "Sounds like the toll was heavy on both sides. Are they still fighting out there?"

"Last I heard they were, but when they cornered us after Wilderness, me and a group of my buddies surrendered. It was either that or be driven back and suffer the fate of so many other men from our corps. Some eight hundred men... burned to death. Brush fires raging all around us. They couldn't... crawl away." He dropped his gaze and pressed his lips together. Then he glanced up and said in a raspy voice, "It's a scene I'll never forget."

"Good God," said Michael. "I'm so sorry." The brutality of the situation nearly overwhelmed him. He took a moment before resuming the conversation. "I'm glad you made it. I know you don't want to be here. Nobody does. But if you have to bide your time as a guest of Uncle Sam, here's just as good a place as any."

"I guess. How long have you been here?

"Couple months."

"Don't look no worse for the wear. I'll tell you one thing," he said, pointing to the mug in Michael's hands, "the prisoners here get better chow than the guys out in the field, that's for dang sure. Didn't know men could exist on beans and weak coffee for months on end, but I was proved wrong."

"It's amazing what a man can do when he has to."

"What unit were you with?"

"18th Arkansas Infantry Regiment, 3rd Confederate Infantry, Company B, under the command of Major General Thomas C. Hindman. Not sure if you're familiar with him, but he had quite the background coming into the war. He was a lawyer, a United States Representative from the 1st Congressional District of Arkansas and was working his way up the ranks of the Union Army before he saw the light and joined up with Lee."

"You've seen one general, you've seen them all," said Joshua wryly. "So, where'd they get you?"

"It's not as dramatic as your tale. After we fought at Ringgold Gap, I was given a four-hour leave to go into Atlanta to see my family."

He paused as he recalled that fateful decision. "Unfortunately, a Union regiment was heading south out of the city to rendezvous with a regiment coming in from the east and there I was, sandwiched between them. There was no place to hide. Just farmland around me as far as the eye could see."

"I can imagine them soldiers were as surprised to see you as you were to see them," said Joshua. "Being a first lieutenant and all."

"Those two bars on my sleeve saved my neck," said Michael, pulling on his collar. "I'm not sure what the going exchange rate is for first lieutenants now, but I imagine there was some calculating going on when they nabbed me."

"So, does that mean you'll be traded for a Union officer?"

"That was the plan," said Michael. "That's why they

shipped me up here. But the exchange has been delayed. Either communications have broken down between the two sides or Lee doesn't have enough bait to get Grant to the negotiation table."

He paused and tilted the mug to his lips to have another swallow of stew.

"Well, at least you have some chance of getting out of here," said Joshua. "I'll be rotting in this place until the war ends. God knows how long that'll take. Thought for sure we'd have those gutless Federal soldiers whupped by now. If we had the same resources they had, we'd have chased those pansies up to Canada by now."

Michael nearly spit his coffee out. He cleared his throat and said, "You got that right." Pushing back from the table, he made his excuse to leave.

"It was a pleasure meeting you, Lieutenant Brown."

"Same here. Hope they get something worked out for you soon, so you can get back on the field and show those Yanks what we Southern boys are made of."

"I'm confident that day is drawing near. Still have some fight in me, that's for dang sure." With that said, he made his way to the door.

Gutless pansies? Not long ago I was saying that very same thing. A man's perspective certainly changes when he's had the chance to experience war from two sides.

Chapter XVII

Josephine would never admit it to her father, but she couldn't wait to go back to the prison. Of course, it wasn't because she enjoyed volunteer work or felt some sort of fulfillment doing manual labor. She was anticipating talking to Michael again.

Heat or no, she had Cecilia dress her in one of her prettiest frocks. It was rose colored with three-quarter-length sleeves, a princess waist, and an embroidered lace collar.

She sat patiently while the girl plaited her hair in an intricate series of tiny braids. A fresh-picked daisy from her mother's flower garden tucked behind her ear was the finishing touch. Josephine dabbed rose water behind each earlobe, inside her elbows and on each wrist before departing from her bed chamber.

She whistled as she descended the stairs to the main level of the house. Spotting her mother in her usual seat by the dining room table, she strolled over and placed a kiss on the woman's cheek. "Good morning, Mother," she said cheerily before taking her own chair.

It took a moment for Mrs. Bigelow to respond. She eyed her daughter suspiciously.

"You haven't gotten into my sherry again, have you?"

"Mother," said Josephine with an air of feigned shock. "Why on earth would you ask such a question? Even if I ever were to touch that evil liquid again, it wouldn't be at seven o'clock in the morning. Besides, it would be completely inappropriate to imbibe in libations when I'm due at the prison soon."

She regarded her mother and shook her head as if reprimanding her for suggesting such a thing. "Can you imagine the talk amongst the staff if I were to start off my day with the smell of spirits on my breath? I'd never be able to show my face there again."

"Magdalene," Mrs. Bigelow called toward the kitchen.

"Yes, ma'am," the woman replied. She hurriedly made her way into the dining room.

"Who is this young lady sitting next to me?" the older woman asked, her brow furrowed.

The servant opened her mouth and no words came out for a couple of seconds. "Well, I, uh... Miss Josephine?"

"She may look like Josephine, but this isn't the Josephine I know."

Magdalene shrugged her shoulders and held her hands palms up. Josephine stepped in to save the woman from her distress. "Mother, you're such a silly goose." She turned and motioned towards the servant. "You may be dismissed, Magdalene. As you can see, it truly is me. Mrs. Bigelow was just being facetious. Weren't you mother?"

"The Josephine that I know neither whistles nor converses before eight o'clock in the morning, unless she's walking in her sleep. What's gotten into you, daughter?"

Josephine waited for Magdalene to vacate the dining room before replying. Not that it mattered. She had no doubt that the woman would keep her ear to the door to see how the conversation unfolded.

When the door swung shut behind the servant, Josephine answered. "I'm just in a cheerful mood, Mother. You can't fault me for that, now can you?"

The woman tilted her head down and perused her daughter. "For the last two days, I've heard nothing but complaints from you about the working conditions to which you've been subjected at the prison. What has brought about this sudden change in attitude?"

Josephine did her best to demonstrate a benevolent attitude. "I had a lot of time to gather my thoughts last night, and I've decided to view my situation differently. Does the Bible not say that we are creatures of free will? We have the power to choose our attitude no matter what happens in our lives. I've decided to adopt a more positive outlook on life."

Mrs. Bigelow pushed herself up to a standing position, slid her chair back and approached Josephine. Bending over to peer at her closely, she gently touched the back of her hand to her daughter's forehead and then to each of her cheeks.

"Hmm, no fever from what I can tell. But, to be certain, you should stay home from the prison today, and we'll have Dr. Hammond stop over and take a look at you."

Had this happened even one day earlier, Josephine would have eagerly accepted such an offer. But circumstances had changed dramatically for her in the last twenty-four hours.

"Mother, I'm perfectly healthy, thank you," she said breezily before brushing the woman's hand from her cheek. "As enjoyable as it has been chatting with you, I need to make my departure now. I don't want to be late."

"You're not helping your case," her mother chided.

"Nonetheless, I need to fly. Charles is waiting for me."

With that, she grabbed a buttered biscuit and two pieces of bacon from her plate, then turned and hurried toward the two-story entryway. Spying the buggy outside, she walked through the door and pulled it firmly shut in case her mother had any thought of following her.

"Is it a crime for a person to be jolly?" she asked under her breath. Charles gave her a sideways glance as he assisted her into the brougham.

I'm just glad that I hid my journal before I came downstairs this morning. The apple didn't fall far from the tree. If she were her mother, she'd be searching for clues, and a journal would be the first place to check.

When Josephine arrived at the prison, she immediately went to the wash house and jumped into the morning routine. She held her whistling in check, not wanting to be subjected to more grilling.

Time passed quickly enough and before she knew it, Agatha was sitting down to eat her midday meal: a thick piece of homemade bread smothered in butter. Josephine had a standing invitation to eat with the officers, so she excused herself to meet with them. The men had told her that the courtesy was extended to her out of deference to her father, who was their commanding officer, but she knew otherwise. Who could blame them for wanting to add a little sunshine to their bland routine? It must have been dreadfully monotonous. Unless a hanging was scheduled. Apparently, that stirred things up a bit around the grounds. She was all for excitement, but that kind of stimulation she could do without.

After Josephine finished her meal with the soldiers, she folded her napkin and put it by her place setting. A general immediately rose to his feet and came up behind her to assist her from her chair. The other men in the room stood as well, and then each politely bade her farewell.

Since it was her third day on the premises, she was allowed to meander about on her own throughout the day. All the guards were familiar with her at this point. They greeted her either with a nod or a verbal acknowledgement as she went from one part of the building to the next.

Walking down the hall leading away from the officers' dining room, she slowed as she reached the intersection. Rather than turning left to go to the back of the building, she turned right and walked to the large foyer. Giving a bedazzling smile to the guard on duty, she proceeded out the front door.

As she had yesterday, she went to the corner of the building and approached the barred window of the ground-floor prison cell. She stood on her tiptoes to peek in. Like bees to nectar, men immediately were drawn to the portal.

"May I be of assistance to you, miss?" asked a man who managed to muscle his way to the front of the group. By this time, half a dozen soldiers stood with their faces framed by the window.

"I desire to speak to the first lieutenant. Would you be kind enough to fetch him?"

"Which first lieutenant would you be referring to, miss?" asked one man.

"Is there more than one first lieutenant sharing this bunk area?" she asked, unable to hide her surprise.

"Actually, miss, there aren't any first lieutenants in this cell," another soldier said.

"You must be mistaken, sir. I spoke with a man of that rank at this very window yesterday."

"That may be true, but there's no one of that rank here today. But I'd be more than happy to step in for him, if you'd care to chat."

"I would think not, soldier," Josephine said indignantly. "I have not come here to shoot the breeze with any Johnny Reb. My business is with that particular officer."

"That fellar ain't here," chipped in another fellow. "He done left early this morning."

"Left? Where did he go?" she asked in exasperation.

"Got me, purty lady."

Josephine whirled around in frustration and stomped her way back into the building. Calls from the men came to her ears as she retreated.

Of all things! She tried to imagine where Michael could have gone. Soldiers aren't just released on a whim in the middle of a war. As a higher-ranking officer, he wouldn't have been reassigned to a room with the foot soldiers. He seemed healthy enough when she saw him last, so she couldn't imagine that he'd be in the infirmary.

As she was wont to do when faced with a dilemma,

Josephine turned to prayer. She wasn't sure if it was appropriate or not, but she called out to a saint to whom she had prayed many a time — usually when searching for a lost reticule or bauble of some sort. *Saint Anthony, Saint Anthony, please look around, there is something* — make that someone — *lost that can't be found.*

Chapter XVIII

"The crow flies at dawn." The message, although faintly printed, had been clear to Michael. There was no packing to do as everything he owned was on his person. He needed only to stay awake and be ready to leave when the guard beckoned him from the bunk area.

When the summons came, Michael followed the guard out of the room. His departure was noticed by some of the other inmates, but no alarm was raised; men came and went from the prison every day.

He knew that firsthand. He'd been in and out of his share of them over the last six months, gathering intelligence. Walking one pace in front of the guard, he ticked them off in his head.

First, it was Fort Delaware, on Pea Patch Island in the Delaware River. Some eleven thousand men were housed there. According to the *Philadelphia Inquirer*, the island "contained an average population of Southern tourists, who came at the invitation of Mr. Lincoln."

Apparently, President Lincoln extended the courtesy to federal convicts, political prisoners and privateer officers as well. Because the structure was originally used as a harbor defense facility, the first inmates were housed in empty powder magazines inside the fort.

Thankfully, by the time Michael arrived, construction was complete on the enlisted prisoners of war barracks, known as the bull pen, and the officers' quarters, where he was assigned.

One of the guests who stayed there before him was the infamous Confederate officer Brigadier General Johnston Pettigrew. He'd been severely wounded at the Battle of

Seven Pines in 1862. A Minie ball from a Union sharpshooter damaged his throat, windpipe and shoulder. While lying wounded, he received another bullet to the arm and was then bayoneted in the right leg. He was imprisoned at Fort Delaware but two months later was back on the battlefield. Last year, a Union cavalryman shot him in the abdomen at close range. He was transported to the southern bank of the Potomac — he refused to be left in Federal hands. He died three days later.

Michael got out of Fort Delaware in decent shape, just before a smallpox epidemic hit the prison. Between that and inflammation of the lungs, typhoid, malaria, scurvy, pneumonia, and the wicked skin disease St. Anthony's Fire, hundreds of prisoners died.

The guard motioned for Michael to take the stairway to the second floor. As he ascended the steps, he wondered where his next destination was. Operatives were never sent to the same place twice, so he knew he wasn't being shipped to Chicago, Illinois.

Last winter, he was holed up there at Camp Douglas. After the Union Army victory at the Battle of Shiloh, the number of prisoners swelled to nearly nine thousand. By the time Michael got there, the conditions in the camp were deteriorating. With scant heating materials, it was frigid most of the time, the yard was essentially unpatrolled, the barracks were crowded and unventilated, and the stench of decaying food and human waste hung in the air.

With all the men in the camp, it wasn't easy for Michael to concentrate on the task that he had been sent there to do. He worked on honing his listening and observation skills and eventually mastered the art of extracting information from unsuspecting marks.

At the end of the hallway on the second floor, the guard came to a halt and pulled a skeleton key from his pocket. He unlocked the paneled door and told Michael to step inside.

The room was empty, except for five bare cots.

"Wait here," the man said.

Michael took a seat on the nearest cot. *A cup of coffee would go down pretty well about now.* That made him think of the one thing that he missed about Camp Douglas. It had sutler stores that sold not only sugar and tobacco, but decent coffee as well. He wasn't a tobacco user, but he had always loved a good cup of coffee. Straight and black, strong enough to put a little hair on your chest, as his mother used to say.

There was no such thing as a decent tin of coffee at Camp Chase in Columbus, Ohio. But, the sheer number of men who passed through its gates made it the ideal spot for gathering intelligence.

That was his last stop before he joined the ranks at Old Capitol Prison. His military career had taken quite the turn since he was with 18th Arkansas Infantry Regiment, 3rd Confederate Infantry, Company B, but his new role suited him well. He was skillful at obtaining information, and he had a deep interest in military history, which was critical when it came time to sort through the bits of material that he gathered each day.

Michael was compensated fairly for his work. He squirreled the money away for when the war was over. From what he could glean, it wasn't that far off. Maybe less than a year.

As odd as it might've seemed, Michael enjoyed what he did: the intrigue, the sleuth work, constantly being on his guard. Other than the shoddy conditions of some of the prisons, his position presented less danger than being on a battlefield. To boot, he was advancing in rank faster than he would have been if he were in combat.

After the next assignment, he anticipated getting a second star added to his sleeve and moving up one rank from major.

United States Army Intelligence Officer, Captain Michael McKirnan, had a nice ring to it.

Chapter XIX

It was nothing short of perplexing. If all the other men were back in the assigned bunk area, where could Michael possibly be?

With little else she could do at this point, Josephine walked back to the wash house. In her mind she listed the other areas of the property, trying to think of another spot in which Michael could be situated. The prisoners were now back in confinement, so he wouldn't be in the mess hall or the prison yard. If he had some reason to be reprimanded, he might be in the front office, but she couldn't imagine a person of his character doing anything that would cause him to get in trouble.

She stopped in her tracks and pictured every area of the facility that she had been shown the day that she arrived. The other enclosures were for the prison military staff and employees. The thought of the infirmary came to mind. Was it possible that he had taken ill or been injured since she last saw him?

The only way to be assured that neither of those things had transpired would be to make a visit to the hospital quarters. So Josephine marched straight ahead. There was no way around it, she'd have to walk right past the wash house. She hoped that either Agatha wouldn't see her or that she would let her pass without calling out to her.

With a purposeful stride, Josephine headed towards the infirmary. She wanted to look confident and appear as though she was authorized to be in the area. *I just need to come up with a plausible reason for being here.* She slowed her pace to think for a moment. When put to the test, she could come up with a fib fairly easily. That's where her stage experience in the school productions came in handy. Some people called it lying. She preferred to use the term embellishing. It sounded much more sophisticated and less like something she would need to confess to Father O'Kelly.

Since she worked in the wash building, she decided to go with that angle and tell whomever she ran into first that she was sent to collect the laundry. With that decided, she stepped up to the door, turned the handle and walked into the building without knocking. Having never been in such a facility before, she wasn't sure what to expect.

The room was rather nondescript, rectangular in shape with about two dozen cots spaced three or four feet apart. To her left, on the far end of the room, an open door led to a smaller room. She could see two waist-high tables and assumed it was the surgical unit. Thankfully, that space appeared to be unoccupied.

To her right, a curtain hung from the rafters, separating another area from the main room. Below the cloth, Josephine could see the legs of several more cots. Why was that area separated from the rest?

Patients occupied seven of the cots in the main area. Some of the soldiers had obvious wounds, like the man with his head wrapped in linen and the fellow with his leg propped up on a folded wool blanket. It was early afternoon and quite warm, so most of the men rested. The two who were awake conversed with the nurses.

Josephine had never seen a military nurse before, but they appeared somewhat how she had imagined them. The year the war started, a woman named Dorothea Dix was appointed superintendent of nurses for the Union forces. She was charged with determining the standards for the women on staff. First off, they had to be at least thirty years old and plain looking. Their dresses, which the women supplied on their own, could be either brown or black without adornment — no hoop skirts, bows or ruffles. The garments had no defined waists and were covered by a plain white apron. Simple white hats completed the ensemble, covering the women's heads and keeping their hair back.

Inspecting them closer, Josephine noticed that the nurses in the room fit the bill exactly. Those two were Plain Janes if she ever saw one, or, make it two. Thank goodness she did not meet the standards that Mrs. Dix set forth for nurses. She had no desire to spend any more time in a hospital setting than necessary.

Engrossed in their conversations, the women didn't even glance Josephine's way. That gave her a minute to peruse each cot one by one to see if Michael was there. As tall as he was, that immediately eliminated the four occupants who were Napoleonic in height. Of the other three men, one had blond hair, the man with the head wound had skin much ruddier than Michael's, and the other had a full beard so, unless Michael had the ability to grow facial hair at an incredible speed, it wasn't him.

Josephine almost let out a sigh of relief but caught herself in time so that she didn't draw the attention of the other women in the room. She considered turning around and going back to the wash building right then, but she felt obligated to peek behind the curtain just to ascertain that Michael wasn't there by some chance.

She skirted her way around the cots and slipped through the space between the wall and the curtain. It was apparent why the area was cordoned off. This was the quarters for the female invalids. In the far corner lay a woman fast asleep. Her face was crimson, so Josephine assumed she had a fever, hopefully not scarlet fever, she thought as she inched closer to the wall.

There was only one other occupant in the area, and when Josephine turned her attention to the woman, she couldn't help but let out a gasp. Bruises covered nearly every inch of exposed flesh. They ranged in color from red to purple to green.

"Oh my," she said out loud, before she could catch herself.

"Does it look that bad, miss?" asked the girl in a raspy voice.

Taking a step closer, Josephine assessed the girl to determine her age and the extent of her injuries. She couldn't have been older than sixteen. It was alarming to see what she surmised was the imprint of four fingers along the left side of the girl's throat. It appeared as though someone had tried to murder her. *How do I respond to her inquiry?*

"It's really not that bad," Josephine said, grabbing the first white lie that came to her head. "I was just startled when I came across you. I didn't expect to find anyone back here."

"Are you a nurse, miss?"

It was far worse than she thought. *The beating must have affected the girl's eyesight.* "No, I'm not," Josephine replied, emphasizing each word in case the girl's hearing was impaired as well. "But, if you need one, I can go fetch somebody."

"No need to bother anyone. I was just going to ask for a drink of water."

"That's easy enough. I see a bucket and ladle on the stand in the corner. I can get you some."

"Thank you, Miss…"

"Josephine."

"Thank you, Miss Josephine."

Josephine hustled to the table and scooped some water. She did her best to keep the ladle steady as she returned to the cot.

"Are you able to sit up?" she inquired.

"I'm not sure. I haven't tried since the orderlies brought me here."

"Here, let me put my arm around your shoulder and help you get a little higher so you can drink without spilling. How does that sound?"

"That sounds fine. Thank you so much, Miss Josephine."

Balancing the ladle in her right hand, Josephine slipped her left hand between the pillow and the girl's back. The chit was so thin that she could feel her rib bones as she assisted her. Once the girl was in a sitting position, Josephine held the ladle to her mouth and let her take a sip.

A sigh escaped from the young lady's parched lips after the first swallow. When the ladle was empty, Josephine lowered the girl to the pillow. She then returned the ladle to the bucket.

The patient's eyelids were beginning to flutter, but Josephine wanted to wish her well before she left. She walked back to the cot, knelt on the floor and proceeded to fluff the feather pillow under her head so it would be more comfortable.

"May I ask your name, young lady?"

"Bernadette, Miss," she said, her voice merely a whisper.

"Bernadette? That's a beautiful name. Did you know that a young French woman a few years older than us bears the same name? She is quite famous."

"No, Miss. Not familiar with her."

The story of the girl had intrigued Josephine the moment she first heard it. She and her friends talked about it at length and tried to imagine what it would have been like to experience what she had.

"Six years ago, when she was just fourteen years old, Miss Bernadette saw apparitions of a beautiful young lady. The woman asked her to have a chapel built at a nearby garbage dump. Can you imagine?" Josephine paused to let the girl absorb what she said.

Bernadette opened her eyes wider.

"Does this sound familiar? It made the news around the world. Surely, you must have heard something of this in school."

"No, miss. I left school after sixth grade. Haven't kept up with the news since then," Bernadette admitted.

"Oh. I see. Well, let me catch you up. This event was quite significant, especially to the Catholic Church. The lady revealed herself to Bernadette as the Immaculate Conception."

The girl gave no indication that she comprehended the import of what Josephine said.

"Have you had no Church schooling either?"

Bernadette averted her gaze and shook her head slowly from side to side.

"The Immaculate Conception is the conception of the Blessed Virgin Mary. She was conceived free from the stain of original sin by virtue of the foreseen merits of her son, Jesus Christ."

"I'm familiar with Jesus. The preacher folks on the corner downtown talk about him."

"Very good," Josephine replied. "He himself was conceived by the Holy Spirit. That's why they call his mother the Virgin Mary."

"Are you saying that his mother got in the family way without having been with a man?" Bernadette asked incredulously.

Josephine nodded in affirmation.

"I never heard of such a thing. Wouldn't that be something if that's how it worked for all of us?" She let out a sigh and put a hand on her abdomen.

Josephine's eyes were drawn to the spot, and it was all she could do to keep her mouth from gaping open.

Good Lord, there was no mistaking what she saw. The girl was with child.

Chapter XX

Michael was escorted off the prison grounds and placed in a Hansom cab waiting near the gate. A Union officer sat inside the conveyance. The driver hopped on the seat and sent the team of horses pulling away at a quick pace toward the center of the city and the New Jersey Avenue Station, or the B&O Depot, as it was more commonly known since it was served by the Baltimore & Ohio Railroad.

The officer remained silent for the first few minutes of the trip. Michael wondered where he would be sent next, but he waited for the man to broach the topic. The prisons he hadn't been assigned to yet were Elmira in New York, Fort Warren in Boston, Gratiot Street Prison in St. Louis, Johnson's Island in Sandusky, Ohio, and the Ohio Penitentiary. If he had to put money on it, he would guess his next destination was St. Louis. It was closer to the front lines now that Sherman and the bulk of the Union troops had converged on Georgia.

Having never traveled that far west before, Michael was intrigued to traverse the path that Lewis and Clark covered six decades earlier to cross into the western portion of the United States during their Corps of Discovery Expedition. He had always wanted to visit the city that was known as the Gateway to the West.

Missouri was an interesting province during the war. Both the Union and the Confederacy claimed the state, so it had two competing state governments and sent representatives to both the United States congress and the Confederate congress.

The Hansom cab rolled through the city, the horses

trotting at a good pace. Old Capitol Prison was long out of view. Michael had never felt anything but relief leaving a prison before, but now... Josephine's sweet smile and the sound of her voice came to mind. It was more than just her looks that attracted him to her. She was engaging, strong-willed, clever and compassionate. He sighed and shifted his gaze to the brick road ahead, the people strolling along the walks, and the storefronts that he may never see again.

Soon enough, Michael found that his prediction about his next assignment was correct. Once they were well on their way, his escort, Captain Jeffrey Van Domelen, began briefing him on his mission at Gratiot Street Prison.

When they arrived at the train depot, Michael and the officer alighted from the conveyance, and the man grasped his elbow and guided him to the train that they would board. From all outwards appearances, Michael was a Confederate officer in the custody of a Union officer. It was a typical scenario at that busy station.

The conductor showed the two to a private car. After a thirty-minute wait, the train finally chugged out of the station. Once they cleared the city, they were able to let their guard down.

"Man, it's great to see you, Jeffrey." Michael slapped his fellow compatriot on the back.

"Likewise, Michael. How've you fared since we last saw each other?"

"Really can't complain. Considering its age, Old Capitol Prison is relatively well kept."

"Glad you liked the accommodations, Michael. Gratiot Street Prison may not have all the amenities of Old Capitol, but there's a wealth of information to be found in its walls. More Rebel officers are being shipped there every day. At this point in the war, there's bound to be some grousing about the state of the Confederate Army. You never know what information you'll pick up there."

"If you could smuggle some whiskey in with me, I bet I could get more folks to talk. Everyone sings better when their pipes are lubricated."

"And risk you getting thrown in the brig? Not worth it," replied Jeffrey.

"How about a sack of decent coffee? Heck, you'd get *me* to sing for a cup of Caribbean brew."

"Sorry, you need to go in empty-handed and come out that way as well. But, if it would make you happy, I can order a cup of coffee for you now."

"Nothing better on a hot day than a steaming cup of coffee," Michael said with a laugh. "But I'll take you up on that."

This was one of those moments where Michael felt fortunate to be traveling by train on Uncle Sam's dime. He could smell the coffee brewing. Whether the coffee beans were from Costa Rica, Mexico or Brazil, it was all fine with him. Most anything would be better than the swill he drank in the Confederate camps. He gave the Rebs credit for their ingenuity because they were known to brew coffee using everything from chicory to acorns, beans, beets, corn, cotton seeds, dandelion root, okra seeds, peanuts, peas, carrots and yams. He scrunched up his nose in distaste just remembering those wicked brews.

When the beverage was delivered, Michael sipped it slowly, enjoying the aroma and flavor. It would likely be a while before he got another decent cup of coffee. As he enjoyed the drink, the captain gave him the lay of the land at Gratiot Street Prison.

The building was a large brick structure with two wings, one of which had been a medical college for the adjoining Christian Brothers Academy. The other wing was a private residence. A three-story octagonal tower stood between the wings. The first story had been used as a recreation room and dormitory but now housed female inmates. The second story, originally the college's amphitheater, had been converted to hospital space, and the third floor had four strong rooms that could hold up to fifteen inmates each. These were the highest-risk prisoners: those sentenced to death, men with a record of escapes, and, at times, ordinary St. Louisans arrested for drunkenness, treasonous comments or for no stated reason at all.

Civilians were held up to eight weeks, after which they were brought before the provost marshal who presented them with the oath of allegiance to the United States, which they were instructed to sign without question.

Confederate prisoners not under sentence of death were put in those quarters as punishment. Michael would not be held there, thankfully, since the last thing he wanted was to be shackled. That would make his job of subterfuge markedly more difficult.

The north wing held cooking and washing facilities on the lower level, and the second level had been converted into a surgical unit, with the attic serving as the morgue. The former McDowell residence now housed guards on the second floor and a confinement area for Confederate officers on the first floor. That would be Michael's quarters.

One area of the prison that Michael hoped to avoid was the dungeon, which was used for short-term punishments. A yard ran along the western side of the prison, surrounded by a fifteen-foot-high fence. Down the middle of the yard was a walkway to separate the various groups of prisoners.

The Christian Brothers Academy was still a school. However, classes were interrupted every so often by prisoners attempting to escape by cutting through the walls in the adjoining prison. The brothers didn't side with either the North or the South, so they allowed prisoners to leave the academy unimpeded if they made it as far as their building.

Since it took a full day to reach St. Louis, Michael and his compatriot had plenty of time to catch up. Jeffrey filled him in on military operations that had transpired over the last several months, plus he talked about things going on in his personal life. He had recently met a young lady whom he believed would be his wife someday.

Michael didn't reveal anything about Josephine. He had no reason to since they had gone their separate ways. But thinking of her made him wonder how she reacted when she discovered him missing.

Trying to shake her from his mind, he thought about St. Louis. He anticipated arriving there. With more than one hundred thousand citizens, it was the largest city west of Pittsburgh and made Chicago seem small in comparison.

The train went to the end of the tracks on the Illinois side of the Mississippi River. Having no rail bridge, ferries hauled the passengers and freight across the water. While others would resume their trips and board The Pacific Railroad on the Missouri side of the river, it was the end of the line for him and Jeffrey.

The traffic on the Mississippi River was a sight to behold. According to his escort, St. Louis was the second largest port in the country by tonnage, surpassed only by New York City. A levee extended down the riverbank, and it was reported that as many as one hundred and seventy steamboats had been counted along that stretch of the river at one given time.

The most impressive sight was the stately boats, or floating palaces, as they were often called. The vessels were luxuriously appointed and constructed and furnished inside and out, using Victorian craftsmanship.

After Jeffrey escorted Michael off the ferry, they made their way to the horse car line on Olive Street. A person could get just about anywhere using the lines in the built-up portion of the city. There was also a stagecoach line headquartered in St. Louis. If the war ended while Michael was still held at Gratiot Street Prison, that stagecoach could very well be his mode of transportation back to civilian life.

He would first go to Atlanta to see how his kin fared. Sherman was on the march, and that stately city stood between him and the Gulf of Mexico. Who knew what would be left of it by the time he got there? For Sherman, contrary to what Michael learned in his years of Catholic schooling, the ends justified the means. The man would burn the city to the ground if he thought it necessary to bring the South to its knees.

Michael prayed that his family, their house and the store would be spared. If that were not the case, he would make his way west. The Santa Fe and National Rails could take a fellow to wide open spaces, from the prairies of Texas to the gold-laden mountains in northern California.

While on the horse line, Jeffrey pointed out the courthouse. The stately building made national news in 1846 when the slave Dred Scott sued for freedom for himself, his wife and their two daughters, who had all been held as slaves in free states. Every phase of the trial, including the Missouri Supreme Court hearing, was held in that building. The case was ultimately decided by the U.S. Supreme Court eleven years later, Dred Scott v. Sanford. It ruled against the Scotts, saying they did not have grounds as citizens to sue.

When the horse line finally pulled up to the neighborhood of Gratiot Street Prison, Michael was surprised by the stately homes. It was a residential neighborhood and a wealthy one, at that. Many of St. Louis' distinguished families, with loyalties on both sides of the conflict, resided here. And for now, until he uncovered the information that he was tasked to find or until the war ended, it was his neighborhood. He just hoped to find it a hospitable one.

Chapter XXI

Josephine wasn't sure what to say — a rarity for her. The girl on the cot was young. Too young to be married and, it went without saying, too young to be with child. Curiosity gnawed at her. What hand had the girl been dealt to land her in such harrowing circumstances?

She bent down and smoothed the sheet covering the girl. While she desperately wanted to remain in the area and interrogate the chit, the shadows beneath her eyes indicated her need for sleep.

"Bernadette," said Josephine softly, as she patted the girl's free hand, "I will leave you now so that you can get some rest. Would you like me to stop by at the end of my shift to check up on you?"

"You would do that?"

"Of course I would," said Josephine.

"That would be nice. I haven't spoken with another female in ages." She bit her lower lip lightly to stop it from trembling and turned her head away from Josephine. "I seem to be forever in the company of men."

While not sure what she meant by that statement, Josephine gave the girl's hand a light squeeze in a show of support. After saying goodbye, she made her way out the front door.

As she strode back to the wash building, Josephine went through several scenarios in her head that could possibly explain how that poor waif ended up in the infirmary of a military prison. It was no accident. The injuries upon her person were dealt by another human and, judging from what Bernadette said, it was a man. An animal, actually. No decent human being would abuse another so.

Instinctively, Josephine started reciting a Rosary in her head for Bernadette. Appropriately enough, it was Friday, the day one traditionally prayed the Sorrowful Mysteries of the Rosary: the agony of Jesus in the garden, the scourging at the pillar, Jesus' crowning with thorns, His carrying of the cross, and the crucifixion of Our Lord. He had been battered by unscrupulous men as well, so it seemed fitting to recite the sorrowful version of the prayers for her.

As she walked, she asked for the intercession of the Blessed Mother in Bernadette's life. By the time she had recited one decade, Josephine reached the threshold of the wash building and so she let the angels complete the rosary for her.

The afternoon flew by. Josephine did the work by rote as her thoughts flitted between Michael and Bernadette. When the men came out to the courtyard for their afternoon exercise, she peeked out the window to scan the grounds for her first lieutenant. As diligently as she searched, she didn't catch sight of him.

She wouldn't be here Saturday and Sunday, so Josephine determined that Monday afternoon she would return to where they'd last spoken and check for Michael once again. If he wasn't there on Monday, she would use the clout afforded her as the daughter of a brigadier general and ask one of the commanding officers about his whereabouts. She would get to the bottom of this one way or another.

As for the girl in the infirmary, Josephine intended to follow through on her promise to visit with her again. This could prove to be just the fodder that she needed to start her novel. Up to this point, all her other ideas had fizzled out.

But, even if the girl had no story worth novelizing, Josephine felt a tug at her heartstrings and guessed that the child could use a little company. A thought came to her. Maybe God led her to this prison for a reason. It would be lovely to think it was to become reacquainted with Michael, but perhaps there was a greater purpose for her here.

The words that the Blessed Mother spoke to the young French girl six years ago came to her mind. "I do not promise to make you happy in this world but in the other." Josephine had spent a lifetime pursuing happiness, but wasn't happiness in eternity the more noble pursuit? How does one attain such a thing? She'd give that more thought later when she had her journal at hand.

Judging from the battered appearance of *this* Bernadette, she had been through quite a bit in the last few days. If the girl would confide in her the name of the man who had thrashed her, Josephine would implore her father to send out his men to apprehend the fiend. The thought of witnessing a hanging from the scaffolding in the corner of the yard was appalling, but, in this case, it would be satisfying to see such a man get his just desserts.

When the last round of laundry was finally hung on the line, Josephine bade good evening to Agatha, stepped out of the wash building, and made a beeline back to the hospital. She had about fifteen minutes before Charles would arrive for her, so she would have to be quick about it if she wanted to get to the bottom of Bernadette's story.

Approaching the doorway, Josephine stopped, brushed her skirt down and lifted her chin in a show of authority. Opening the door, she stepped in and almost ran into one of the nurses.

"Excuse me, miss," said the woman apologetically. "May I be of service to you?"

"Thank you, but I'm fine, miss, um...ma'am." *How was one to address an old maid, again?* She was forever trying to keep the rules of etiquette straight. "I have a task to complete for the prison staff. I won't be here but a moment."

With that said, she turned away from the woman, whose eyes had widened at her remark, and made her way through the partition to the females' ward. Once on the other side of the curtain, Josephine noticed that the cot under the window was empty. Whether that was a good or bad sign, she couldn't ascertain, but as long as Bernadette was exactly where she had left her some three hours before, it was fine.

The girl was awake and stared up at the wood-beamed ceiling, apparently deep in thought.

"Miss Bernadette," Josephine called in a low voice.

The sound must have caught her off guard. She pulled back in fear.

"It's me, Josephine," she said, coming around the cot to make herself visible.

"Oh, Miss Josephine, you startled me," Bernadette said. "I must confess, I'm a bit jumpy lately."

"I can imagine," Josephine replied as she visually inspected the bruises on the girl's arm. She dropped to her knees next to the cot to be eye level with the lass. "I came back, just as I promised. Is there anything I can get for you?"

"That's terribly kind of you, but the nurse was just here to attend to my immediate needs, so I am fine for the time being."

"I'm glad to know they're taking care of you adequately."

A moment of silence lapsed between them. Josephine wanted to hear the girl's story but didn't want to seem like a snoop, so she wasn't sure how to get her to open up. Perhaps the best way was to share a bit about herself with Bernadette. Then the girl might return the favor and talk about her own life.

"It has been such a pleasure to meet you, Bernadette. I'm volunteering at the prison. Even though I was born and raised in Washington, D.C., this week was the first time I was ever in this compound."

"It sounds like we have something in common," noted Bernadette. "This is my hometown and it's my first time here as well. Actually, it's the first time I've seen the inside of any prison, to tell you the truth."

"Same here." Josephine flashed the girl a smile. It was difficult not to stare at her. She was so pretty. Even with the bruises on her face, it was apparent that she had attractive features: high cheekbones, dark eyebrows with matching dark eyelashes that framed deep brown eyes, and a dainty nose sprinkled with light freckles. The combination of blond hair and brown eyes was unusual and quite striking. It was no wonder that men were attracted to her.

Josephine had to ask the question that she'd been wondering all afternoon. "Bernadette, I think we're close in age. On the twenty-ninth of December, I will turn eighteen. How old will you be on your next birthday?"

"If my calculations are right, I'll turn seventeen in November. I'm not sure of the exact date. My mother wasn't much for numbers."

Josephine scrunched her face in disbelief. *What mother would forget the date of her own child's birth?*

"But, thanks to President Lincoln, my birthday is now a national holiday," Bernadette exclaimed.

"Really? How's that?"

"Last year the president proclaimed a national day of thanksgiving and praise for our beneficent Father who dwelleth in the Heavens, according to the preacher folks. The day of thanksgiving is to be celebrated the last Thursday in November each year. So, I decided that would be just as good of a day to celebrate my birth as any."

"How clever of you," exclaimed Josephine. "You get to commemorate your birthday on a different day every year, and the entire nation celebrates with you." It was actually so clever that she wished she had thought of it herself. *Would it be possible to amend the date on my birth certificate to New Year's Eve?* It was truly the most festive night of the year, in her opinion. She'd have to remember to research that.

"Bernadette," said Josephine, ready to steer the conversation to the topic that she'd come here to discuss, "I don't mean to sound forward, but may I ask what happened to you?"

The bruises on her face were instantly shrouded in pink.

"It's really nothing, Miss Josephine."

"*Nothing*? It's apparent that someone used you as a boxing bag. What would cause a person to treat a young lady in such a manner?"

The girl rolled her eyes upward as though searching for a plausible answer. After a moment, she replied. "It was my fault, actually."

"Your fault," Josephine exclaimed incredulously.

Realizing that the volume of her voice had risen, she leaned closer to the girl, stared straight into her eyes and whispered, "You could never have done anything to anyone that would warrant such abominable treatment as this."

A tear came to Bernadette's eye.

"But there is, miss." She hesitated before adding, "I disobeyed my man."

Josephine looked at her in shock. "Your *man* did this to you? What kind of man beats an innocent girl?"

Bernadette didn't answer.

Trying to make her words as gentle as possible, Josephine continued her questioning in a less confrontational tone. "You call this person your man. You're married then?"

"No, miss."

This time it was Josephine's turn to bite her bottom lip. "If I'm reading this picture correctly, you found yourself expecting and your *man*, the father of your child, is somehow blaming you for this predicament?"

Bernadette opened and closed her mouth and then twisted it to one side as if not sure how to answer. With an air of resignation, she blurted out. "Not exactly, miss. He doesn't blame me for conceiving the child. H-he blames me for not getting rid of the child." Tears pooled in her eyes.

The gasp that came from Josephine's lips was audible. She raised her hand to cover her gaping mouth. The only words that came to her mind tumbled out of her mouth.

"Good God, that man is dastardlier than I even imagined — he's in league with the devil."

Chapter XXII

Michael was impressed by the stately neighborhood that housed Gratiot Street Prison. As he and Jeffrey drew closer to the penitentiary, they passed the Brant Mansion, where General John C. Fremont had his headquarters.

Fremont, an explorer, politician and soldier, was quite the storied gentleman, from what Jeffrey said. During the 1840s, Fremont led four expeditions into the American West and was given the nickname The Pathfinder. The reports and maps produced from his explorations significantly contributed to massive American emigration overland into the West.

He was the first presidential candidate of the new anti-slavery Republican Party but lost the 1856 presidential election to democrat James Buchanan when the Know-Nothings split the vote. Democrats warned voters that if he were elected, it would lead to civil war. Despite the loss, the country still plunged into the war. Fremont was given command of the Department of the West by President Lincoln. After Fremont's emancipation edict, which freed slaves in his district, the president relieved him of his command for insubordination, despite the fact that Fremont was the only general to produce a Union victory in 1861. Following a brief tenure in the Mountain Department in 1862, he moved to New York and retired from the Army.

Fremont had recently entered politics again. He was currently running for president as the candidate of the Radical Democracy Party, which was an abolitionist and anti-Confederate party made up largely of disaffected radical Republicans who felt that President Lincoln was too moderate on the issues of slavery and racial equality.

As impressive as Fremont's dwelling was, it was overshadowed by the building across the street from Gratiot Street Prison, the family home of Judge Harrison, who was widely known as a southern sympathizer. The brick structure was massive and stately, just as one would imagine the home of a prominent judge would be.

As the vehicle pulled up to the corner of Gratiot Street and 8th Street, Jeffrey went over a few final points with Michael. A mix of more than two thousand people were housed in the compound. The Confederate soldiers held at Gratiot were mostly those captured during battles in the Mississippi River region or those who fought in Missouri and Arkansas and were sent north for processing before being moved to Alton Military Prison and other eastern facilities.

It was not yet determined how long Michael would be ensconced there. The only prisoners held for an extended length of time were spies, smugglers, officers found recruiting behind the lines and political prisoners.

Many of the most dangerous criminals in the Trans-Mississippi passed through the doors of Gratiot Street Prison. Some escaped in dramatically risky ways. Others who tried and failed lost their lives at the end of a Union rope or before a firing squad. Michael was determined to avoid that fate.

Squaring his shoulders, he brought himself to his full height and prepared to enter the prison gate. Michael went over the story he would share if any inmates asked about his military background and how he ended up at Gratiot Street Prison.

A good portion of the story — up through his capture near Atlanta — was true. The rest would be fabricated to protect his guise.

In reality, after he was apprehended, Michael thought that Fort Delaware would be his home for the duration of the war. He was perplexed when he was singled out one day and escorted to the prison superintendent's office. That puzzlement turned to astonishment when he walked into the room and was met by his old roommate's father, Brigadier General Matthias Bigelow.

Automatically, Michael saluted the superior officer. But, for the life of him, he couldn't figure out how the man knew that he was here and, more importantly, why he wanted to meet with him. He found out soon enough. Their conversation was short but to the point. He'd never forget it.

"First Lieutenant McKirnan," said the officer, as he returned the salute to his subordinate, "welcome back to the Union." That greeting could have been interpreted two ways, so Michael had chosen to remain silent.

His thoughts were interrupted as Jeffrey escorted him into the building at gunpoint and then directed the nose of his revolver toward the doorway of an office. "Intake."

Michael stepped past an armed guard and into a sparsely furnished room. A desk was positioned near the far wall and a dozen wooden straight-backed chairs lined the near wall.

The man at the desk glanced up when Michael and Jeffrey walked in. "Take a seat," said the harried soldier. As there was only one empty chair, Michael walked to the end of the room and took the last spot. "Paperwork?" the man asked, holding his hand out.

"Yes, sir." Jeffrey pulled a packet from the inside pocket of his single-breasted Prussian-blue coat and handed it to the officer.

"We've got it from here. You may be dismissed. Thank you."

"Thank you, sir," said Jeffrey. He saluted the man and then turned and gave a slight nod to Michael.

With eleven other prisoners in front of him, it would be some time before Michael's name was called. He tried to get as comfortable as possible on the hard seat and leaned his head back against the whitewashed wall.

The room resembled the one where he encountered Brigadier General Bigelow last December. That man possessed a booming voice but had spoken in hushed tones that day to keep their conversation private.

"You made quite the impression on me the day you graduated from West Point," said the general. "Same fire in your belly I had at your age. It was a shame I couldn't convince you to come under my command right then and there. But you were young and stubborn as the day is long. And no doubt brainwashed by those radical professors hired under Beauregard's watch."

There was some truth there, but Michael didn't say that out loud. He kept his eyes trained on the older man, wondering where the conversation was leading.

"I heard you attached yourself to the 18th Arkansas Infantry Regiment. They've got some fine men in command, including a couple fellows from my graduating class at West Point."

"Yes, sir, they do."

"That being said, you're a bright young man, and I'm going to guess you can see the tides of war have shifted substantially since you joined up."

Michael nodded in agreement.

"McKirnan, President Lincoln wants to bring this whole affair to a conclusion in the next twelve months. He is prepared to take more... aggressive action to do so."

At those words, Michael narrowed his eyes.

"I'm not going to beat around the bush, son. I've been tasked with recruiting men to act as emissaries for the Union Army. First man I thought of was you."

It took a moment for the words to register in Michael's head. "By emissaries, you mean spies."

"We prefer not to use that verbiage," said the general. "But you get the picture. We need someone to infiltrate a few key prisons and cozy up to inmates who might have information that can help us map out our adversaries' positions."

His heart began to thump so hard, Michael wondered if the general could hear it. How could the man possibly know that the idea of changing allegiances had crossed his mind?

It all went back to his brother, James. After his senseless maiming, Michael was so enraged that he was prepared to bring the war to a conclusion single-handedly if he had to. With the scales tipped in favor of the Union, he considered how he could use his military training to benefit the North.

Common sense prevailed after he realized two things. First, there was little any one man could do to make a significant impact on something as large as a civil war. Second, there was no practical way to change sides even if he wanted to.

That was until Brigadier General Bigelow made his proposition. The man looked at him as though he were staring into his soul. "Are you up for this?"

"Sir, may I have some time to think it over?"

"The fact that you didn't say no at the get-go tells me you're considering this. How about I give you the lowdown of how this process works, what our expectations are, and the benefits for you?"

"I would appreciate that, sir."

Brigadier General Bigelow spelled out in detail the assignment that he had in mind. Michael listened to the man's words but couldn't stop the questions running through his mind. Would James hate him if he sided with the army that crippled him? How would he bring himself to target the men whom had once been his comrades? Would he forever be known as the Benedict Arnold of the Confederate Army?

"You're going to have to go with your gut, son. I need a decision."

Normally, in such a situation, Michael would put paper to pen and write a list of the advantages and a list of the disadvantages to help him make a proper determination. There was no time for that now.

The general broke the silence. "To sweeten the deal, we're prepared to commission you as a captain in the U.S. Army. While in prison, you will still pose as a Confederate first lieutenant, but you will receive the pay of a Union captain."

Michael did his best to hide his surprise. He considered how to answer to the man's offer.

"I'll give it to you, you're a negotiator, McKirnan," said the general, shaking his head. He reached into his overcoat pocket and pulled out a stack of neatly folded Greenbacks and pressed them into Michael's palm. "Here's an advance."

Michael eyed the stack of bills. The bill on top had "United States" printed on the paper in green ink, a picture of Lady Liberty, and the inscription, "Payable at the Treasury of the U.S. at New York," running along the bottom. On either side of the bill it noted the denomination: twenty dollars. If all the bills were twenties, he could be in possession of a couple hundred dollars.

Mistaking his silence for another negotiating tactic, General Bigelow spoke again. "Fine. After you complete your first successful mission, you will be promoted to major. That's my last offer."

Truth be told, Michael had made up his mind before the negotiations began. As much as it went against his grain to make an unvetted decision, he did as the general suggested. He went with his gut.

Michael brought his head up and looked his superior directly in the eye. "I'm in, sir."

A satisfied grin stretched across the general's face. He gave a salute to the newly minted captain, which was returned sharply, and then took his leave. When Michael was escorted to the bunk area a few minutes later, he caught one of the guards peering his way. The man discretely tipped his cap. That was the signal he had been told to watch for.

His training began that very day. Michael's assignment was to befriend fellow prisoners and pump them for information that might be pertinent to the architects of the Union Army. In due time, he learned that if he confided something about himself to another inmate, they felt obligated to reciprocate — and fell right into his snare.

Chapter XXIII

"How on earth did that man expect you to dispose of the child?" Josephine put her hands on her hips. "Once a baby is conceived, unless there is a miscarriage, you have no other option than to let nature take its course."

"Not necessarily," said Bernadette hesitantly. "There are ways to get rid of it."

"I have never heard of such a wicked thing. While I may not know a lot about birthing, I do know that you can't just pull an infant out of the womb like a magician pulls a rabbit out of a hat. Babies arrive when they're ready to arrive."

"Miss, I'm no expert on this topic either, but there are herbs that can be mixed together" — her voice dropped to a whisper — "that will make a baby shrivel up and die inside its mother."

Josephine couldn't believe her ears. "What malevolent person would concoct something of that nature? Other than a witch doctor!"

"Not witch doctors but real doctors — or at least men who call themselves doctors."

"I was under the impression that doctors swore an oath to do no harm." Josephine shook her head in exasperation. "That is horrible! I'm just glad that you didn't do such a thing. But still, I cannot fathom why a man would want to kill his own child."

A tear trickled from Bernadette's eye and slid down her cheek and onto the pillow case.

Josephine wiped it away. "It's okay. You can tell me. I won't share this with anyone."

Bernadette cast her eyes down as the red crept back to her

cheeks. "To be honest with you, he wasn't sure it was his child."

It was a good thing that the girl was looking away because Josephine's eyes widened in shock. *This is much more complicated than I could have anticipated.* Such a scandalous tale from so young a girl. If she hadn't seen the evidence herself, she would have thought that Bernadette was making it all up.

Silence hung between them, and when the girl began to cry in earnest the only thing that Josephine could think to do was to wrap her arms around her. She held her close and rocked her back and forth, just as her mother had done for her when she was a child and inconsolable over one such slight or another. Her heart filled with compassion for the poor creature.

When the tears finally dried up, Josephine patted Bernadette on the back. "Everything will be fine."

It was obviously the wrong thing to say because the tears started again.

"Everything...won't...be...fine," Bernadette stammered. "He beat me when I wouldn't drink that vile concoction. I guess he thought he'd take care of the problem himself." Despite the heat, the girl shivered. Then she took a breath and continued. "When it became apparent that the baby was still growing inside me, he told me I had to go back to work. If I refused, he said he'd put me out on the street."

"Pardon me for asking so many questions, but are you saying that you share a residence with that man?" The story was getting darker by the minute.

The girl nodded once in affirmation.

"And your parents allow this?" Josephine asked with a disbelieving tone.

"I have no parents, miss," Bernadette said sadly. "My mother died last year, and I never actually knew my father. He passed away when my mother was carrying me. My mother told me he died a hero's death defending the Alamo alongside Davy Crockett and James Bowie."

Math may not have been Josephine's strong point, but she did a quick calculation and realized what Bernadette said could not possibly be true. The Battle of Alamo happened in 1836, nearly thirty years ago. She had no idea why the girl's mother would have concocted such a story, but she felt no need to set the matter straight and add disillusionment to the list of the girl's woes. So, she chose to go along with Bernadette's tale.

"Oh my, your father must have been quite brave," said Josephine. "It's been said that one hundred Texans held off more than fifteen hundred Mexican soldiers until the fortress was breached that fateful day."

A slight smile crossed Bernadette's lips. "Oh, he was brave. My mother was so proud of him. She also told me that he witnessed Francis Scott Key pen the poem, 'The Star-Spangled Banner,' while the British attacked Fort McHenry."

Fort McHenry? That was during the War of 1812. There was no doubt about it, the girl had been lied to. "So, your mother raised you on her own?" Josephine asked.

"Mostly. She had benefactors that supported us."

Josephine wasn't sure what she meant by that.

"Unfortunately, when she passed, I was left to fend for myself."

"I'm so sorry to hear that. What caused her death?"

"The doctor told me she suffered from sift less."

"Sift less?" The wheels turned in Josephine's head. "Do you think he may have said... syphilis?" she asked, arching her eyebrows.

"Yes, that was it." Bernadette appeared thoughtful for a moment before continuing. "Actually, I believe it was the mercury that killed her. They were using it to treat her disease."

"Oh, my goodness, that is so sad," said Josephine sincerely.

"It was difficult losing her. We didn't have an easy life, but she did what she could to raise me properly." Bernadette let out a slight sigh. "I'm anything but proper now. My mother's last benefactor took me in. He said he was going to take care of me. He was a perfect gentleman at first and I grew to trust him. But after several weeks at his house, one night he enticed me to share a drink with him. I couldn't think straight after two glasses of wine and before I knew what was happening, he forced himself on me."

Bernadette seemed like she didn't want to proceed with the story. Josephine didn't know if she wanted her to either, but the girl took a deep breath and went on. "Unbeknownst to me, an acquaintance of his was at his house that night and witnessed the act."

This story was so harrowing, it would be too disturbing to put in a book. Josephine just hoped that she would be able to block it out of her mind once she left the prison.

"After he-he stole my innocence" — her voice broke — "he told me I was tainted goods. I'd never find a man who'd want me." Bernadette turned her head away from Josephine.

A moment later, the girl picked up where she had left off, her voice barely a whisper. "But he was wrong... His friend wanted me, and since he'd seen with his own eyes what I'd done, he threatened to report me to the constable if I didn't accommodate him." Josephine pursed her lips to keep from voicing her thoughts of that despicable man.

Bernadette's thin shoulders began to shake as sobs overtook her. "O-once my benefactor realized this could be a profitable venture... h-he made me available to other men."

Josephine's blood began to boil. She stepped to the other side of the cot, knelt down and gently pulled Bernadette's hands into her own. "That horrible man took advantage of a young, innocent girl and then let other men do the same. How could he treat you so poorly?"

"Please, Miss Josephine. I don't want to paint Marcel in a completely bad light. When he's of a mind, he can be quite kind to me."

The ogre's name had slipped from Bernadette's lips. Marcel. Josephine committed it to memory. If he ever laid another hand on the girl, she would see to it personally that he was strung up.

"He took me to the dressmaker for all the pretty gowns that I have."

Josephine glanced down at Bernadette's dress. The material was as thin as tissue and the craftsmanship was sorely lacking. *I could have constructed something better than that myself.*

"Pshaw! Purchased by him to lure more males to your door, I'd wager."

"That's not necessarily so. He said a pretty girl like me needs pretty dresses. And he actually told me more than once that he cared for me."

"Cared for you?" Josephine was fuming. "Like a plantation owner cares for a slave!"

"It wasn't that bad."

Josephine shook her head. She couldn't believe the girl was defending the lout. "Not that bad? Did you have freedom? Were you allowed to be on your own or spend time with your friends?"

"I... I'm not permitted to have friends anymore," she acknowledged quietly.

That statement struck Josephine. As if the girl's life wasn't tragic enough as it was. She couldn't imagine life without the company of friends or loved ones. "Well, you have one now," said Josephine, squeezing the girl's shoulders. "And, as a friend, I want to help you. I really do."

"I appreciate that, Miss Josephine, but I don't know how you can possibly do that. When I am released, it will be into... his care. He told the staff he was my guardian."

Josephine shook her head. "We'll make other arrangements."

"Please, miss, no." Fear flashed in Bernadette's eyes and she grabbed Josephine's arm. "I appreciate your offer, but you mustn't get in the middle of this. I cannot cross him."

"You're not a possession," Josephine said firmly. "You're a human being and God has given you the gift of free will. You can do what you want with your life."

"Maybe you have the gift of free will, but I don't." Bernadette waved her hand in front of her face. "You've seen what happens when I disobey him. He told me if I ever crossed him again, he'd kill me."

If ever there was a time to stand up for a fellow woman's rights as a true feminist would, this was it. A line from Miss Alcott's speech came to Bernadette. "Strong convictions precede great actions."

"Then we'll just have to make sure that he doesn't find you."

Bernadette shook her head. "He knows every street and alley in this town."

"That may be true, but he doesn't know every street and alley in every town in the United States. Do you by any chance have relatives living in another city or state?"

"The only relative that I'm aware of is my mother's mother, but she lives halfway across the country. I haven't seen her since I was a child."

"Do you remember where she lives?"

"I'm not sure. My mother and I visited her once. We traveled by train all the way to the Mississippi River. This city was on the far banks of the river."

Josephine thought for a moment. "Was it New Orleans?

Or perhaps Memphis or Baton Rouge?"

"It wasn't in the South."

"Minneapolis?"

"That doesn't sound familiar. I remember seeing numerous boats docked by the shore. Some were brightly painted and had fancy passengers on board."

"St. Louis?"

"Is that in Missouri?"

"Yes, it is."

"That's it!"

"Fine," said Josephine with conviction. "We'll make arrangements for you to travel to St. Louis to be with your grandmother."

"After all these years, I'm not sure that she's even alive anymore," Bernadette said in a worried voice.

"If that's the case, we'll come up with another plan. At least you and your baby will be out of danger."

"Can you really get me there, Miss Josephine?"

"With a little help from my father, I can," she said confidently. "I must go now. Get some rest and something to eat so you can regain your strength. With any luck, we'll have you onboard a passenger train to St. Louis by Monday."

"I don't know how I will ever be able to thank you enough, Miss Josephine. You're the nicest person I've ever met."

She looked askance at the girl. Josephine received her fair share of compliments. Her friends, and even some of the bolder young men, admired her striking green eyes, pretty smile, and figure with curves in all the right places. But those things were all superficial. If, as they say, it's what's on the inside that truly counts, then the compliment from Bernadette was one of the nicest ones Josephine had ever received. She could only think of one way to respond.

"Thank you," she said, her voice heavy with emotion.

Chapter XXIV

When the intake process was finally complete, Michael was escorted through the main building to get to the quarters for the Confederate officers. He surveyed the facility as they walked. Jeffery's description was spot on.

In reality, if you've seen one prison, you've seen them all. Make that seen, heard or smelled. The sounds of talking, laughter and snoring came to his ears. A stale mix of cigar smoke, decaying food and body odor assaulted his nostrils.

No matter the setting, people were still people, Michael thought as he passed numerous soldiers and prisoners. The same cast of characters was in every show whether the setting was a school, church, military academy or penitentiary.

Hippocrates wrote of the four temperaments. With that knowledge, Michael found it easy to sort people by their primary characteristic, to serve his purposes.

Vocal men craved adventure and strove to be the center of attention. They were the ones always planning their great escape. In between time, they regaled the crowds with stories of their various endeavors on the field of battle. Those men were always his first mark. They loved nothing better than the sound of their own voices and, when new arrivals came in, it was a fresh audience for them.

Every setting had the nurturers, the folks who sought peace and harmony above all. How they fared in the middle of a civil war was beyond Michael. But they'd talk after they warmed up to a fellow.

Then there were the analytical types, who valued structure and authority, and the academics who lorded their superior intelligence over their peers. Getting information from either of those types was a trick. Michael could attest to that since his personality skewed that way. To his advantage, he knew what it took to get people like himself to let their guard down. If they felt they had a chance to educate someone, they'd speak up.

In the officers' bunk house, groups of men stood talking, a six-handed game of cards was being dealt, and a handful of other prisoners lounged on their cots. People barely glanced up when Michael was handed off to the guard inside the door.

"Grab a cot," the soldier said.

Michael didn't know if the beds were assigned or not, so he took the first open one. He removed his Richmond Depot jacket, folded it neatly and laid it at the head of the cot. Taking a seat, he worked to remove his Wellington boots. *What I wouldn't give for a boot jack right now.* It took some maneuvering to pull the calf-height footwear off unassisted.

No one stepped forward to introduce themselves, so Michael laid back to relax for a bit. As was usual when he had a moment to himself, his thoughts turned to Josephine. What Hippocratic temperament defined that young lady?

She's definitely one who basks in the limelight, he thought as a slight smile came to his lips. *A spitfire like that would make the perfect balance for a person of my demeanor.* He pictured her to be of the nature to jump into things with both feet and not overanalyze decisions, as he tended to do.

He couldn't help but wonder how she reacted when she realized that he was missing. Knowing her, she'd turned the place upside down searching for him. The thought made him feel a pang of guilt. If he could have told her that he was being transferred, he would have.

It was apparent that she was sweet on him. Maybe when peace finally prevailed, he could return to Washington, D.C., make his intentions known to her father, and court

Josephine properly, as a young lady of her status deserved.

In the meantime, he needed to concentrate on his assignment. Michael covertly surveyed the room, determining the ideal person to approach first.

The bell rang for supper, so Michael tucked his observations into his mind before leaving the area. He had an eye for detail and a knack for memorizing, skills which would prove to be valuable in his new endeavor.

Over the next two days, Michael encountered scores of prisoners and staff members and struck up dozens of conversations. The third night in, Michael reclined on his cot and sorted through bits of information he'd picked up since his arrival.

His ears perked up when he overheard two inmates talking about The Citadel. Apparently, one of the men was a graduate. The Military College of South Carolina was established just twenty years ago. It wasn't as old as West Point, but it had a stellar reputation for producing fine soldiers.

The information wasn't relevant to his assignment, but it was interesting to hear that fellow's memories from his four years there.

Michael thought with pride of his alma mater. West Point Military Academy was founded in 1802. The man known as the Father of the Military Academy, Colonel Sylvanus Thayer, became superintendent fifteen years later. The colonel was responsible for upgrading the school's academic standards, instilling military discipline for the cadets and emphasizing honorable conduct. His biggest contribution to the academy may have been his creation of the Thayer Method of teaching, which emphasized self-study, small class size, and daily homework — much to the chagrin of many of Michael's classmates, including George Custer Armstrong.

The foundation of the curriculum was civil engineering, thanks to Colonel Thayer. The U.S. Military Academy's graduates were largely responsible for the construction of railway lines, bridges, roads and harbors across the country over the last four decades.

The other conversation drifted off, so Michael turned to face the wall and resumed going through his own recollections.

Thayer forged many of the traditions and the culture of the academy. West Point was the predominant source of commissioned officers for the United States Army, and, times being what they were, the Army of the Confederate States of America, as well.

During Thayer's tenure, West Point was the first university in the United States to issue class rings. Michael and all his classmates had them. It showed loyalty to their school and loyalty to their brotherhood. If a West Point graduate fell during a time of war, the ring was returned to the academy and ensconced in a case with the rings of other graduates who had suffered a similar fate. Michael prayed that someday he would be able to gift his ring to one of his children — not have it enshrined on his former campus.

Out of habit, Michael felt for his ring. His hand was bare and he was glad of it. Before he joined up with his regiment, he had given the ring to his sister, Amara, for safekeeping.

He wondered if Robert E. Lee wore his ring on the field. Lee was an 1829 West Point graduate and was superintendent of the academy the year that Michael applied for admittance. By his decree, candidates had to be nominated to the academy by members of the United States Congress. Only one young man could be admitted from each congressional district. Thomas Howell Cobb nominated Michael as a prospective cadet before he left congress to take the position of Secretary of Treasury under President James Buchanan.

Michael hadn't seen the man in years, but he could still picture him in his finery, wearing his long wide-lapel jacket and matching checked trousers, meticulously starched white shirt, double-breasted vest, and a silk necktie.

Cobb was one of the founders of the Confederacy, having served as president of the Provisional Congress of the Confederate States for two weeks between the foundation of the Confederacy and the election of Jefferson Davis as president.

On the recommendation of Mr. Cobb, Michael was accepted at West Point. He began his studies there in 1857, the year the new barracks, with modern gas lighting, were built.

Life was wasn't easy at the military academy, by any means. The staff had the task of turning boys into men over the course of five years, or four in his case. With only about fifteen pupils in each classroom, the young men got ample individual attention from their instructors. The coursework was challenging and the competition fierce. The higher one graduated in his class, the better assignment he'd be offered after graduation.

A yawn escaped Michael as he thought back to his classes. Using the Thayer Method, they were assigned to go over their reading material before class, including the *New York Times*, and during class were encouraged to talk with their classmates and go in depth about the various articles or texts that they read.

They were taught to think, not just regurgitate facts. But it was more than book learning. The cadets were exposed to new ordnance and tactics training, incorporating the most current rifle and musket technology.

When they weren't in the classroom, they spent a fair amount of time on the grassy plain in front of the main hall. Each day started with physical training, then an insufferable amount of time drilling. When they weren't drilling or studying, they did ruck marches throughout the area, hiking fifteen to twenty miles at a time, wearing heavy sacks over their shoulders.

Honor and leadership were emphasized throughout their time at the academy. The first-year students had no charges under them, but when they advanced to Yearlings, they got their first taste of leadership overseeing a few Plebes. The Cows, who were a grade older, were in charge of both Yearlings and Plebes. The Firsties, as upperclassmen, oversaw all the underclassmen.

They did get some reprieve from the drudgery of life in a military academy. The students shared meals in the mess hall, and even though the Plebes were not allowed to look down at their plates, they could eat their fill. Everyone anticipated attending campus balls and parties. Young ladies from nearby colleges, including the Academy of Mount Saint Vincent, were sent formal invitations to the social gatherings, which, much to the disappointment of the cadets, were closely supervised.

Thinking of supervision, the bunk room door was swung open. *Wonder who's checking up on us now?* Out of curiosity, Michael turned to see and instantly was wide awake.

It was dark in the room, but the light from the hallway illuminated the figure of the guard in the doorway. In profile, the man bore an uncanny likeness to one of Michael's schoolmates from West Point, Edward Appleby.

The young man was a bully through and through. Between his size and his seniority, he could coerce Plebes to do his bidding, whether it was shining his boots or taking on his KP duties.

He and Michael had been about the same height, so physically Appleby didn't intimidate him, but, as an underclassman, the man was his superior.

They'd had no classes together, so, for the most part, Michael ignored him. There was no use looking for trouble. That was, unless the man pushed things too far with a fellow Plebe.

Michael went toe-to-toe with Appleby a number of times. Upperclassman or not, he wasn't going to let that tyrant physically abuse his classmates.

Appleby was smart enough to know when he met his match and, inevitably, backed down. That didn't engender feelings of admiration toward Michael, by any means.

The brute was probably enjoying a stellar career in the Union Army, Michael thought. He had the perfect disposition to be a career drill sergeant.

"Move it!" A new prisoner was hauled into the room and sent crashing to the floor by the guard. "Take a cot, maggot!"

Michael would know that voice anywhere. *God bless it!* It wasn't just a soldier who resembled Appleby, it *was* Appleby. Michael pivoted his head toward the wall. *If that man spots me, my goose is cooked.*

Chapter XXV

Josephine strode away from the infirmary. Now, in addition to wondering where Michael went, she had to worry about Bernadette. Not being one to bide her time until every duck was in a row, she immediately began to formulate a logical — make that *viable* — game plan.

By the time she got to the main building, she had something in mind. She strode to the prison superintendent's office. A young soldier manned the desk in the antechamber.

"Excuse me, sir," said Josephine briskly. "I'm here to meet with the superintendent."

The man jumped to his feet, knocking his chair back to the wall.

"Do you have an appointment, miss?"

"No, but that is of no consequence. The superintendent will see me."

"He will?" The soldier scrunched his brow. "I meant to say, I'm sure he will, but I must check to see if he is indisposed."

"No need to do that, Private. I'll just step in and look for myself."

Before he could say another word, she barged past his desk, gave one rap on the door frame and walked into the adjoining room.

"What do you need, Jones?" asked the man, not bothering to glance up from the paperwork spread out before him.

"It's not Jones, it's Bigelow," said Josephine.

The man's head shot up and he sprung to his feet.

"Pardon me, miss. I thought you were my assistant."

"No harm done." Josephine extended her hand to the man. When he hesitated, she grabbed his hand and gave it a vigorous pump. "Nice to make your acquaintance, sir. Josephine Bigelow."

"William P. Wood," replied the man with a note of consternation in his voice.

She dropped her hand from his. "You may not remember me, but we met in passing Wednesday when I received a tour of this facility."

"How could I forget such a lovely face?"

Brushing off the compliment, Josephine plowed on. "I'm here to inquire about the status of one of your prisoners."

The man's eyes widened briefly before he resumed his professional demeanor. "This is highly unusual. May I ask why you would have need of such information?"

"Certainly."

He looked at her expectantly. With no answer forthcoming, he picked up the conversation. "I wasn't seeking your permission. I want to know *why* you need such information."

"Oh, of course. That is certainly a fair question, so I will tell you. One of the soldiers ensconced in this prison happens to have been my brother's roommate at West Point Military Academy. I spotted him the first day I was here. Yesterday I had the chance to speak with him for a moment."

His gaze narrowed on Josephine. "Miss Bigelow, you were informed, were you not, that we have a policy forbidding volunteers from interacting with the prisoners?"

Josephine stopped short of rolling her eyes and continued determinedly. "I was made aware of that. But this case is different. I wasn't speaking to a random inmate. I was conversing with my brother's friend."

"Are you saying that your brother is a Confederate sympathizer?"

"Heavens, no. Why on earth would he hold anything except contempt for those traitors?"

"Didn't you just say that they were friends?"

"They *were* friends," Josephine said in exasperation. "Now that we're in the middle of this abominable war, they're sworn enemies. But, when all this nastiness is behind us, I would imagine they'll pick up right where they left off."

The man raised his eyebrows. "*Undoubtedly*. But that day isn't here now, so why is this man of interest to you?"

"I didn't declare that he was of interest to *me*," she exclaimed indignantly. "I'm asking on behalf of my brother, of course."

"Of course."

Josephine did not care for the man's condescending tone but kept talking anyhow. "The soldier I'm inquiring about, his name is First Lieutenant Michael McKirnan. I had every intention of picking up our conversation from where we left off yesterday, but when I went to the area in which he was housed, I found neither hide nor hair of him."

The warden eyeballed her without replying.

"Out of concern for my brother's friend, I'm checking on his welfare." Josephine did everything she could to keep the sound of desperation out of her voice. *What if he won't cooperate?*

"No need to worry, miss. I'm sure the first lieutenant is fine."

A sense of relief washed over her. "He's been moved to another area?"

"You could say that."

"Then I will be able to find him on this property?"

"He is on prison property, just not *this* prison," said the warden with finality.

"Not this prison?" Josephine's stomach tied in a knot. "To

where has he been moved?"

"I am not authorized to disclose that, miss."

"Says whom?"

"Says my commander."

"Then I shall need to speak with him directly," she said emphatically.

"That won't be possible, miss. His office is in the White House."

"The White House, say you." Josephine glanced away as she considered that statement. "My father is Brigadier General Bigelow, and he also happens to work at the White House. If he heard that you refused to answer my question, he would be quite displeased."

"Miss, I don't care if your father is President Abraham Lincoln. I'm not allowed to disclose that information to you. You may be attractive, but you're not worth risking my neck."

She crossed her arms and looked down her nose at the man. After giving him an extended glare, she deigned to conclude her business with him. "Very well, then. Thank you for your time."

With that, she spun on her heel to make her leave. As she headed out the door, she heard the man muttering. "God help First Lieutenant McKirnan if she ever gets her claws in him."

"Hmpf," she exclaimed before stamping her way out of the anteroom and into the hall. *Men think they know everything* — just like her father. But, in this instance, she could use the brigadier general's knowledge to her advantage. He'd be able to help her.

She was dying to figure out where they'd shipped Michael. Was it far away? What if the conditions in the new prison were unbearable? Or unsafe? Perhaps his life would be at risk. The thought of never seeing him again was agonizing.

Josephine prayed for Michael as she made her way back

to the wash building. A thought sparked in her mind. If her father was able to track him down, when the war was over... yes, she could travel to where he was imprisoned and meet him upon his release.

Or even better, maybe I can help him obtain an early discharge! There was talk of prisoner exchanges. Michael was a first lieutenant, so he must be worth something.

A glimmer of hope came to Josephine. *If I could save First Lieutenant McKirnan from a life of misery in the federal prison system, he'd be indebted to me forever!* She smiled, thinking of ways that he could pay off his debt.

That thought kept Josephine's spirits uplifted as she went back to her chores. At the end of her shift, she bade Agatha a good evening and walked down the cobblestone path to the main building.

Josephine glanced at her left hand as she went and imagined a wedding band adorning her ring finger. Maybe Michael would splurge and have a diamond set into it. Or a blue zircon. They were all the rage lately and blue was her favorite color — particularly the deep blue shade of Michael's eyes. How fitting would that be? She may need to drop a hint when the time got closer. Unlike women, men were oblivious to the little details in life.

Charles was stationed in the entryway. He escorted her to the brougham, where she gave him orders to drive to The White House.

When the carriage turned the corner, Josephine could see the infirmary through the prison fence. It made her consider Bernadette's situation again.

From her conversation with the attending nurse, it sounded as though the girl would be discharged Monday morning. Josephine would make it her duty to see that Bernadette was whisked away before word reached her man that she'd been released.

Charles could fetch her with the buggy. Josephine had money set aside in her armoire; she would purchase a one-way ticket to St. Louis for the girl. There'd be enough left over to cover her expenses in the city for a month or two.

Josephine had been saving the money for a new reticule, since her father refused to let her discard her current handbag every time a new season came around. That could wait. There would be more seasons and more handbags. She could live without that particular one she'd been eyeing up in *Godey's Lady's Book*.

As they rolled up First Street, Josephine noticed couples walking arm in arm, the gentlemen walking nearest the road for the safety of their companions. That sight tugged at her conscience. She couldn't just put Bernadette on a train and send her on her merry way. Sixteen-year-old girls didn't ride conveyances unescorted. It was not only unseemly but potentially dangerous, considering that civility had gone out the window as of late.

She wouldn't mind accompanying her. Anything better than spending her summer working in the wash building. However, while two might seem better than one, a pair of teenage girls traveling alone might actually cause twice the problems.

The lawn of The White House came into view. Josephine had just another minute to get her talking points in line before she was in her father's office.

Charles pulled up to the guard station and Josephine leaned out her window to address the man on watch. After hearing that she was there to see her father, they allowed them to pass.

"I shan't be long," said Josephine breezily as they pulled up to the main entrance of the neoclassical style building. "You may park the buggy under that beech tree along the drive while I'm inside."

"Yes, miss," Charles replied. When the horses came to a

halt, he jumped down from his seat to assist Josephine as she stepped to the ground.

"Shall I accompany you into the building, miss?" he inquired.

"No, thank you, Charles. I know right where I'm going."

She turned and breezed up the steps and into the building. Once inside, she picked up her skirts and swiftly made her way down the long hallway. The sound of her wooden heels tapping against the marble floor echoed through the grand space.

Doors on either side of the hall led to offices, and Josephine encountered several soldiers as she went. They seemed to be in a hurry themselves but greeted her politely as she passed.

Turning the corner at the end of the hallway, she entered the West Wing. A desk was positioned a few yards past the intersection. A soldier sat on the edge of the wooden seat of an iron swivel chair, engrossed in a document set before him.

"Good afternoon, Hubert."

"Hello, Josephine," the man said without bothering to bring his head up. "Just one second." He scanned the sheet of paper, then put the stack together, carefully aligning the edges. Josephine tapped the toe of her boot impatiently. With the papers arranged, Hubert opened the top desk drawer and put them inside, neatly tucking the stack into the back corner. He then stood and turned his attention to his sister. "Aren't you supposed to be volunteering at the prison?"

"I'm done for the day, thank you for asking." *Or if I play my cards right, done forever.* "Is Father in his office?"

"He's just finishing his meeting with the senator from *Maine*," Hubert said with authority.

"Ought I be impressed by that?" Josephine queried.

"It just so happens that William Pitt Fessenden is the chairman of the Senate Finance Committee." He leaned closer to his sister and lowered his voice. "Word has it that President Lincoln will be nominating him for Secretary of the Treasury because of his intimate knowledge of the nation's wartime finances."

"Well, isn't that something," said Josephine, not even bothering to feign interest. The capitol staff probably considered it juicy gossip. It meant nothing to her.

"I have news that you might find even more interesting than treasury chitchat," she said conspiratorially. "Yesterday, I spoke with an old friend of yours."

"Really?" said Hubert. "Where?"

"At Old Capitol."

"The prison? Was it one of the guards?"

"This gentleman doesn't work there. He's actually a guest."

"A guest?" Hubert echoed in astonishment. "By that I assume you mean he's one of the inmates?"

Josephine nodded in acknowledgement.

"I'm not sure what shocks me more — that someone with whom I'm acquainted is incarcerated there or that you were conversing with someone incarcerated there. But knowing you, I'll go with the former."

The only response she gave was an eye roll.

"Well, don't just stand there. Tell me who it was. For the life of me, I can't even begin to guess whom it could be."

"It was your old roommate from West Point."

"George Armstrong Custer? Impossible. He's newly married, just promoted to the rank of major general. Last I heard, he was engaged in the Overland Campaign."

"Not George, you silly goose. Your other roommate."

"Michael McKirnan?

"Uh-huh."

"Michael McKirnan." Hubert shook his head. "I haven't

laid eyes on him since graduation day. Heard he joined up with the Reb Army. Guess my sources were correct. What did he do to land himself in prison up here?"

"How would I know? The only thing that I am certain of is that I saw him Wednesday and Thursday, and he was gone today. I inquired with the superintendent as to his whereabouts, but all the boorish man would reveal was that he had been transferred to another facility."

"Which isn't all that surprising; it's a fairly common practice," noted Hubert. "Regardless, what interest is it to you?"

"I was just looking out for the welfare of your friend."

It was Hubert's turn to roll his eyes. "How noble of you. You sure it wasn't for some other, more personal reason? It seems to me you were sweet on that fellow back in the day."

"Hubert! I was thirteen years old the last time I talked to him. I was just a child."

"First loves are last loves, don't they say?"

Heat crept up Josephine's cheeks. "Think what you'd like, but I was just checking on him. Seeing that you were bosom buddies back in the day."

"I'm sure he's fine. Uncle Sam will provide for him."

With a bit of hesitation, Josephine pushed the conversation further ahead. "That being so, are all the Union prisons similar? Old Capitol Prison isn't a castle, but it isn't horrible either."

"Actually, depending on the population, the conditions in each prison vary. Old Capitol is probably the top Federal facility. It helps that it's here in D.C. because politicians stop in there once in a while to assess the facilities. It assuages their guilt if they see prisoners being treated humanely. I'll wager the facilities outside the range of their vision are considerably less hospitable."

A feeling of lightheadedness came over Josephine. She

was genuinely getting worried about Michael. "Hubert, can you do me a tremendous favor?"

"What's that, sis?"

"Can you find out to which prison Michael has been assigned?"

Hubert's eyes homed in on his sister's face. "Michael? I didn't know you two were on a first-name basis," he said smugly. "So, I was right. You're harboring feelings for him, aren't you?"

"What if I am?" Josephine said indignantly. "Liking a boy isn't a crime."

"It is if the boy is a Reb soldier and the girl has sworn her allegiance to the Union."

Josephine crossed her arms in front of her and stamped her kid leather boot on the marble floor. "I haven't sworn my allegiance to anybody. Besides, this war can't go on forever. When it's all said and done, it won't make one bit of difference what color uniform a man wore during the conflict. The country will be united once again."

"If only it were so simple," Hubert said, letting out a sigh.

She gazed at him imploringly.

"Don't give me that look, Josephine! You know I can't say no to you when you're staring at me like that."

A smile lit Josephine's face. "Does that mean you'll find out for me?"

"It means I'll try. It might take a bit. I'll have to dig through the records in an office in a different wing. But, let me ask you this. Say I do find this needle in the haystack, what will you do with this knowledge?"

"Oh, I won't be doing anything with it," she said with confidence. "Father will."

Hubert appeared skeptical. "How's that?"

"I shall have Father arrange a prisoner exchange between Michael and an officer of equal rank from the Union Army. He's First Lieutenant McKirnan now, don't you know, Second Lieutenant Bigelow?"

Chapter XXVI

Michael stared at the wall, holding his breath as he waited for Appleby to exit the room. Having someone who knew him working in the prison would make it next to impossible to go about his duties. The place was relatively large, but there was no way of avoiding the man twenty-four hours a day. There weren't enough hiding spots.

The door slammed shut and Michael heard heavy steps walking away from the bunk area. He let out his breath. Thinking of Edward Appleby brought back countless memories for Michael — mostly bad. Appleby was a Cow the year that Michael enrolled at the military academy as a Plebe. As a third-year cadet, Appleby seemed to feel that it was his personal duty to make sure the new cadets were broken in, or more apropos, *broken.*

As the self-proclaimed head of the devilers, he put his leadership skills to the test, getting his buddies to follow his example and make life a living hell for the young men new to the campus. What would have gotten him expelled from a secondary education facility went unquestioned at the university level. The administrators turned a blind eye to it. The practice had gone on since day one and would go on long after their terms there were over. "Boys will be boys," as they said.

The Plebes traditionally suffered abuse at the hands of the upperclassmen. They forced the young cadets to do double time around the barracks at a hundred or more beats per minute, squaring the corners like tin soldiers. At mealtimes the underlings were told they had to eat and walk so erect that their chins would push into their gullets. The intent was to teach the younger men discipline, but Michael felt it was just a show of power from the older students.

Once settled in their bunks for the night, instead of telling ghosts stories, the Plebes related horror stories passed along to them of hazing incidents, such as fellows being forced to sit on bayonets or slide naked down splintered boards. One young man was said to have fallen unconscious after three separate groups of upperclassmen forced him to perform deep knee bends over broken glass.

The older boys had the right to approach any first-year student wearing a crooked cap or whose brass buckle needed a shine and literally shout the proper rules of conduct in his face. These practices, permitted by the fourth-class system, were supposedly instituted to improve the character of tenderfoot officer candidates.

Under the guise of leadership, the Plebes had to learn not only military history but pages of other non-vital material that was, in effect, the equivalent of taking another entire academic course. Unfortunately for some men like Edward, he spent so much time harassing the Plebes that he hadn't enough time left over to work on his own character.

At one point, deviling had become such an issue on campus that an academy superintendent advised the Plebes standing guard duty to use their bayonets against their upperclassmen tormentors if they needed to.

From his bunk, Michael heard Appleby in the hallway, chewing someone out. Apparently, the man had found his calling. As a prison guard he could abuse men and get paid for it. *Glad to see that all those years of practice paid off for him.*

There certainly had been no love lost between the two of them at the academy. While Michael went along with some of the harmless pranks, he put his foot down when it came to participating in idiotic things that could be harmful to his person just to humor some jackass upperclassman.

He was one of the few people that Appleby couldn't push around. Even though Michael never outright refused an order from him, the look in his eyes said it all — "Make me." That was a line Appleby had never been willing to cross. He couldn't care less about the safety of the Plebes, but he had great concern for his own wellbeing.

Appleby had the upper hand again. Michael gritted his teeth in frustration. He wouldn't dare stand up to a prison guard. The stakes were too high. Knowing Appleby, he probably moonlighted as the prison executioner as well.

Michael had no desire to be his next victim, so he decided to make himself scarce and keep his eyes open for the first opportunity to get word to his protector that he needed out of this facility immediately. Where in God's name was Jeffrey's plant when he needed him?

Chapter XXVII

The door opened and Brigadier General Bigelow appeared, ushering Senator Fessenden out of his office. "We will proceed with that," he said, finishing up their conversation. "Have a good evening, Senator. Say hello to the missus for me, if you will."

"Of course, General. Give my best to your family as well."

"Conveniently enough, two of them are right here," said the general when he noticed his children standing outside his office. "Senator Fessenden, may I introduce my daughter, Josephine."

Josephine nodded her head to the man and gave him a slight curtsey. "How do you do, sir?"

"I'm quite well, thank you, miss."

"And you remember our oldest, Hubert," said the officer, waving his hand towards his son.

Hubert extended his hand to the man. "Nice meeting you again, sir."

"Same here, boy. Glad to hear you've followed your father's footsteps into military service. A West Point graduate, too. Impressive. Keep up the good work and someday you'll make a name for yourself like your father has."

"Thank you, sir. That would be an honor."

The senator gave a final nod and turned to go.

"And to what do I owe the pleasure of this visit today, Josephine?" asked the brigadier general.

"I was in the area and thought I'd stop by to say hello, Father."

"I'm sure you were, dear. Would you like to step into my office? I suspect you have something on your mind. It's not every day that a father gets a visit at work from his favorite daughter. Actually, it's not any day. Hubert, will you excuse us?"

Josephine turned towards her brother and mouthed the words, "Find those orders."

Hubert gave her a nod.

Assured that he was starting his task, Josephine followed her father into his office. She sat in the Chippendale chair he offered her.

He proceeded to the other side of the desk and sat down in his upholstered Federal armchair. "How was your day working in the wash building, dear?"

"It was relatively the same as the two previous ones. You've seen one pair of drawers, you've seen them all."

Her father frowned at her before leaning back and crossing his arms. "Let's cut to the chase, young lady. I assume you aren't here for a social call."

"Not exactly, Father, even though it is a pleasure to see someone as important as you hard at work helping President Lincoln."

"Buttering me up? That's never a good sign. Out with it; what do you need?"

Josephine stiffened, strengthening her resolve. "Actually, it's not what I need, it's something of which an acquaintance is in need."

"How altruistic of you. Proceed."

"I had the pleasure, through my duties, of meeting a young lady around my age who has found herself in an unsafe situation and needs to temporarily relocate."

"And that concerns me how?"

"I'll get to that in a moment. But first, from talking to her, I found that she has a grandmother residing in St. Louis, Missouri. I told her that I would help her travel there."

"Help her? In what fashion?" her father inquired.

"I intend to fund her travel," she replied, assuredly.

The man's eyebrows shot up. "I shall presume this is where my assistance comes in," he said.

"No. I am prepared to put up the money myself."

"That's quite generous. But, how do you know that if you give money to this young lady that she'll travel to see her *alleged* grandmother? What if her intent is to fleece you?"

Who was he to question her judgment? "Father, if you met Bernadette, you would know that her intentions are pure. She never asked me for help. I offered it completely unsolicited."

"Fine then. If you want to wager your money on this risky venture, so be it. I'm still not clear how this involves me."

"I'm getting there," said Josephine brightly. "Being that you're such a caring and concerned father, if I were to have need to travel halfway across the country via rail, would you let me go unaccompanied?"

"Of course not. You know that."

"Exactly," said Josephine. The man was following her lead precisely as she planned. "Bernadette has no loving father like I have, so she has no one to watch out for her welfare. I would never be able to forgive myself if I sent her off on that trek alone and something happened to her."

Her father viewed her askance and then jumped in before she could utter another word. "No!"

Josephine's heart sank. "What do you mean, 'no'? I haven't even asked a question yet."

"There's no need to. I know where this conversation is going. I will not even allow you to escort that girl across the street. We're in the middle of a war, in case you've forgotten. It's not safe for females to travel anywhere unescorted, no matter how many of them are in the gaggle."

"But, Father."

"Don't, '*But, Father*' me. If you had a trusted male to escort you, it would be one thing, but you cannot do this on your own."

Thinking on her feet, Josephine sweetened her tone. "Father, would you consider being our escort?"

His eyebrows shot up. "Didn't you just hear what I said about being in the middle of a war? President Lincoln would not approve of one of his cabinet members abandoning his post to gallivant across the country chaperoning two young ladies on an adventure. There will be plenty of time for travel when this uprising is tamped down."

Josephine gripped the seat of the Chippendale chair. "This cannot wait that long!" Pulling out another weapon from her arsenal, she put on her best pouty face. "What if I were to find a male escort for us, someone who would be above reproach?"

"The only men who fit that description are my men, and they're on the battlefield fighting for this great nation."

She scrunched her nose is frustration. A knock on the office door interrupted their conversation. Hubert walked in and approached them. It was providence. Josephine's face lit up. "Not all of them!"

The brigadier general glanced from his son to his daughter and back again. He shook his head in resignation. "Fine. But the two of you had better return within two weeks, or I'll send a battalion after you."

"It's a deal." Josephine clapped her hands in elation. She got up, scampered around the desk and threw her arms about the general's neck. "Thank you! You're the most wonderful father a daughter could ever ask for."

"Hrmph."

Focusing on Hubert, the man shook his pointer finger at him. "This child is your responsibility. If so much as one hair on her head is harmed, you'll find your desk moved from the West Wing to the West Lawn. Do I make myself clear?"

The young man looked between the two of them. "Am I missing something here?"

Josephine sprinted across the room, grasped her brother's arm and tugged him to follow her out the door. "I'll explain everything to you in a minute."

"Goodbye, Father," she threw over her shoulder. "We'll be back before you know it."

"You darn well better be."

"Goodbye, Father?" Hubert stopped in his tracks. "Just a moment, where are we going?"

Still hanging onto her brother's arm, Josephine tugged him through the doorway.

"St. Louis," she answered.

"St. Louis," he repeated. "How did you know? I didn't have a moment to get a word in edgewise."

Josephine stared at him in confusion. "How did I know what?"

"That your first lieutenant was sent to the federal prison there?"

Chapter XXVIII

Michael threw a glance over his shoulder, scanning the hallway. Men were scattered throughout the area, but no one matching Appleby's size was present. He was beginning to think that he was in a game of cat and mouse, or make that rat and mouse, considering his foe. He was on pins and needles constantly, whether in the yard, mess hall or even lying on his cot in the bunk area. The hypervigilance had him on edge. It was annoying as all get out.

While he waited for his contact to approach him, he kept his eyes open for men who might have information that could be useful to the Union cause. He could obtain the most helpful intelligence from the men lower on the chain of command. They never seemed to suspect that he was pumping them for information. If they did, they likely found it flattering to be in the confidences of a first lieutenant.

Commanding officers rarely asked subordinates their opinion on anything, but surprisingly, a number of them were not only intelligent but had keen insight as well. Not enough to know that they were being played, but enough to serve Michael's purposes.

With the coast clear, he started a conversation with the man behind him in line as they were led to the yard. Like most of the Confederate soldiers with whom he interacted, the man seemed to be a decent fellow. Michael had to keep reminding himself that what he was doing would benefit soldiers on both sides of the conflict. Life would be better for everyone in the United States when the South finally conceded.

Interestingly enough, Rebel soldiers, for the most part, bore little animosity toward their foes from the North.

When the imaginary lines had been drawn, partitioning off their country, some found themselves on one side of the conflict and some on the other. And it wasn't always the side on which their friends and family stood.

Perhaps, like himself, other soldiers were beginning to feel like pawns in an oversized chess game. The players were Lincoln and Davis, Grant and Lee, or perhaps men so far behind the scenes that most people would never know.

It had come as quite the shock to the nation when war was declared. Valiant efforts had been made to stop the conflict from erupting but with so many forces pushing for war, the tide couldn't be turned.

Like most people, Michael was flabbergasted by how long the hostilities dragged on. After more than three years, neither side seemed ready to give up. There were rumblings of Sherman and his dedication to all-out war to bring the fight to an end. Michael was concerned about the collateral damage such an endeavor would bring. Particularly, the loss of innocent lives and destruction of property.

Michael glanced ahead as the man was just about to answer the question he'd posed of him.

"Gotta go," said Michael abruptly. Damnation! The goliath was walking with another officer toward the line of prisoners.

"What?"

"Need the facilities," Michael said, a true note of urgency in his voice. He made a quick right into an adjoining hall and double stepped it toward the back of the building.

Please God, help me get out of here!

Chapter XXIX

She didn't want to make a spectacle of herself in front of the people walking in the vicinity of Hubert's desk, so Josephine dropped her voice to a whisper. "My first lieutenant?" Her eyes widened as the gears began to turn in her head.

The thought of reuniting with Michael caused her heart to nearly burst. She imagined the gentle touch of his hand on hers as she listened spellbound to him speaking in that genteel Southern accent.

"We need to go back to the house now," she said to Hubert.

"I beg your pardon?"

"No time for questions. Charles is waiting." Josephine picked up her skirts and made her way down the hallway toward the exit. She heard Hubert rummaging through his desk drawers before hustling to catch up with her.

Josephine's mind hopscotched to other thoughts about Michael's situation. Maybe she could volunteer at his new prison for the summer if it wasn't too far away. Or perhaps an early release could be facilitated. The thought nearly made her stop in her tracks. Were there any palms that could be greased? Or a commanding officer who would yield to the pleadings of a prisoner's loved one?

That was it! She could pose as Michael's wife and set up a meeting with the prison superintendent to beg for his release. It would just be a matter of concocting some sob story about how she was destitute without her husband working the farm or some gibberish or other.

For most women, such a charade would be difficult to perform, but Josephine knew that she had what it took to pull it off.

As she approached the double doors, she went through the scenario in her mind. To start, she'd have to find a dress that was flattering enough to get her in the door of the superintendent's office, but not so fine that her story would be put to question.

Should I walk in authoritatively or with the demeanor of a timid chit? Perhaps something in between. If she had to, she could squeeze out some tears. Occasionally that worked with her father. They both knew that the sobs were ingenuous, but the last thing her father wanted to hear was some female caterwauling. Mayhap this officer would be of the same disposition.

Josephine waited for Hubert to catch up and open the door for her. She surveyed her bare finger. Where was she to find a wedding ring? It wasn't like she had such a thing sitting on her mirrored vanity tray. Getting one on short notice could pose a problem, but she wouldn't let that obstacle stop her.

She, Hubert and Bernadette would be on a train heading west tomorrow morning, come hell or high water. The plan might need tweaking. Maybe instead of being his wife, she could be Michael's fiancée. That would eliminate the need to show documentation of their wedding vows. That would take care of the ring issue as well.

That settled, she turned her attention to Hubert. She wanted to tell him about Bernadette before they got to the carriage and had an audience.

The story was brief. Bernadette was a young woman who had been accosted by a maniac in the city and wanted to return to the safety of her grandmother's arms in St. Louis. Josephine skimmed over a few minor details, such as the fact that the madman considered Bernadette his possession and she was carrying a child whose father was unknown to her.

She spelled out the situation to her brother in no

uncertain terms. "Miss Bernadette is a female, in distress, and you need to step up as an officer and a gentleman and get her out of harm's way.

The two of them walked through the doorway, into the late afternoon sun. Much to Josephine's surprise, Hubert seemed amenable to the idea of helping the girl. "There's one glitch, though," he noted.

"What's that?"

"Francine."

"Francine? What about her?"

"I don't see my fiancée approving of me escorting a young lady to another state."

"Approve? Who gives a rat's rear end if she approves or not!" exclaimed Josephine. "We are talking about two, maybe three days of travel, at the most. It's not like you'll be alone with her. I'll be there too."

"I realize that. But Francine isn't quite as understanding about such things. She doesn't even like it when I address other women, let alone travel with them."

"Seriously, Hubert, that woman has got you under her thumb. Maybe a few days apart is exactly what the two of you need. It could be a nice break from her harping on you night and day about setting a wedding date."

Hubert inclined his head. "Well, you do have a point there. But I cannot leave town without letting her know that I'm departing."

"Fine, if it makes your conscience feel any better, tell her that you're traveling under orders from Father, which is actually true." She tapped her chin. "Let's see... it's a top-secret mission so you can't disclose any details. She'll find that quite intriguing, I'm sure."

"That would be telling a lie," he said.

"A white lie. Just a venial sin. When you get back in town, you can confess it to Father O'Kelly if it would assuage your guilt. Probably be the most scandalous thing you'll have to confess the entire year. He may actually be somewhat impressed."

"And what of the sin of presumption?" Hubert asked. "To decide to sin because one knows that he can be forgiven is to sin twice."

Why did he have to be so well-versed in catechism? "I'm leaving it up to you. Tell Francine whatever you want," Josephine snapped.

"I'll come up with something. But, speaking of confession, I want you to go with me when we get back."

"It's bad enough that I have to go to confession when I find myself in Mother's crosshairs on a Saturday. Now you're gunning for me as well."

She never knew what to tell the priest in confession. How people went every week confounded her. Especially men and women in religious orders. They swore vows of chastity and poverty. If you take those two temptations away, what was left?

Hubert assisted her into the carriage. "Agreed?"

"Fine." She turned to address the driver. "Charles, bring me to the house. After you drop me off, Hubert needs to go see Miss Francine."

Hubert tilted his head. "What's the rush?"

"We're departing tomorrow."

"Tomorrow? We haven't even secured the train tickets yet."

"Good reminder. Pick those up on the way to Francine's house," said Josephine. "Here." She held her hand out to him. "Father passed this to me as I was leaving his office."

Seeing a neatly folded twenty-dollar Greenback, Hubert shook his head. "You really are the apple of his eye, aren't you?"

"What can I say? He adores his only daughter."

The next few hours passed by in a whirlwind. Even with

Cecilia helping her pack for the trip, it took a good deal of time to figure out what to bring. For one thing, Josephine wasn't sure how many days she would be gone. It was a large city; who knew how long it would take to track down Bernadette's grandmother? Plus, she needed to meet with the prison superintendent, and there was no guarantee that would happen immediately.

On top of that, she had to pack for two. Bernadette was about her size, and she needed clothes for the trip. Even if the girl had a complete wardrobe at Marcel's house, which Josephine highly doubted, it would be unsafe to sneak back there to get her things.

Another item on Josephine's agenda that evening was telling her mother about the trip. She had to frame the story in such a way that it would seem like she and her new-found friend, Bernadette, were taking an excursion to see the great city of St. Louis... and Hubert was kind enough to offer to be their chaperone for the week. There would be no talk of prisons, unplanned pregnancies or any other kind of subterfuge.

As she anticipated, her mother ate the story up. Mrs. Bigelow only wished that she hadn't committed herself to helping out at the Ladies Aid Society that week to knit socks for the troops. She would have loved to join in the fun. *As if that would happen.* Goodness gracious. *What teenage girl would want to go on an adventure with her forty-year-old mother?*

All the busyness wore Josephine out or it would have been a struggle to fall asleep that evening. Finding slumber was never easy for her as she tended to hash through things in her mind when she finally took to her bed.

Thankfully, that night, she slept soundly. It seemed as though she had barely closed her eyes when Cecilia gently tapped her shoulder to awaken her. What would normally have been a ten-minute process, happened instantaneously. When Josephine recalled why she was being roused at such an early hour, she immediately sprang up in bed.

She hurried through her morning ritual, ran down the curved steps to the first floor, joined her mother for a quick repast and was standing on the front porch, reticule in hand, when Charles pulled up in the carriage.

Hubert was already on ground level when she walked out.

"Very punctual this morning, Josephine." He nodded in approval.

"There's a first time for everything."

"That there is." He held his hand out to help Josephine into the vehicle.

"Where's your bag?" he asked.

"I don't have one."

He gave her a puzzled look. "You're bringing nothing other than your reticule?"

"Oh, I'm bringing something, all right. The steamer trunk is in the back hallway. Can you help Charles load it onto the carriage?"

"A trunk? Exactly how long do you plan on being gone?"

"I'm not sure, so I felt it best to be prepared for whatever circumstances we may face."

Hubert rolled his eyes before signaling the driver to follow him into the house. "And to think I actually want to marry one of these creatures," he said to the man as they walked up the steps.

"It doesn't get any better once they have you in their trap," the older gent replied with a note of wisdom in his voice.

Men, they're as bad as women, always complaining about something, thought Josephine. Of course, *Michael* wouldn't be that way. At least she didn't think he would. She didn't actually know him that well, but he didn't seem to be of that mien.

After she and Michael spent the entire summer together,

they would certainly be well-acquainted. She predicted that she would then find him to be even more perfect than she already did.

Once the trunk was hoisted onto the carriage and the men returned to their seats, the trio took off on the short drive to the prison. When they got there, Hubert accompanied Josephine into the building. Before walking in, she noticed other vehicles lining the street, their drivers perhaps waiting for other female inmates.

The women accused of misdemeanors were released every morning at half past eight. Josephine witnessed it the other day. They would be grouped in the entryway, given their belongings, instructed to stay out of further trouble and then sent on their way.

Bernadette was surrounded by six other women when Hubert and Josephine arrived at the prison. Thankfully, the girl had enough sense to wrap a shawl around her shoulders to hide her midsection. It would be quite unfortunate if Hubert spied her profile and had second thoughts about his role in their escapade.

After the other women stepped through the gate, Josephine approached Bernadette and gave her a quick hug, doing her best not to cause the younger girl any pain. "Good morning! You appear much better today."

It was a fib. The bruises on her face had subsided, but they took on deeper shades of yellow, green and blue as they healed. Josephine glanced at her brother out of the corner of her eye.

His eyebrows climbed up his forehead and his mouth hung open. *Maybe I should have been more forthcoming about her physical state.*

Bernadette gave her a slight smile, revealing nice teeth. Surprising, considering the poor circumstances of her childhood.

Since Josephine had never seen the young girl standing, she noticed that they were about the same height. Surveying her more closely, under the bruises, the girl had quite refined features: high cheekbones and full pink lips. The finishing touch was that blond hair. She must have bathed this morning. With her hair clean, the color was closer to gold. The wavy locks hung loose halfway down her back.

Josephine glanced at Hubert. His mouth still hung open and his eyes were glued on the chit. Apparently, she wasn't the only one perusing the girl.

"Hubert," said Josephine, raising her brows and opening her eyes wide as she looked at him. He seemed caught in a trance, so she elbowed him in the ribs.

"Yes, Josephine?" he replied, snapping to attention.

"I'd like you to meet Miss Bernadette Taylor. Miss Taylor, I'd like you to meet my brother, Second Lieutenant Hubert Bigelow."

"How do you do?" said Hubert, giving the girl a slight bow.

"Very well, thank you, Lieutenant."

"You may call me, Hubert, Miss Taylor. It sounds as though we're to be traveling companions for the next few days. That being the case, it would seem acceptable to dispense with the formalities."

"Thank you, *Hubert*," the girl said in a soft, sweet voice. "You may call me Bernadette."

"Bernadette, such a saintly name," he replied.

Josephine rolled her eyes. This child was about as far from sainthood as anyone she knew. Besides that, the Bernadette who saw the Marian apparitions in France was not a saint yet, unless Hubert knew something that she didn't.

With his interest in the litany of saints, perhaps he should have studied for the priesthood instead of taking up the military life. Of course, watching him stare at the girl before him, she had a feeling that religious life would not have suited him well. He'd always had an eye for attractive women.

Apparently, the girl appreciated fine specimens of the opposite sex as well. Her dark brown eyes seemed to shimmer as she stared at Hubert.

Those darn uniforms will get a girl every time, fumed Josephine, knowing all too well. First Lieutenant Michael McKirnan immediately came to mind.

As much as she hated to break up the mutual admiration society, they had a train to catch and needed to vacate the premises posthaste.

"Come along, shall we?" Josephine prompted.

"Of course," Hubert replied. He held his arm out for Bernadette. She placed her petite hand in the crook of his arm, and the two walked through the front gate.

"Don't worry about me," Josephine said acerbically as she followed closely behind.

They were the last to exit the building and their carriage was the sole vehicle parked alongside the prison. The only other vehicle in sight was a wagon pulled over a block down from the building. A man sat in the driver's seat. His eyes were hooded by a cap, but Josephine sensed that he was watching them. Something about him was unsettling. She was happy to vacate the area. There were too many shady characters in the vicinity for her liking.

By the time they covered the few yards to the carriage, Hubert came to his senses and helped Josephine step up to her seat. He then turned to assist Bernadette. She winced as she attempted to bring her right foot up to the step. Noticing that, Hubert swept her into his arms and placed her in the seat across from Josephine.

After positioning himself next to Bernadette, Hubert instructed the driver to go to the depot.

Josephine raised her eyebrows at him. *It hasn't even been twenty-four hours, has he already forgotten his fiancée?*

Chapter XXX

Michael stepped outside and headed toward an inmate who stood alone on the far side of the grounds. Not wanting Appleby to notice him if he happened to step outdoors, Michael turned his back to the prison building as he greeted the loner.

The man offered an amiable smile. He barely appeared old enough to shave but, according to the insignia on his sleeve, had somehow reached the rank of sergeant in the Confederate Army.

The fellow was in Major General Benjamin F. Chatham's Division, Maney's Brigade, led by Brigadier General George F. Maney and Colonel Francis M. Walker, 41st Tennessee. They got swept up in the Chattanooga Campaign in the Battle of Missionary Ridge as well.

From what the sergeant said, Johnston's Army of Tennessee was on the verge of withdrawing toward Atlanta because of the successive flanking maneuvers by Sherman and his army. It sounded as though the hostilities would come to a head at Atlanta.

The Union Army needs to move as many troops there as they can, Michael noted to himself. He'd have to relay that information to his contact, once he located the man. He was told to watch for a soldier wearing a West Point class ring on his left hand, as opposed to the right hand that the graduates traditionally wore them on. The distinct oversized stone set in a gold band made the rings recognizable.

Michael had been on the lookout for the man since he arrived but realized he needed to search more aggressively.

He had intelligence to relay, and he had to move on before he was spotted by Appleby. It took some artful dodging, but Michael managed to stay a step ahead of his adversary.

One afternoon, as the guards escorted them back to the bunk room, the prisoners walked past the lounge where the officers took their breaks. Sunlight glinting off an object caught Michael's eye. He stopped dead in his tracks. Sure enough, the flash of light came from a West Point ring adorning the left hand of one of the officers.

Michael stepped aside to let the other prisoners pass him and tried to catch the man's eye. Not five seconds later, he felt a rough tap on his shoulder. Pivoting around, he stood eye to eye with a ghost from him past — or rather a *goblin* from his past.

God bless it! I lower my guard for one minute and this is the punishment I receive? He stood face to face with none other than Edward Appleby. The next thing he knew, he was slammed against the stone wall.

"Well, my eyes aren't deceiving me after all," said the man in a malevolent tone. "I swore that I saw something yellow slithering around this prison. If it isn't the high and mighty Michael McKirnan."

Regardless of his utter infuriation with himself for letting his guard down, Michael showed no emotion and stared directly into the man's eyes.

"I see you decided to side with the lowlife Rebs," Appleby said contemptuously. "Guess you weren't man enough to fight for the federal army with your classmates."

Michael held himself in check. What he wouldn't give to haul off and take his frustrations out on this malefactor.

"You spent all those years in the Union State of New York, you took advantage of Uncle Sam by letting him pony up for your schooling, and then how do you repay him? You spit in his eye and jump in the sack with the enemy."

Appleby grabbed the points of Michael's collar and shook

him to emphasize each word. "You know what I call a man like you?" he asked threateningly. "I call you a traitor. And do you know what we do to traitors in this prison?"

Still Michael didn't flinch.

Lowering his voice to a whisper, Appleby finished. "We string them up. You better get out your rosary, church boy. Your day of reckoning is here."

Chapter XXXI

The temperature in the train was moderate, yet Hubert offered his jacket to Bernadette. He made an attentive chaperone for his young charge. Too attentive, for Josephine's comfort. Hubert couldn't seem to take his eyes off the girl. From the minute he escorted her onto the train, he was completely entranced.

Josephine wasn't normally the odd man out. It was disconcerting to say the least. Not that she needed attention from her brother, but she swore he was having a more in-depth conversation with that young lady, even though he'd only recently made her acquaintance, than he'd ever had with his sister of seventeen years.

Bernadette was enwrapped in her conversation with Hubert. Josephine could see what was transpiring before her eyes. The child was becoming enamored of her brother. Between his good looks, attentive demeanor, and his rank and position in the government, the man *would* be hard to resist. On top of that, she'd obviously elevated him to the status of savior — her very own knight in shining armor.

Hubert glanced up, smiling about something Bernadette said, and when his gazed connected with Josephine's, she mouthed the word, "Francine." As though swishing away a bothersome mosquito, he dismissed her and turned his attention back to Bernadette.

It wasn't that Josephine liked Francine better than Bernadette. As a matter of fact, it was quite the opposite. Francine Causten was insufferable. She acted as though she was the queen bee of Washington, D.C., and her friends swarmed around her like worker bees, doing whatever it took to stay in her good graces and maintain their coveted status in the community.

Whereas Brigadier General Bigelow rose to a place of prominence in the capital through years of hard work, dedication to the United States military, and his fierce loyalty to President Lincoln, Francine's father was given his spot. He came from money.

The Causten family had roots in the United States, dating back to before the War of Independence. Francine's great-grandfather was said to have attended the Second Continental Congress in Philadelphia, where he voted in favor of Richard Henry Lee's motion for independence. Francine boasted that he was one of the signers of the Declaration of Independence. Josephine had no way of determining if that were factual or not, having never seen the document herself.

It was true, however, that Francine's grandfather was an international lawyer and the consul to the nations of Chile and Ecuador. His job as a diplomat brought him to Washington, D.C. When the Causten family was united with the Shriver family through marriage thirty years ago, their rank in the community soared even higher.

Josephine had resigned herself to the fact that she and Francine would never be bosom buddies, and she would not be getting the sister that she had always longed for. But the woman and Hubert were engaged, and, even if they had no date set, at some point they were going to get married.

Hubert could not let Bernadette wrap her pinkie finger around him and make him forget his obligations. There would be hell to pay if he broke off his engagement with Francine. It would be career suicide. He'd never be able to show his face in the city of Washington, D.C., again.

Attempting to nip the situation in the bud, Josephine stood up from the bench seat and announced to Hubert and Bernadette that she was going to walk to the dining car to get an early supper.

Hubert immediately got to his feet and offered to escort her to the other car.

"That is so kind of you, Hubert, but I'm perfectly capable of making my way through the train to the dining area. Since we just had lunch a few hours ago, I would imagine neither one of you is hungry yet, but I had my eye on the *crème brûlée* and I'd like to secure a dish of it for myself before they run out."

Both Hubert and Bernadette nodded.

"Then, sister, that's exactly what you should do," said Hubert amicably.

"And so I shall," she said, gracing them both with a smile. "While I'm gone, it may be a good opportunity for you to get to know each other a little better. I'll give you a conversation starter. Hubert, why don't you tell Bernadette about Miss Francine who awaits your arrival back in Washington?"

The smiles froze on their faces, but Josephine's grew brighter. "Tootaloo! I'll see you both soon."

She turned and flounced out of the car, sliding the door shut behind her. *Oh, to be a fly on the wall in that state car now*, she thought mischievously. We'll see how Bernadette likes Hubert when a chink appears in his shining armor.

An hour should give them enough time to chat. Josephine proceeded to the dining car and ordered a four-course meal that included the coveted *crème brûlée*. When the food arrived, she savored each bite, imagining the delicious conversation that was going on just three cars down from her. She stretched out her dinnertime as long as she could and then sauntered back to the state car. Excited to see the fireworks, she took a deep breath and opened the door.

There were fireworks, all right. Hubert held Bernadette's face in his hands and planted a gentle kiss on her bruised forehead just as Josephine walked through the door.

The gasp that escaped her caused the two to break apart.

"What in God's name is going on here?" she said in a raised voice. "That was not what I instructed you to do when I left. Did you not have the conversation I suggested?"

"That and more," said Hubert, keeping his eyes and hands locked on Bernadette's face. "Through our dialogue, I have discovered that Bernadette is one of the most courageous human beings that I've ever met. She has gone through more in sixteen years than most women, or men, for that matter, have endured in an entire life."

He dropped his right hand and gently turned Bernadette's face toward his sister with his other hand. "Yet, look at her; she has managed to retain her beauty inside and out."

Josephine placed her hands on her hips in exasperation. "Wait, did the topic of your *fiancée* come up *at all*?"

Bernadette stared down at her hands, which were folded demurely in her lap.

"Of course, Josephine," said Hubert as though he was talking to a youngster. "It would have been quite ignoble of me not to share my story after Bernadette was so willing to be open about her life."

Without even thinking, Josephine stamped her foot on the train floor. "And what is to become of you and Miss Taylor, then?"

Hubert reached for Bernadette's hands. "We'll see how this plays out. If God hadn't meant for our lives to intersect, they wouldn't have. For the time being, we'll enjoy each other's company. When we reach our destination, I will do everything in my power to help Bernadette find the whereabouts of her grandmother."

Josephine huffed. "It's your life," she stated before plopping down on the bench furthest away from them. "I'm washing my hands of this whole affair," she threw back over her shoulder.

She remained sitting alone in the front of the car until they pulled into the station in St. Louis. After the three of them descended the train steps, Hubert went off to fetch a horse-drawn cab. That left her and Bernadette alone. The silence hung between them until Josephine could stand it no longer. She clenched her fists together in exasperation.

"How could you?" she asked the younger girl in exasperation.

Bernadette shrugged one shoulder up. "I couldn't help it, Josephine. I've met a lot of men in my life but none like Hubert. He's kind and smart and caring and devilishly handsome."

Devilishly was certainly a fitting description of the man at this moment.

"He has offered to take care of me," Bernadette continued. "No man has ever done that before without dubious intentions." She hesitated and then began anew. "I am not foolish enough to think this will last forever, but I mean to enjoy it while it does. God knows that I've taken care of myself for long enough. It's nice to be able to pretend that I've found myself an honorable man who will do right by me."

Young girls, they can be so foolish — falling head over heels in love with the first handsome man who catches their fancy. The irony of that statement hit Josephine between the eyes. Of course, *her* situation with Michael was entirely different.

"I guess I can't blame you, Bernadette," she replied after a moment of thought. "Hubert truly is a remarkable man. As long as you see this for what it is and don't get your hopes up, I guess there's no harm in playing the charade that you two are a couple for a few days."

"Thank you, Josephine." Bernadette reached out to her, and the two embraced.

When they pulled apart, Josephine had a lump in her throat. "If dreams really did come true," she said with sincerity, "after this war is over, not only would I marry the man that I've always pined for, but I'd have the sister I've always wanted as well."

Bernadette smiled at her warmly.

Josephine turned away so the younger girl wouldn't see the tears forming in her eyes. Glancing to her right, she saw Hubert hurrying towards them with a cabbie on his heels. He directed the man to their railcar, and the two went to get Josephine's trunk.

After everything was loaded onto the waiting vehicle, the group set off for Planter's House Hotel, a massive four-story building on Fourth Street with three hundred rooms, two of which were secured for their group.

Once they freshened up, the three of them met in the lounge on the first floor to determine the game plan for the next day or so. Hubert suggested taking Bernadette to the courthouse first to search for records of her grandmother. It had been so long since she'd been in the city that Bernadette couldn't even remember the neighborhood in which the lady lived.

While they did that, Josephine would have a cabbie take her to Gratiot Street so she could go to the prison and make an appointment with the superintendent. Her brother showed concern about her traveling to such a place on her own, but she assured him that she would have the driver escort her into the building. She would pay him to wait outside until her business was completed.

With everything squared away, Josephine and Bernadette went to their room on the third floor and Hubert went up another flight of stairs to his room.

The next morning, they met in the lobby at nine o'clock. Hubert already had a carriage lined up and the driver was waiting inside the building for Josephine. They all said their goodbyes, and the women exchanged a quick hug before they went their separate ways.

Squaring her shoulders, Josephine let the driver escort her to the buggy and help her in. As they drove the few blocks to the prison, she rehearsed her part several times to make sure she had it down pat.

As promised, the man escorted her into the building and then parked within eyesight to await her departure. Approaching the first guard that she saw, Josephine asked for his assistance. "Would you kindly escort me to the superintendent's quarters?"

"Absolutely, miss. It would be my pleasure."

The soldier brought her to an office on the main floor. After he excused himself, she walked up to the gentleman manning the wooden desk in the antechamber.

"Pardon me, sir," said Josephine. "I need to see the superintendent today."

"Do you have an appointment, miss?" the man asked solicitously.

"I'm afraid I don't, but I'd be more than happy to make one."

"Of course," he said, going over a ledger set before him. "The first open appointment is tomorrow morning at eleven o'clock. Does that work for you?"

"As a matter of fact, it doesn't. I need to see him today."

"Miss, I would like to be able to accommodate you, but the superintendent is not available. He has appointments scheduled throughout the day at the prison and an engagement tonight in the city."

"Certainly, he must have some free time during the day," Josephine said sweetly. "I really only need a moment of his time."

Making a show of inspecting the ledger closer, the man picked it up and glanced down at the notations.

Seeing him momentarily distracted, Josephine scooted past him and hurried toward the superintendent's office. The younger man wouldn't dare lay a hand on her. However, just in case, she quickly made her way through the portal and slammed the door behind her.

The noise caused the officer to snap his head up. He peered over the rim of his reading spectacles to see who had barged into the area unannounced. Noticing that it was a person of the female variety, he immediately got to his feet.

Josephine could hardly believe her luck. That was twice in one week that she had used her womanly guiles to get in front of a prison official. *With security as lax as this, it's a wonder any of them have survived this far into the war. What if I had been a person of ill intent?*

That was beside the point. She had found the man she wanted to see, so she started her spiel, planted in front of the door to stop the entry of any unwanted guests.

"Pardon me, sir," she began. The doorknob clicked behind her. Josephine did her best to appear nonchalant as she leaned her weight into the door to keep it from opening.

The officer raised his eyebrows as Josephine dug her heels into the Persian carpet to keep from sliding toward his desk. It was a useless endeavor. She didn't have the strength to stop the man on the other side of the door.

"Sergeant," said the superintendent with a tone of amusement, "you may resume your duties."

"Yes, sir," came a muffled voice from behind the door. Josephine shifted her weight as the pressure behind her ceased.

"Colonel Bristol Brady," the man said. "And to whom do I have the pleasure of addressing today?"

"Miss Bigelow, Colonel. Josephine Bigelow."

"And what brings you to my office this fine day, Miss Bigelow?"

"I took a train from Washington, D.C., to St. Louis just to

visit this very prison. I'm here on official business."

"Oh. And what business is that, may I ask?"

She folded her hands behind her back and pulled her shoulders back.

"I'm here to arrange for the release of my fiancé."

The man's eyes narrowed. "That is a highly unusual request, Miss Bigelow. If your fiancé is a guest at our facility, I assume he's here for a reason. We generally don't release prisoners on a whim."

"This certainly is not on a whim, Colonel Brady. I've put a good deal of thought into this."

"I'm sure you have, Miss Bigelow. But what would make you think that I would release a criminal to you?"

"My fiancé is no criminal," Josephine replied indignantly. "He's a fine gentleman and a graduate of West Point Military Academy."

"Well, if that's true, then may I ask why he is incarcerated?"

"He was captured during a battle."

"He's an enemy soldier?"

"That's one way to view it," said Josephine, innocuously.

"And that certainly begs the question again, why exactly would I release him?" the officer asked.

"*Release* may be the wrong word. Trade may be more apropos."

"Trade? Trade him for what?"

"Not for what. For whom," replied Josephine. The man looked at her askance. Josephine had a moment of discomfit, wondering if this trek may have been all for naught.

"Trade him for another officer, of course," she said with renewed conviction. "There must be some Union officer holed away in a Confederate prison that you've been hoping to repatriate."

"Miss, where did you get the impression that soldiers can be traded like checkers on a checkerboard?"

"From my father," said Josephine.

"Your father? And whom might that be, miss?"

"That would be Brigadier General Matthias Bigelow."

The man's bushy eyebrows shot up. "*The* Brigadier General Matthias Bigelow?"

"None other," said Josephine sweetly.

Colonel Brady viewed her thoughtfully. "You're the daughter of a Union Brigadier General and you're engaged to a first lieutenant in the Confederate Army?"

"Uh-huh." Josephine crossed her fingers behind her.

"And your father approves of this match?"

"He actually financed this trip. *And* sent my brother, who's a second lieutenant in the Union Army, to accompany me." That may have been stretching the truth but, for all practical purposes, wasn't a lie.

"Hmm. If this trade you propose cannot be worked out, what do you intend to do?"

"I'm sure something can be hammered out. It's just a matter of time. If it can't be done today, I'll just make myself at home in your antechamber until it can be. I have a room at Planter's House Hotel booked for a week."

A smile lit her face.

The man pulled a pocket watch from his overcoat and checked the time. "I have five minutes before my next appointment. What's the name of your fiancé?"

Chapter XXXII

Appleby put his hand under Michael's chin and slammed his head against the wall. "What you got to say for yourself, boy?"

Michael's head was swimming. As much as he wanted to make some clever retort, he couldn't put together a coherent thought.

The commotion caused men to gather around them. Michael blinked hard as the lack of air had him on the verge of passing out.

"Where's that tough guy now?" Appleby said, his head so close that Michael could smell his foul breath.

He couldn't reply if he wanted to. The next thing he knew, the grip on his neck loosened and he was dropped to the floor.

On his hands and knees, Michael sucked in air. He only had time for one deep breath before Appleby grabbed his arm and twisted it behind his back. He yanked him onto his feet.

"How about we go check out that dungeon, Benedict Arnold?"

Michael felt the color drain from his face. Even though Appleby had no idea of the implications of what he said, it was a slap in the face to hear that slur hurled his way.

Appleby pushed him past the door of the officer's lounge. Michael glanced in the room. All eyes were on him, but no one said a word. He was still looking in that direction when a voice called out behind them.

"Halt."

Appleby released his arm and spun around. The crowd

split to allow room for a man to walk through. Appleby's hand shot up in a salute.

The insignia on the officer's shoulder indicated that he was a captain. He addressed Appleby. "Is there a problem here?"

"No, sir," replied the second lieutenant. "Just keeping the prisoners in line, sir."

"There is no reason to exhibit such force on an unarmed man, lieutenant. If I see such a display again, you'll be court marshalled. Do you hear me?"

Appleby's faced registered surprise. He clenched his teeth and replied crisply, "Yes, sir."

"I'll take it from here."

"Yes, sir," said Appleby. He saluted the man again and stepped past the captain.

The officer turned to Michael. "First Lieutenant Michael McKirnan?"

Michael straightened up. "Yes, sir."

"Follow me."

"Yes, sir."

Appleby paused when he heard the interaction. Their eyes locked. Appleby mouthed the words, "I'll kill you," before storming away.

The officer walked in the opposite direction and Michael quickened his step to keep up with him. How did the man know his name? Was he another contact? Perhaps it was fortuitous timing and he was being reassigned to another prison.

Choosing to think positively, he held onto that thought as he was led downstairs to the superintendent's office. On arrival, the captain rapped on the door and was then ordered inside.

Peering into the room, Michael saw the officer who had addressed the new prisoners the day that Michael had arrived at Gratiot Street Prison. The colonel dismissed the captain. When the man left the room, Michael took a step toward the commanding officer. The man sized him up for a moment and then inclined his head towards the right side of the room. Following suit, Michael glanced that direction as well.

His eyes snapped wide open and his feet felt rooted to the wood plank floor. *What in tarnation is she doing here?* If anyone had asked him to guess who he'd find in the colonel's office at a federal prison in the heart of St. Louis, Missouri, the last person that would come to mind would be Josephine Bigelow.

The woman in question, on the other hand, didn't seem surprised at all. She jumped up from a straight-backed chair, crossed the floor to where he stood, and threw herself into his arms.

"Oh, Michael!"

Michael wrapped his arms around her, albeit in a brotherly fashion. He wasn't sure what reaction was called for in this situation. "Josephine?"

Pulling back from the embrace, Josephine titled her head to gaze directly at him. "Michael, my love, our prayers have been answered." She stepped back and piously crossed herself before continuing. "I feared that I would never see you again." Her eyes bore into his. Making a show of holding back a sob, she opened her reticule, grabbed a lace monogrammed handkerchief and proceeded to dab the outer corners of her sparkling green eyes.

An award-winning performance if I've ever seen one, thought Michael. He looked at Josephine questioningly. *What in the devil's name was she up to?* He'd find out soon enough, but for now, it was time to see if he could match her thespian skills.

He gently took hold of her free hand. "I can say the same thing myself, Josephine," he replied with uncharacteristic emotion in his voice. "Can this actually be real?"

Josephine bit her lip and nodded.

"That's some fiancée you have, First Lieutenant McKirnan," interjected the commander.

It took every bit of willpower for Michael to keep from snorting. His eyes narrowed on Josephine. The longer he stared at her, the bigger her smile grew, and the more furrowed his brows became.

"Fiancée?" he said with a hint of a question in his voice. Feeling a set of manicured fingernails digging into his palm, he repeated himself with more conviction. "Fiancée. Yes, she is something, isn't she?"

Josephine smiled in approval.

"Miss Josephine is one determined little lady, I'll say that about her," the officer added. "She tells me that she took the train all the way from Washington, D.C., to see about your welfare."

"Well, what do you know? A person could have knocked me over with a feather, I was so taken by surprise," exclaimed Michael.

"This little lady was bound and determined to camp out in my office until I took action on her petition."

Josephine shoved her handkerchief back into her reticule and held her hands out to Michael. Without pause, he grabbed onto them. He could feel her steel herself as she waited for the officer to continue. She squeezed his hands in anticipation.

"Petition?" Michael peered down at Josephine. Her expression was unreadable, so he turned his head toward the colonel.

"Yes. It seems as though she has inherited some of her father's negotiating skills."

"Really," said Michael. "And how's that?"

"She has requested that I broker a deal with the commander of a Confederate prison to trade you for a

Union officer of equal rank."

Michael's head snapped back towards Josephine. His mind raced as he considered the implications of such a deal. Meanwhile, the chit looked like a cat who had just swallowed a canary.

Searching for an appropriate response, Michael inquired in an even tone, although he already knew the answer, "Is such a proposition even allowable? I was under the impression that the prisoner exchanges had ended."

"Officially, they have, but there's always a bit of negotiating that goes on behind the scenes."

With his hands still locked in Josephine's grip, Michael kept his eyes on the man, curious as to where the conversation would lead.

The officer pulled himself up to full height, which was considerably shorter than Michael. "You may think I've got a heart of stone, but I was a young buck once too. I know what it's like to be head over heels for a pretty young gal. Miss Josephine reminds me so much of my wife, Edwina, back in the day. I just couldn't deny her request."

He paused for effect. "You're in luck, First Lieutenant McKirnan. By chance, a Confederate delegate is coming to the prison in the next week or so. I will make arrangements to exchange you for a Union prisoner, or prisoners, depending upon the deal that we strike. Your former regiment is engaged in the Atlanta campaign. We'll ship you to the front by the first of the month."

Chapter XXXIII

It actually worked! Michael was to be freed from prison. Josephine was tempted to squeal with delight but opted to fold her hands together gleefully until she was sure the colonel was out of earshot. Her plan couldn't have worked out better if it had been mapped out weeks in advance, instead of being concocted on the fly.

As if getting Michael freed from prison wasn't enough, the officer allowed them to have five minutes alone so that they could make their goodbyes. When the man's footsteps echoed away, she eyed Michael expectantly.

He looked back at her. His expression was unfathomable. After a few discomforting moments, he finally broke the silence. "Fiancé? Is there something that you know that I don't?"

That wasn't exactly the response Josephine had anticipated. But the conversation would get back on track once she explained the situation. She shrugged her shoulders. "I had to come up with something to convince Colonel Brady to let me see you."

"Fair enough. The next rational question should be, 'How did you discover my whereabouts?' but let's start with a different one. Why are you following me?"

Josephine bit her lip so Michael wouldn't see her pouting. The man was insufferable. *Where was his gratitude?* Was it impossible for him to show some emotion before the interrogation began? That was exactly why she steered away from men who viewed life so logically. She found them terribly boring. She could put up with it from Michael; she could never find him dull. A man with his remarkable features would keep her interested for a lifetime.

Holding her emotions in check, she decided to appease him and answer whatever silly questions he posed. "You speak as though I were stalking you. That most certainly is not the case. Did you not comprehend what I requested of the commanding officer? I came here to secure your release from prison."

"So I heard. We'll get back to that in a moment. How did you know my whereabouts?"

"I went to the White House and inquired," she said matter-of-factly.

"Of course. Where else?" he said sarcastically. "Are you telling me that your father, a brigadier general with the Union Army, disclosed classified information to you?" Michael looked at her intently.

"I didn't say that," Josephine replied defensively.

"Then who gave you that information?"

"What difference does it make? The bottom line is, I found you and I came here to rescue you."

He didn't seem appeased. Actually, he appeared the opposite, perhaps agitated?

Waiting a moment, Michael resumed his line of questioning, much to Josephine's chagrin. "Am I to understand that you got on a train, by yourself, and trekked halfway across the country to find me?"

"Would it make you feel better if I told you that I had an escort?"

"Potentially."

"That being the case, I will tell you that I was in safe hands. My brother was my guardian."

"Your brother?" Michael asked with a genuine note of surprise in his voice. "Hubert?"

"The one and only."

"Wasn't he commissioned to serve at The White House?

What in God's name would convince him to run this fool's errand?"

"Fool's errand? I beg your pardon!" Josephine said forcefully. "A fool's errand has no hope of success. As you and I both know, my mission has been accomplished. You heard the man. You're to be released back to your regiment."

She set her arms akimbo and glared at him. "To think I put my life on hold for a whole week to journey from Washington, D.C., to the Mississippi River in a godforsaken, teeth-rattling, stuffy train, and then traipsed through this city to a flea-infested prison to save your life. And this is all the thanks I get?"

Michael locked eyes with her. "Save my life? You have no idea what you've set into motion."

"What in the name of God is that supposed to mean?" Josephine spat back. "What I've set into motion is your chance to be free. From what I can see, this seems rather cut and dried. Am *I* missing something?"

"From your perspective, I'd say not."

She examined his countenance, trying to decipher his words.

"To be clear, I'm sure that your intentions were honorable, Josephine."

His words left her somewhat mollified.

"There's little chance of stopping what you've started. Only God knows how this will play out."

A sigh escaped from Josephine's lips. She hated cryptic statements.

Michael reached out and put his hands on her shoulders. "Our time here is almost up, my darling *fiancée*."

Josephine could not move a muscle. He was being facetious, but at this moment she couldn't care less. His touch burned through the fabric of her gown and her face grew more flushed by the moment.

"Godspeed to you, Michael," she finally choked out. "I only want what's best for you."

"I'm sure you do, Josephine. That's my wish for you as well."

Footsteps could be heard approaching the office.

"Ready to put your thespian skills back to the test?"

She looked at Michael in confusion.

"The word will soon be out that we're engaged. Let's convince the colonel that it's true."

He could have asked her anything at that moment and she would have agreed. The conspiratorial tone, the charming Southern accent, that handsome face, it was too much to resist. She nodded in agreement, though unsure of his intentions.

Michael pulled Josephine into his arms. He slid one hand to the back of her head and dropped his other hand to her waist. The he dipped her back and pressed his lips to hers in a fashion that was anything but brotherly.

His kiss took her breath away. The whole Union Army could have walked into the room at that very moment and Josephine wouldn't have noticed.

Chapter XXXIV

Once again, Michael found himself in Georgia. He stared into the campfire, half listening to the conversations between the other soldiers, while he thought back to that last encounter with Josephine.

The kiss was meant to close the iron door between the two of them before they went their separate ways. The ploy misfired. Much to his dismay, instead of being the clean break that he had hoped for, it actually intensified his feelings for her.

During his time at West Point, Michael had snuck a peck from a girl here and there, but never in his life had he tasted lips as sweet as Josephine's. *Lord have mercy. The last thing I need is to be as addled as a schoolboy over some silly girl.* With the turn of events in his life, it was critical to maintain a stellar focus, not have his mind adrift in the clouds.

He wasn't adept at reading the feminine brain, but he had a hunch that Josephine had been as affected by the kiss as he had been. That is, unless she was a much better actress than he had given her credit for. When the officer had walked back into the room and cleared his throat, the two of them reluctantly disengaged from each other. Yet, he felt compelled to keep his arm wrapped around her.

Josephine's knees seemed to buckle as she tried to step away. Her cheeks were flushed, and her breath caught in her throat. Staring into the depths of those olive-colored eyes, he'd felt a connection to another person unlike anything he had ever experienced in his life. He would have given just about anything for a few more minutes alone with her.

But that was not meant to be. The colonel handed him off to a guard who was waiting outside the door. That man walked him to a different part of the prison, where he was to stay until the negotiations were complete. Michael could have been in solitary confinement for all that he cared, as long he was out of sight, and arm's reach, of Appleby.

The transaction didn't happen as quickly as he'd expected it would. As he and the other men awaited news of their respective transfers, Michael had a good deal of time to replay in his mind the last interaction he'd had with Josephine. How had she gotten embroiled in his situation? How much did she know of his background? Did her father actually send her to St. Louis to facilitate the transfer? It seemed highly unlikely that a brigadier general would involve his own daughter in state affairs, but in these times, who knew?

From what he figured, things would turn out one of two ways for him. Either the original plan was still in place, and he would be assigned to another prison or, by some macabre twist of fate, he would actually be sent back to Company B.

When the conveyances finally rolled up to transport the prisoners, Michael scanned the area, looking for a messenger. Surveying the space several times, he concluded that he was on his own. That was a bit worrisome. Most of the men were anticipating reuniting with their company mates but that was about the last thing on earth that he wanted to do.

When they arrived at the depot, Michael boarded the train as directed and moved to the last car to get a bench seat to himself. He wanted to keep the war, soldiers, intrigue and everything of that genre out of mind for the trip. There was nothing he could do at the moment to change his path, so he was going to let things unfold and come up with a plan from there.

In the meantime, he had Josephine to daydream about. Starting from the top of her head crowned with honey-streaked hair to the tip of her dainty toes, he admired every part of her. She was a work of art, no doubt. He thought back to the stories that she shared of her growing up years. It made him wish that he would have stayed in touch with her after graduation. But there was no going back, only forward. When the war ended, he intended to make up for lost time. If it took the rest of his life, then so be it.

The plains streaked by as the train lurched toward the south and the longer that they were on board, the more apparent it became that he truly was going to the battlefront. They could string him onto any regiment since every commander was hurting for men at this point.

If he was shipped to Company B, he stood a good chance of encountering someone that he had fought alongside before. The last those men knew, he had been captured after the Battle of Ringgold Gap. He would let them assume that he had been holed up at Fort Delaware since then. A person might wonder why, after eighteen months, Michael was eligible for a prisoner swap, but the workings of the military remained a mystery to the ordinary enlisted man. Chances were, they wouldn't think twice of it.

Who knew, maybe he would arrive at his old camp and not recognize anybody. Various diseases had been running rampant through the Confederate ranks. His company could have been one of the unfortunate ones wiped out by a dysentery or chicken pox epidemic. If that were so, he would just assume his role with the rest of the men when he got there.

Now to address his major concern. What would he do once he got back to the front? He had done his share of killing and wasn't keen on shooting Union soldiers, seeing that he was now on their side. When he defected from the

Confederate Army, his goal was to save lives. His former comrades might see it as betrayal, but it really was in their best interest if his actions helped the war conclude sooner. If they survived, they would thank him in the end.

He stood fast by that decision, but now he faced another dilemma. Once assigned, or reassigned, to a company, he would be expected to fight. Conscientious objection was not an option.

Should he take up arms against his newfound allies? Should he put on a show of firing upon the Union troops but conveniently find his aim lacking? Should he try to escape or surrender? It was a moral dilemma. *If only this war would finally come to its inevitable conclusion.* Despondently, he let out a sigh.

At that moment, the engine brakes made an ear-piercing squeal and the train slowed to a crawl. Michael peered out the smudged window and saw the name "Atlanta" painted in block letters on a sign tacked to the side of a worn wooden building.

The soldier guarding the front of the railcar stepped to the platform, and the prisoners were instructed to disembark. After they assembled on the wooden deck, a group of officers approached them. Each man called out a name or two and the soldier or soldiers went to stand before them.

Michael recognized one of the men and, sure enough, he was the one to call his name. Captain John H. Crump seemed like he'd aged considerably since they saw each other last, but he'd survived, unlike a good deal of others from the regiment, Michael guessed.

The captain took a step towards him and instinctively Michael saluted.

"McKirnan?" the man asked, giving him a hard look.

"Yes, sir, Captain Crump."

"I couldn't believe my ears when I heard you were

rejoining us. When you disappeared, I thought sure you'd deserted. Or worse, you became a turncoat and sided up with the Yanks."

"Oh no, sir. I would never do that," Michael said as sincerely as possible despite the discomfort of lying to a commanding officer. "Nothing could make me relinquish my allegiance to the Confederate cause. I'm in this for the long haul." *Those acting lessons from Josephine were paying off.*

Chapter XXXV

After Michael had been escorted away, Josephine thanked the officer and left the room as well. Once out of the man's view, she leaned against the stone wall — punch drunk from her intoxicating encounter with that Adonis.

Once her heart rate subsided and she got her breath back, she exited the building. She dismissed the driver so she could walk back to the hotel. Josephine wasn't much for introspection, but she wanted to take a few minutes to consider the entire situation from a broader view before she reunited with Hubert and Bernadette.

Josephine was puzzled by Michael's reaction to her efforts on his behalf. Shouldn't a person be grateful to another person who facilitated their release from prison? She couldn't fathom why he hadn't prostrated himself at her feet after what she had done for him.

Perhaps she needed to consider the situation from Michael's perspective. "Hmm," she said to herself as she walked. "Let me think once..." *I am a man — make that a very handsome man — and I graduated from the top military institute in the country. Seeing that I hail from Georgia and my state defected from the Union, I chose to fight on the side of "President" Jefferson Davis.*

It's a losing proposition, but my loyalty to my state and my fellow combatants runs deep. After putting up a harrowing fight, I am captured and sent to a foul Union prison to rot my life away. Then a beautiful — make that stunning — young lady feels moved by my plight and pulls every string possible to secure my release.

Well, that certainly didn't help. It all sounded acceptable to Josephine. *What could it be?* She thought harder. Maybe his pride was hurt from being rescued by a female... Not likely. Could it be that he didn't want to return to the battlefield? That would be hard for Josephine to imagine. In her eyes, Michael was the bravest, strongest and most skilled man to ever grace a Confederate uniform.

When the hostilities first erupted, all the boys from town bragged about their enlistments. They seemed excited about the prospect of going to war and vowed to make the girls back home proud. Isn't the battlefield where young men proved their manliness?

Josephine stopped at a corner to let a buggy pass. She saw a soldier in full dress uniform seated next to a young lady who wore a fashionable off-white day dress with emerald green piping. The couple looked refreshingly carefree. When she was growing up in Washington, D.C., such as sight was commonplace, but it no longer was.

There were fewer young men in the city every day. Unfortunately, not all the boys who marched off to war would come home. *What have I done now?* She'd wanted to make life easier for Michael, but instead she might have put his life in further jeopardy. The idea was sobering.

But the die had been cast. And, as she was wont to say, *everything happens for a reason.* Josephine picked up a stick from under a pecan tree and ran it along the wrought iron fence she passed.

Michael was going to the front and she couldn't follow him there. What was she to do? Josephine hadn't thought any further ahead than securing Michael's walking papers.

She'd consider that in more depth after Bernadette was taken care of. If she and Hubert located her grandmother — and the woman agreed to take in her granddaughter and future great-grandchild — then Josephine and Hubert would board the next available train to Washington, D.C.

He may be a bit infatuated with Bernadette, but once Hubert was back in the city, he would be engulfed in his work and in keeping Francine happy once again.

My task when I get back will be to weasel my way out of working the entire summer at the prison. After three days there, she had already chipped a fingernail. The situation was unacceptable.

Josephine tilted her head up and saw the courthouse. It made her wonder how Hubert and Bernadette's search had gone. They planned to check that building first for any records of Bernadette's grandmother.

She was only a couple blocks from the hotel, so she quickened her steps to get there sooner. By chance, when she turned the final corner, she ran into Hubert and Bernadette.

"Any luck?" she asked her brother.

"The courthouse was a bust. But the clerk gave us a good idea. He suggested checking with churches in the area for any records. Apparently, those are more detailed than the government ones."

Bernadette had mentioned that she went to church with her grandmother as a child, so the idea seemed sensible to Josephine. "Did you visit any yet?"

"A few near the hotel. So far, no luck. It could take a while to get to all of them. Here's the list."

Josephine surveyed the piece of paper he held out to her. "With this number of churches in one city, sinners don't stand a chance around here! There are at least a dozen Catholic churches..." She skipped down to the other entries written in Hubert's neat scrip. "Then you've got the Methodist, Baptist, First *and* Second, Presbyterian, Episcopal, Evangelical and Unitarian, whatever those are. It would take a week to visit every one of these."

Hubert shrugged and Bernadette bit her lip to hold back a smile.

"Oh, no, little missy," said Josephine, looking the

younger girl straight in the eye. "I am not going to bide my time in a hotel for the next seven days while you and Hubert gallivant around St. Louis. I have much better things to do."

Whatever those things were, she didn't really know, but her tone of voice was intended to tell the two of them that she meant business.

"Have you a better suggestion, Josephine?" asked Hubert.

Josephine gave the question a few seconds of consideration. "As a matter of fact, I do," she said, snapping her fingers. "To start, let's narrow the list down. We can cut it in half by determining if Bernadette's grandmother was Catholic or something else. Do you know, by chance, Bernadette?"

"I'm sorry, Josephine, I don't."

"All right, then. What's your grandmother's name?"

"Lula Taylor." That was Bernadette's last name, so this woman was her paternal grandmother. But, if she was her maternal grandmother, that would indicate that Bernadette's parents had never married. The poor thing really did come from a disadvantaged background.

Josephine considered that information before replying. "If I had to make a guess, I would say she wasn't Catholic."

"What makes you think that?" asked Bernadette.

"There's no Saint Lula. No priest in good standing would christen a child with that name. Unless, of course, it was a nickname. But the surname Taylor sounds British or Swedish, which makes me believe that she was a Protestant."

Bernadette shrugged her shoulders.

"We can clarify this further," noted Josephine. "You said that you attended church with your grandmother when you visited St. Louis. Did the church have a crucifix upon the altar?"

"I don't know what a crucifix is."

"You know, a cross. One with the body of Jesus hung upon it."

"I recall a large cross but it was plain."

"Did your church have stained-glass windows?"

"Not that I remember."

"Well, there you go. Every Catholic church that I've been in has stained glass windows," Josephine noted. "I would say that our best bet is to start with the Episcopal Church. That sounds like a place an elderly lady might attend. What's the address, Hubert?"

He glanced at his list. "Corner of Fifth and Chestnut Street. What do you say we have lunch and then walk over there? The road that runs along the river intersects with Chestnut."

"A stroll would be lovely," said Bernadette. She glanced at Josephine imploringly.

"Fine," Josephine replied, rolling her eyes. "But I will warn you, my new kid leather boots are not broken in. If I get so much as one blister on my foot, I shall hold you both responsible."

"It's a chance we'll take," said Hubert with a chuckle.

After a lunch of lightly grilled shrimp and root vegetables, the three of them set out. The women held parasols over their heads to protect their skin from the early summer sun. They passed numerous other folks enjoying the river walk as well.

Turning down Chestnut Street, they noticed that the neighborhoods were less refined. The further south they walked, the more dilapidated the buildings were.

Several blocks from their destination, Josephine noticed a group of children walking at a distance behind them. When the trio stopped at an intersection to let a buggy pass, a male child, possibly six years old, scurried up to Josephine and tugged on her skirt.

"Miss," said the boy politely.

"Yes," said Josephine, scrutinizing the child from head to toe. The little urchin was filthy. She quelled the urge to brush the spot where he had touched her clothing.

"Spare a penny, miss?" He looked at her beseechingly. "Me and my little sister, we ain't eaten since yesterday."

The boy was stick thin, and the little girl who stepped out shyly from behind him was just a wisp of a thing. Josephine had no reason to doubt his story.

"Don't your mother and father feed you?"

"Ain't got no father," mumbled the boy, staring down at his bare feet. "Ma gets us grub when she's around but when she's gone, we have to fend for ourselves."

Josephine could hardly believe her ears. She had heard of children living in poverty but had never spoken with such a creature before. The downtrodden folks in Washington were cordoned off from her neighborhood, so she never interacted with them.

Moved with pity, she reached into her reticule and pulled out two nickels. "Here's one for each of you. This should tide you over until your mother returns."

"Thank you, miss," the two said in unison before running off.

She, Hubert and Bernadette resumed their walk but hadn't gone more than ten feet when they sensed that they were being followed again. Turning around, they discovered a group of children gathering behind them like a gaggle of goslings traipsing behind mama and papa goose. Having garnered their attention, they all began imploring them for money, each sharing their own sad story.

The little ones pressed in on them, overwhelming Josephine.

"Hubert, gather your change." She reached into her reticule and grabbed her remaining coins. "Now, hand me yours," she said to her brother. The children looked at her hopefully.

Checking to see that there were no oncoming vehicles, she flung the money into the street. The children ran into the roadway to gather the coins. Seeing their opportunity, the girls picked up their skirts, each grabbed one of Hubert's hands and scampered the last three blocks to the church.

Once there, they hastened through the large wooden doors, quickly pulled them shut and leaned against the wood panels to catch their breath.

It was Josephine's first time inside a church that wasn't Catholic. She peeked around in curiosity. It had pews on each side like her parish, albeit sans kneelers, and the main aisle ended at the altar, which was elevated two steps. But it was rather plain, as there were no statues of saints, no font with holy water inside the door, no Stations of the Cross depictions on the wall, and no stained-glass windows, just double hung, glass-paned windows like most houses had.

"May I help you?"

Josephine's head swung toward the doorway near the front of the church. A gentleman dressed in a black robe with bell sleeves approached them. He didn't have the white clerical collar of a priest, but he did have a white lace tie of sorts around his neck, so she assumed that he was a clergyman.

"Hello, sir," said Hubert, stepping forward and extending his hand. "Hubert Bigelow." He nodded toward the two girls. "Josephine Bigelow, my sister, and Bernadette Taylor."

"How do you do?" replied the man. "I'm Pastor Schultz. How can I be of assistance to you?"

"Sir," Hubert said, "My sister and I are helping Miss Taylor in her quest to locate her grandmother, Lula Taylor. Would she, by any chance, be a member of this church?"

The man shook his head. "I'm sorry to say, she isn't. But, having been pastor at Christ Episcopal Church for thirty years, I've met a good number of St. Louisans. The name does sound familiar. Perhaps you could try First Presbyterian Church; it's just one street over from here."

"We'll do that. Thank you for your time, sir," said Hubert.

"It was my pleasure. May God bless you with success in your endeavor."

The pastor showed the trio out the back door and instructed them to cross the yard to Fourth Street. They'd see the church from there.

As the man said, a simple wooden steeple with a cross affixed to the top was visible from the next street. As they walked closer, the whole building came into view. It was a simple white-washed clapboard structure with a single door in the front. The lawn was neatly manicured and daisies lined the walkway leading to the wooden porch.

"This building seems familiar," said Bernadette.

"Let's hope so," said Josephine sincerely. Her feet were starting to ache. They got closer and approached a man sweeping the wooden plank sidewalk in front of the church.

"Excuse me, sir," said Hubert. "Do you belong to this church?"

"You could say that," he replied. "I'm Reverend Artemas Bullard."

"Pardon me, Reverend," said Hubert. He offered his hand to the man. "My name is Hubert Bigelow, this is my sister Josephine, and Josephine's friend Bernadette."

"How do you do?" said the girls politely.

Hubert took up his speech. "We traveled here from Washington, D.C., because Bernadette recently lost her mother. The only family that she has left is her grandmother, who lives in this city. She can't remember her address but recalled that she was a church-going woman. We're trying to find the church that she attends."

"That seems like a logical idea," said the older man. "Miss Bernadette, what is your grandmother's name?"

"Lula Taylor."

A look of sorrow crossed the pastor's face wrinkled face. He laid the broom aside and pulled Bernadette's hands into his. "I'm very sorry to hear that you've lost your mother," he said compassionately. "The timing is so unfortunate. I hate to say this, but your grandmother just passed last month. I conducted her funeral services myself. We buried her in the paupers' graveyard near the river."

Bernadette's face blanched, Hubert's eyes widened, and Josephine's mouth gaped open. *What in the world are we going to do with her now?*

Chapter XXXVI

Michael was assigned to patrol duty with Captain Crump. As they paced the perimeter of the encampment, the man caught him up on the company's last encounter. The story centered on Confederate General Joseph E. Johnston.

"Johnston was getting hounded by Sherman and had just fallen back to a new defensive position close to Atlanta," said the captain. "On the twenty-sixth of May, Sherman sent Major General Oliver O. Howard's Fourth Corps on a flanking mission around our right. We were entrenched west of Marietta. The next day Howard ordered an assault against our works. He was surprised to see ten thousand of our troops under the command of Major General Patrick Cleburne waiting for him," said Crump with a chuckle.

"The fighting took place near the Pickett family farm and grist mill. When the smoke cleared, we still held possession of the field. It was Sherman's worst defeat in his foolhardy campaign to take Atlanta." A stream of chewing tobacco expelled from Crump's lips hit a tree trunk, punctuating his declaration.

It was a lot for Michael to take in. He was under the impression that there was no holding Sherman back. But if the Confederate Army got a new lease on life, the war could go on forever. How anyone would survive this debacle was beyond him. He kept his thoughts to himself as they completed their rounds.

When their shift was over, Michael meandered through the camp, making his way between pine trees. He walked past groups of men gathered around campfires, cooking beans or boiling water for coffee. Wedge tents were scattered throughout the area. The commanding officer's walled-tent and the hospital tent were pitched toward the edge of a clearing.

Michael searched for anyone familiar from when he had last been with the company. In time, he ran into a fellow with whom he'd always had a cordial relationship. After glancing at the man's overcoat, he noted that the former sergeant had been promoted.

Quartermaster Sergeant Beau Blue was nothing less than astonished to see him. "Lordy, Lordy, look who's back from the dead!" he exclaimed when he recognized Michael. The man, affectionately known by his friends as B.B., pushed himself up from the tree trunk that he was perched on and offered his hand to Michael.

"Where the heck you been? Haven't seen hide nor hair of you since late last year."

"Uncle Sam invited me to stay with him up in Delaware. It was an offer I couldn't refuse," said Michael sardonically.

"Barrel of a gun pointed at your chest when he was being all hospitable like?"

"How'd you know?" Michael asked in jest.

"Just a good guess. How'd you ever end up back here?" B.B. asked earnestly.

"Well, the Union Army must have been hurting for replacements. I was part of a trade between the two sides."

"What'd they git for you — a sow and two steers?" joked B.B.

"Something like that," said Michael.

"I'd say we got the better end of the deal." His voice turned serious. "Been a long winter and spring. Our forces are depleted. Gonna take a lot more manpower to mow those Yanks down. Glad to see you back."

Michael nodded noncommittally, but a voice resounded in his head. *Enough is enough.* He was sick of dismemberment and death. The last thing he wanted was to be the cause of more misery for anyone, regardless what side they were on.

"You're probably raring for some action. Sorry to disappoint you, but you're gonna have to wait," said B.B.

"How's that?"

"We'rc in a holding pattern for a few days. Both sides are regrouping."

"That's fine by me," said Michael earnestly. "I can use the time to work on my shot or do a little hand-to-hand sparring. I'm a bit rusty."

"Well, there you go."

The two men finished their conversation and B.B. invited him to bunk with him in his two-man pitch tent. Michael readily agreed. No use asking what happened to the previous tentmate. He really didn't want to know.

Chapter XXXVII

As much as Hubert and Bernadette may have wanted to extend their time in St. Louis, they had no reason to stay there any longer. Consequently, Josephine hatched a new plan. Never one to let grass grow beneath her feet, once the pastor delivered the disheartening news to Bernadette, Josephine asked the man to point them in the direction of the train depot.

She then set off at a rapid pace, leaving the other two hustling to keep up with her. When they arrived at the station, Josephine purchased three tickets and handed one to Hubert and one to Bernadette.

Hubert reviewed the ticket. "Atlanta?"

Bernadette didn't question the move, but Hubert voiced his misgivings. "Listen to me, Josephine. The most reasonable thing for us to do is return to Washington. There's a war going on, you remember that, don't you?"

Josephine rolled her eyes. "Why do you and Father feel compelled to keep reminding me of that?"

"Okay, then. Are you aware that the battlefront is centered near Atlanta?"

"I know that, Hubert." Josephine was ready to recite a list of reasons why it made sense for them to travel toward Atlanta and away from Washington, D.C., but decided to get to the point quicker. "We need to put as much space between Bernadette and her abuser as possible."

Hubert seemed as though he considered arguing his point but simply said, "Fine."

It was just as well that he didn't ask for more reasons. The list was rather short. It started with Bernadette escaping Marcel and ended with Josephine getting in the vicinity of

Michael. However, she preferred to keep that information to herself.

With Hubert on the same page, she emphasized why Atlanta was the ideal destination. "It's a large city and undoubtedly has a Catholic church somewhere. Once we locate the church, more than likely we'll find a Catholic school nearby. And if we find a school, there will be a convent on the same grounds, housing the sisters who teach there. What religious sister, in good conscience, would turn away an unwed mother?"

It all sounded aboveboard, but in truth she was only using Bernadette's situation as a means to get what she wanted. Josephine knew that Michael was being sent to the frontlines near Atlanta. She had convinced the superintendent to tell her the regiment and company to which he was assigned, under the premise that she wanted to correspond with him, as would any devoted fiancée. It may have been a bit underhanded, but the subterfuge was necessary to get closer to Michael.

The trip to Georgia took nearly two days. Twice the time it would have taken to travel east. The condition of the train tracks worsened the further south they traveled. When they finally reached Atlanta, they spotted a Catholic church immediately. They only had to scan the cityscape and keep an eye out for the tallest steeple. Upon seeing it, Hubert hailed a Hansom cab. As they pulled up to Hunter Street, they saw a stone marker near the walkway with the words *Immaculate Conception Church* chiseled into its surface.

As soon as the conveyance pulled over, Josephine jumped out, not even waiting the extra few seconds for the driver to hand her down. Impatience was getting the best of her. She was anxious to talk to the priest and see if he could help find accommodations for her and Bernadette.

Fr. Thomas O'Reilly was a compassionate man. He listened as Josephine began her story and then graciously greeted Hubert and Bernadette once they made their way to the door of the rectory. She hadn't quite gotten to the part about the young lady's delicate condition, but the priest was able to draw his own conclusions when he laid eyes on the girl with her hand centered on her protruding midsection.

Evidently, Bernadette wasn't the first female to reach out to Father O'Reilly with this particular problem. Within minutes of their arrival, he directed them to the convent on the far side of the grounds, with instructions for Sister Francis Ann to welcome their new guests.

The sisters received the trio, Bernadette in particular, with open arms. They were keenly interested to learn of her lack of religious training. It was something they intended to rectify as quickly as possible.

With the assurance that his charges would be well taken care of, Hubert fondly, *too fondly* for his sister's peace of mind, said farewell to Bernadette. He then gave Josephine a hug and a kiss on the cheek.

She pulled him aside and gave him explicit details of what to say to their father when he got back to the city. She wanted him assured that his only daughter was in good hands and would be returning in due time — *due* being the operative word.

Since she claimed to be Bernadette's guardian, the sisters were more than happy to have Josephine stay at the convent until the baby arrived. *Guardian or relatively new acquaintance, it was a horse a piece.* All that really mattered was that she could remain in the area where Michael was positioned. When the Rebels finally came to their senses and laid down their arms, she would be close at hand to greet her returning hero.

Josephine vowed to find him, regardless of what it took. If she had to purchase a personal ad in the *Atlanta Daily Examiner,* she would. If it took following his retreating regiment back to Arkansas, she was prepared to do that as well. There was no way on God's green earth that she was going to lose the man of her dreams, now that she had finally found him.

Until she and Michael could reunite, Josephine planned to bide her time at the convent. She could help the sisters and keep an eye on Bernadette.

Besides its location, there was something about the convent that appealed to her. While religion had always been a part of her life, she realized that she hadn't appreciated the gift bestowed upon her at her baptism. Something stirred in her heart and caused her to want to learn more about her faith. Residing with the sisters for a while might be the ideal way to do that.

With a chapel on site and the cathedral next door, she'd have ample opportunity to give thanks to God for all the blessings granted unto her this year. She'd managed to graduate from Georgetown Academy for Young Ladies, she discovered the intriguing career of a feminist undercover author, and she was reintroduced to Michael. That in itself was nothing short of a miracle.

Oh, and I was able to save a girl from a conniving, murderous cur. That certainly was worth noting. The icing on the cake… she was free from her obligation to volunteer at Old Capitol Prison. Her laundry days were finally behind her!

Chapter XXXVIII

What Michael thought would be a forty-eight or seventy-two-hour break turned out to be nearly four weeks of down time. As the days went on, the anticipation and restlessness grew in the ranks. Everyone knew that Sherman and his troops were out there and that they stood between him and his prized possession of Atlanta.

The call to arms came on the twenty-sixth of June. Company B was ordered to march towards Kennesaw Mountain. Reaching their destination, they entrenched themselves around the mountain. A day later, all hell broke loose. As the first rays of sunlight crested the eastern horizon, the Union Army launched their attack.

Wave after wave of men came at them. Michael and his fellow soldiers had the advantage because the Union troops were attacking uphill. Having had plenty of time to think through his plan, Michael decided the best way to engage in this battle without compromising his conscience was to put his shooting skills to the test and aim at the oncoming soldier's extremities and forgo the kill shot.

From what he could tell, his plan was working well. His accuracy was dead on, and he winged a couple dozen soldiers. At one point, he pulled back behind a tree to reload his firearm. As he shoved the ramrod into the barrel, he glanced up and did a double take. Several Yanks had infiltrated the Rebel line.

Within seconds, he was thrust into combat with a soldier who approached him from the left. The man was too close to shoot and had a wicked-looking bayonet affixed to his rifle. Michael used his gun to block the bayonet each time it was thrust his way and soon had the man down on his knees.

A shot rang out behind him. It grazed Michael's leg but hit his opponent in the center of his gut. The soldier crumpled forward, his weapon still in hand, and before Michael could get out of the way, the man toppled over, and the tip of the bayonet sliced into Michael's thigh.

The searing pain hit him immediately. It felt as though his leg was on fire. Blood trickled from the superficial wound but gushed from the spot where the bayonet pierced his skin.

Michael heard a swooshing sound in his skull and then fell forward head first to the ground. He had the oddest sensation of being asleep and yet being aware of what was going on around him. A bugle blasted and then an eerie silence came over the area as men retreated to their respective camps.

"Does someone out here need help?" The words floated through the fog to Michael's brain. A few moments later, he felt himself being rolled over. The next thing he knew, an object was being secured around his thigh.

"Sir, I've put a tourniquet on your leg to stem the bleeding," said a soldier wearing a blue uniform. "It looks like you have a nasty lesion there." Michael struggled to open his eyes, squinting to block the midday sun.

"Have I been captured?" he asked the man.

"No, sir. Both sides are regrouping. They'll be coming to collect the casualties soon."

Forcing his eyes open further, Michael noticed the man staring at him intently with a puzzled expression on his face.

Michael had no idea what was going through the Yankee's mind, but he felt befuddled himself. His eyebrows furrowed and he managed to choke out a few words.

"You've saved my life. Perhaps I'm confused from the blow I took to the head, but isn't it the job of Union soldiers to take Confederate lives, not spare them?"

"Sir, I am not a butcher. You are no threat to our side in your present condition. There's no reason for you to die on this field today. Enough have passed here as it is." Voices barely audible from the south of their position alerted the two to the presence of soldiers drawing near.

"Your men are coming. You'll be back to camp in no time. I need to depart before they catch sight of me."

"I am eternally grateful for your help, sir," said Michael, mustering the energy to give the man a brief salute. "I only wish I had the means to repay your kindness."

"If you want to repay me, take care of yourself and get home to your family when the hostilities are over and done."

"Yes, sir," said Michael, giving another salute to the retreating major, who was dashing through the trees. Lacking a belt, the soldier held his pants up with one hand as he went.

"That's exactly what I intend to do," he said out loud, even though the man was beyond hearing range. "Come hell or high water, I am going to get back to Josephine. We aren't family yet, but I intend to rectify that situation the moment I see her."

Chapter XXXIX

Carrying an empty laundry basket and humming, "Salve Regina," Josephine pushed open the back door of the convent and stepped out into the fresh air and sunshine. Apparently, God had a sense of humor. The sisters felt that it would be a good idea for Josephine to keep occupied while Bernadette received tutelage in the Catholic faith. With a noticeable lack of skills in cleaning and cooking, she had been assigned to the laundry area.

Thus, for the past two weeks, she found herself outside on most days, hanging loads of wash on the rope lines behind the convent. Sheets, towels, habits, undergarments, and veils flapped in a gentle breeze. It was hard to imagine how a group of no more than thirty women, who wore the same thing every... single... day, could accumulate so much wash each week.

The lines filled up with the never-ending row of monochromatic fabric, dotted by the occasional pastel of one of Josephine's garments. In the sea of black and white, the bright fabrics stood out.

Josephine set the basket in the grass and reached overhead to unpin the white tunic on the end of the clothesline. The sisters had graciously offered to loan lightweight tunics to the young women. The white garments were more practical and cooler than what the girls wore. While Bernadette accepted the offer, Josephine politely declined.

Josephine had worked diligently her whole life to maintain her porcelain skin tone. She avoided exposing her bare skin to the sun; the last thing she wanted was to be mistaken for a field hand. With a complexion so fair, white was not her color. It completely washed her out so she refused to wear it, whether it was in season or not.

Of course, when it came to her wedding day, that would be a different matter. White was the color of purity, after all. Following the adage "something old, something new, something borrowed, something blue," she would wear the vintage diamond bracelet passed down to her from her grandmother, a new wedding gown, the garter that her mother wore for her wedding, and Josephine's neck would be encircled with brilliant blue sapphires. She had her father commission such a necklace from a local jeweler for her sixteenth birthday, and it had been safely tucked away in her cedar hope chest ever since.

An eerie sensation caused her musings to grind to a halt. For the past two days, she had the strangest feeling that someone watched her as she performed her daily chores. As was now her routine, she woke every morning when the sun rose — along with the sisters and postulants — got dressed and then proceeded to the chapel to begin her day reciting the Liturgy of the Hours with the other women.

They said Lauds at dawn, Prime at six, Terce at mid-morning, Sext prior to lunch, None at three o'clock, vespers before supper and Compline before bed.

Between the first two morning prayers, Josephine generally started the laundry, and after Terce she hauled baskets to the backyard of the convent to hang the clothes. By the time None was complete, the items were dry enough to gather and bring back to the laundry area for ironing, a new chore that she had mastered with only a few scorched items to her credit.

Josephine unpinned a veil from the line and brought it to her face. She inhaled the aroma of sunlight and fresh air as she turned to scan her surroundings. It was so quaint with the white picket fence lined with hedges, the fruit trees sprinkled across the lawn that provided both shade and produce, and the gardens occupying the rest of the space.

Turning back to the lines, that sense of peacefulness came to a sudden jolt. Josephine felt eyes upon her as she took the clothes down. For the life of her, she couldn't imagine what anyone would find so interesting about a woman doing laundry. But whomever it was, they chose to remain out of sight. With the waist-high picket fence encased by shrubs and the numerous trees along the perimeter of the yard, there were multiple places in which a person could stay concealed if they chose to.

The thought of someone spying on her sent shivers down Josephine's spine. Spending day after day on her knees in the chapel was beginning to affect her in a positive way. She found comfort in the words that the women repeated in group prayer. Once again, daily Mass had become a part of her routine as well. The Latin words from her school days came back to her. Before long she could follow along and repeat the prayers by rote, as she once could.

It wasn't so much the idea of being observed while she worked that bothered her, but she sensed that the observer had dishonorable intentions. Needing to complete her chores, Josephine did the only thing that she could think of. She started praying to her patron saint, St. Joseph the Worker. Considering her life as of late, he had been her daily confidant. The other saint whose ear she bent was St. Michael the Archangel. During her daily routine, she prayed for him to watch over her own Michael.

Josephine couldn't take the perusal any longer. Back in the day, she would have dropped her work, sprinted to the trees and jumped the fence to confront the scoundrel, but with Bernadette under her charge, she acted uncharacteristically prudently. As she bent to place a sheet into the basket, she pretended to drop one of the clothespins. As she crouched to pick it up, she pivoted and shifted her eyes to see if she could spot anyone near the fence.

Sure enough, she saw someone. It was a man dressed from head to toe in black. He melted back into the shadows, but Josephine caught a glimpse of his figure. The hair on her arms stood on end. There was something eerily familiar about him.

Chapter XL

Just as the Union major had told him, Michael's men were on their way to help. He was placed on a stretcher by two soldiers and quickly transported back to camp. Thanks to the tourniquet that the Union soldier had applied above the wound, his condition was stable and so he was placed in a holding area while the surgeon dealt with the more urgent cases.

After biding his time for half an hour, Michael noticed a priest walk into the tent. An orderly pointed out several men to him, and he walked to their cots to quietly administer Last Rites. Out of respect for his fellow soldiers, Michael shut his eyes and listened as the priest intoned the Latin prayers over the men. He went through the ritual four times, working his way through the tent.

Michael cracked his eyes open just to make sure the priest wasn't stopping in front of him. If he did, things were a lot worse than the orderly had made them out to be. He could sense the priest bending over him. *Good Lord, why isn't he moving along?*

"Is it really ye, Michael?" the man asked. His brogue was likely as thick as the day that he stepped foot off the Emerald Island.

Immediately, Michael snapped his eyes open wide. "Father O'Reilly?" He looked at the man incredulously. "What are you doing here?"

"That be exactly the same thing I was going to ask ye," said the priest.

Indicating his blood-soaked trousers, Michael said, "I used my leg to stop a wayward bayonet."

"Aye. If yer opponent was meanin' te fillet ye, he had a good start," said the man with a chuckle. "No need to worry. I believe the surgeon's assistant is set to work on ye next. I see him threading his needle."

Michael glanced in the direction the priest indicated and his head grew light.

"He's got a delicate touch, lad, ye'll be fine," assured the priest. "But back to me initial question. How did ye come to be here with Company B again? The last I knew, yer name was on the list of men missing in action. I read it meself in the town square."

"Was in action all right, Father, just not with my company. I had the misfortune of stepping into an enemy trap late last fall and found myself captured by the Union Army."

The priest raised his eyebrows.

"I've been a guest of President Lincoln since then," he added. *No fib there.* It was bad enough confessing the sin of lying, but it would be twice as hard to confess that he'd lied to the priest himself.

"It can happen to the best of us, son. I be glad to see yer injury isn't any worse." He offered his hand to Michael. "Take care of yerself, hear me? I'd like to spend more time with ye, but I need te make me way to the Union camp te see about some souls over there." He clasped Michael's hand between his two hands. "If ye can find me before ye head back to the field, I'd be happy to hear yer confession."

"Yes, sir," replied Michael, shaking the proffered hand. "I'll see what I can do."

Father O'Reilly said a prayer over him and then exited the tent.

Encountering the priest from his home parish was such an odd coincidence. After the man left, Michael thought back to their conversation. *Was Father O'Reilly really serving both armies?* When the hostilities were all behind them, they'd have to sit down and swap stories. It sounded like they had more in common than just their Irish heritage.

The casualties from the battle were horrific, particularly for the Union Army, which was said to have lost some two thousand men. It would take a good week to bury the dead, so the combatants on both sides were in for a reprieve. The timing was ideal for Michael. It would give his leg time to heal before they resumed their march.

As much as the men claimed to abhor the fighting, it didn't take long for tedium to set in when they were encamped in one spot for any length of time. There were only so many times that a man could clean his gun, march in formation around the square, or swap the same stories with his bunkmates.

If a company stood still long enough, word would get out and occasionally a coach carrying ladies of negotiable virtues would stop by to entertain the troops for a few days. Michael had no intention of imbibing on a sweetmeat such as that, but seeing someone of the feminine persuasion wouldn't be the worst thing in the world. The tedium was getting to him as well.

Chapter XLI

Did the man know that she saw him? Regardless, Josephine wanted to get back into the convent as hastily as she could. Clothespins flew as she ripped the last few things off the line. With the wicker basket balanced on one hip, she scurried toward the back door of the building.

She hadn't gone more than ten feet when someone stepped out in front of her from behind a tall hedge. It was the man that she had seen moments before. Josephine froze.

Everything about him was dark: his greased back hair, his narrow-set eyes and his complexion. Some women might consider him handsome, but he was the devil incarnate in Josephine's view. He appeared precisely as she had pictured the villains in the numerous mystery novels she'd read through the years.

She tried to keep her imagination in check. For all she knew, the man could have some connection to the church and was at the convent for a valid reason. While her gut told her to throw the laundry basket at him and run, she didn't want to alarm the sisters inside or appear to be a crazy woman.

"May I help you?" Josephine asked guardedly.

"Perhaps," replied the man in an unfamiliar accent. His eyes raked down Josephine's figure. She felt as though he were sizing her up, which was worrying, to say the least.

"I am missing something, miz. Perhaps you know where it is."

Josephine drew back and eyed him warily. What could he have possibly lost that she would know about? "I highly doubt that," she said haughtily. "To what are you referring?"

"It's something about this high," he said, holding his hand level with the top of Josephine's head, "with a shape like this." His put his hands about a foot apart, then moved them down, making an hourglass figure in the air.

If she was interpreting correctly, he was indicating the shape of a woman's body. *What in God's name was he getting at?* She let silence hang between them until he continued.

"She goes by the name of Bernadette."

Josephine's heart dropped from her chest to her stomach. This could only be Marcel, the man who had harmed Bernadette. Knowing what he was capable of scared the wits out of her, but she did her best to keep a neutral countenance. "I don't know what you're talking about," she replied firmly. "And I have no more time to waste on this conversation." She attempted to step around him.

"Not so hasty, young lady," said Marcel as he roughly grabbed her elbow. "Let me refresh your memory a bit."

Josephine attempted to yank her arm from his grasp. He was surprisingly strong for a wiry man. She could not wrestle away from him.

"I came to collect Miz Bernadette the day she was released from Old Capitol Prison, but alas, what did I see? Some woman and a dandy Union soldier in a fancy carriage whisking *ma cherie* away. I couldn't imagine my Bernadette leaving with strangers willingly, so I followed to see where she was being taken."

The conversation made Josephine highly uncomfortable, but she pursed her lips and remained silent as the man went on.

"I saw you purchase train tickets at the New Jersey Avenue Station. It was unwise to cause a — how do you say — commotion at the depot, so I kept an eye on the three of you as you boarded the train. It didn't take much convincing to get the ticket man to tell me your destination." He paused as a devilish grin crossed his face. "I then returned to Old Capitol Prison. The soldier in the outer office was more than... accommodating when I made my inquiries about the woman who accompanied Bernadette from the prison grounds."

He chuckled. "What can I say? I have a way with words."

Josephine highly doubted that. More likely he had a way with weapons. She stood motionless, waiting to see where the conversation would lead next. If she had to guess, it would be nowhere good. She had no choice but to hear him out since his hand was wrapped around her arm like a vise.

"The next day, I find myself on a train, heading toward the Mississippi. Quite the enchanting town, St. Louis, wouldn't you say?"

Josephine stayed mute.

"Fortunately for me, *stupide* people that you are, you failed to cover your tracks. I stayed on the scent and, voilà, here we are — at a convent, of all places. Who would have thought that *ma petite* Bernadette would land here, considering the condition in which she has found herself?"

Marcel sighed, as though he pitied the poor girl — which was ironic to Josephine, considering that the child was in her predicament because of him.

"I haven't seen the soldier on the grounds since my arrival. Thus, I shall presume it is just you, Bernadette and the harmless spinsters in residence here."

Josephine refrained from educating the man that the women were not spinsters. They were, in fact, brides of Christ. But that was beside the point at this moment. Back to the matter at hand, there was no use bluffing any longer, so she came directly to the point. "What do you want?"

"That's more like it," he said. "I didn't travel this far to go home empty-handed."

It was exactly as she feared. The man intended to bring

Bernadette back to Washington, D.C. The reality chilled her to the bone. She saw what he did to the girl the last time he laid hands on her. Josephine's mind raced as she tried to figure out how to stop him. Her first thought was to get free of him and hope she could outrun him to the door of the convent.

The man seemed to read her mind. He tightened his grip on her arm to the point where Josephine was losing circulation in her fingertips. "Don't even think about it," he said menacingly.

It was hard for Josephine to hide her fear. Judging by the position of the sun in the sky, she guessed the sisters would be in the chapel for mid-afternoon prayers. They would certainly notice that she was missing from her usual seat. *Why hasn't anyone come searching for me?* If even one person came outside, they would sound the alarm and the man would, likely, slither back to his hiding spot. That would give her the time that she needed to figure out how to get Bernadette to safety.

The man shook her arm to get her attention. "Drop the basket now. We're leaving."

Josephine looked at him in confusion. Hearing a clicking sound, she dropped her gaze to the man's free hand.

He held a knife, the blade gleaming in the sunlight.

Her eyes widened in genuine fear.

"No need to worry about Miz Bernadette any longer."

Her head began to spin. Had he finally succeeded and killed the poor girl? It was too much to fathom. She felt as though she was going to faint.

"Oh no, you don't," he said in a steely voice. "You will remain steady on your feet, and you will walk with me to where the horse is tethered. If any passersby see us, you are to act as though you are with a beau."

"Why on earth would I do that?" Josephine exclaimed.

"It will be in your best interest to do as I say. I would hate to see such a pretty frock stained with blood."

The knife was still visible in his hand, so Josephine knew that he was serious. Her level of bewilderment matched her degree of alarm. "Where are you taking me?"

"You shall find out soon enough."

If her concerns about Bernadette were correct — that he had murdered Bernadette — then she was in serious trouble. Josephine had to fortify herself for what she might soon face, so she asked the question that was foremost in her mind.

"Why are you doing this?"

"Why not?" he countered. "Let us talk as we walk, shall we?" He pulled Josephine through the gate and set off at a quick pace on the wooden walkway.

"I will make this brief," he stated, as they strode away from the grounds. "You and that soldier stole something that belonged to me. Though its value has decreased substantially as of late, nonetheless, it is my property."

Bernadette was alive. God be praised. That thought didn't ease Josephine's concerns for her own well-being. She instinctively tried to pull away from Marcel.

"Oh, not to worry, my little one. Bernadette is still tucked away with the sisters, just as you last saw her. In her present condition, she is of little interest to my customers. I shall let her sit on her roost until the child arrives and deal with her after that."

A shuddering breath escaped Josephine's lips. She was more than relieved to hear that Marcel hadn't harmed Bernadette any further, but the state of the girl's health once he returned was disconcerting. However, at this moment, the more pressing concern was her own safety.

"Ah, yet business must go on. I've become accustomed to a certain lifestyle which takes a considerable amount of money to maintain. That's where you come in, Miz Bigelow.

Since Bernadette is..."— his eyes shifted upwards — *indisposed* for the next several months, I need to supplement my income."

Josephine's eyes widened in distress. The situation was getting more calamitous by the moment.

"I will need to change things up a bit. Obviously, we can't have you walking the streets of Washington, D.C. When word gets out that you are missing, your father, the esteemed brigadier general, will have his men scour every square inch of this country hunting for you."

Josephine didn't know whether to be outraged by the street walking comment, relieved that it wasn't viable, or scared about what else the scoundrel had in mind. As she quickly discovered, it was the latter.

"That being the case, I have made up my mind to pass you along to the highest bidder. You would be amazed what a piece of unsullied goods will go for in a camp of soldiers starving for female companionship."

"You wouldn't dare," ground out Josephine.

"Oh, wouldn't I?" Marcel replied nonchalantly.

"When I tell them that my father is one of President Lincoln's trusted generals, no soldier would dare lay a hand on me."

"*Au contraire*, my pretty one. When these *Rebel* boys catch wind that they have a Union female at their disposal, they will be throwing their money at me to get their hands on you."

Chapter XLII

Michael rubbed the barrel on his revolver with a piece of scrap cloth as the sun lowered in the sky. It seemed a never-ending task as he bided his time waiting for the next call to action.

Soldiers conversed throughout the camp as they shot dice, drank coffee or worked on their own chores. Out of the blue, the guard on watch duty announced that a horse with civilian riders was nearing their encampment.

The word "woman" rippled through the crowd. A feeling of excitement took over the camp. After two weeks of inaction, the men finally had something to relieve their ennui.

The prospect of seeing females was enough to get most of the men to their feet. They hustled toward the clearing as the man pulled the horse to a halt some twenty feet in front of the gathering crowd. With nothing better to do, Michael followed the other men.

"One?" he heard someone say.

"That ain't enough for everybody," said another man.

More voices came from the crowd. "Where's the passel of women like we had last time?"

"Not even worth stickin' around." The crowd started to disperse. Most of the married men went back to their tents, Michael noted.

"Ain't one better than none?" A few heads nodded in agreement.

The crowd of men opened to allow the horse to be walked to the center of the group. A female passenger sat sidesaddle in front of the driver. Michael couldn't see her face but seeing the grip that the man had on her, Michael assumed that she wasn't there of her own volition.

When the horse stopped, a good number of men rushed forward for ringside seats. Michael, however, kept his position on the outer edge of the group.

The man threw one leg over the rump of the horse and jumped to the ground. He then grabbed the woman by the elbow and forced her down in a less than gentlemanly fashion. When her feet were planted on the ground, he lifted the veil adorning her fashionable bonnet to reveal her face. He put his finger under her chin and swiveled her head from side to side so that the men could get a better view of her. She yanked her head away and scowled at her escort.

One soldier after another whistled and expressed their admiration for the comely female.

"We done struck gold," said one of the soldiers. "This gal's a whole lot pertier than any of those other ladies that come pay us a visit," another man said in agreement.

Looking past the soldier in front of him, Michael gained an unobstructed sightline of the couple. Instantaneously, every muscle in his body constricted. His heart caught in his throat when he recognized the girl.

How in the name of heaven did Josephine end up in a Confederate camp in the middle of a war zone? Knowing her, she'd have a perfectly "logical" explanation, but that didn't dismiss the fact that she was in imminent danger.

Michael clamped his jaw and willed himself not to spring forward and beat the living daylights out of that wretched excuse for a human being who had his hand on her. With his anger barely in check, he worked his way through the crowd so that he could hear what pronouncement came from the blackguard. If Michael had anything to say about it, those would be the last words that viper ever muttered.

"Good evening, *messieurs*," the man began. The murmuring in the crowd died down as the soldiers strained to hear what the stranger said. "It is my understanding that the Confederate Army just won a vital engagement against the Union troops."

A cheer went up from the crowd.

"In appreciation of your diligent efforts, I have come bearing a gift for your company." The men nodded and yelled in approval. "This fine piece of female flesh, courtesy of Uncle Sam, has been shipped all the way from Washington, D.C., to entertain the victors." Most of the men broke into raucous applause, but some turned and walked away in disgust.

Josephine didn't utter a word. The daggers she threw with her eyes at the crowd of strangers spoke volumes. It didn't bother the men. Once the word *entertain* was mentioned, with the exception of Michael, all the men's thoughts seemed to take off in the same direction.

In his mind, Michael was going through various options that he could use to free Josephine. He would fight to the death for that girl if he had to. His hands balled up in fists as he continued to survey the situation.

"Listen up, my good men," the man said in a raised voice. "As you can see, this property, it's quite valuable."

Hearing those words used to describe a white woman struck Michael. How many times had he heard that same term applied to a Negro? His family had never owned slaves, but he knew many people who did. He had been surrounded by the institution of slavery most of his life. The thought now sickened him.

The salesman was getting to the heart of his pitch. "To be fair to all you fine men, I am going to auction this young lady off." A few boos were heard but the rest of the crowd cheered in approval.

At that point, most of the officers left the clearing. Michael assumed they wanted no part of this fiasco but didn't want to risk a mutiny by stopping the proceedings.

"Top bid gets her." Scuffles broke out here and there as a couple men attempted to intervene on the lady's behalf. The man was not deterred from his task. "Just to be clear, I'm not opposed to pooled bids as long as you gentlemen are... amenable to sharing the young lady." That idea gathered a positive reaction from potential bidders. Men gathered in small clusters and started digging through their pockets.

Like a trained auctioneer, the man began the bidding. Michael listened as the numbers rose but remained in his spot. There wasn't more than one hundred dollars between the lot. As the bidding wound down, a group of four men licked their chops. It appeared no one had the means to outbid them.

"Going once... Going twice..."

"Two hundred Union dollars," Michael yelled from where he stood. He waved overhead the stack of twenty-dollar bills that Brigadier General Bigelow had given to him all those months ago.

Immediately, all heads swiveled in his direction, including Josephine's. Voices rose from the crowd, expressing disbelief that anyone had that much money — or, if he did, what a fool he was for wasting it all on one female. Some wondered aloud how a Confederate soldier came upon such a sum of Federal bills. But, for the seller, money was money.

"Sold, to the man over there."

Michael nodded and stepped through the throng to claim his prize. When he reached for Josephine's arm, she slapped it away.

"Keep your filthy paws off of me, you swine!"

The men shouted their approval. "She's a feisty one, lieutenant!" There were more catcalls. "You'll have fun breaking that little filly!"

Josephine's response was not what Michael expected, but it was of little consequence. As far as the others were concerned, she now belonged to him. He took a step closer as she backed away.

"Not so fast, soldier," said the salesman, putting himself between the two. "I need to see the cash before the transaction is *fini*."

Michael glanced towards Josephine and then handed over the stack of bills. The men around him whistled in admiration as a show was made of counting the money. It was doubtful that any of them had ever seen that much money at one time.

The money counted, the man grabbed the horse's reins and instructed Michael to follow him and the girl.

"Not to worry, men," the man said, before leaving the clearing. "There are more women where this young lady came from. Seeing that you are such a hospitable group, I plan on returning with more delightful tidbits soon." The men applauded in approval.

"Sir," he said to the highest-ranking officer still present, "if you wouldn't mind allowing this soldier a little privacy to *inspect* his purchase, we'll make our way to that grove of trees just down the way. I can't imagine it will take more than a few minutes."

The officer snorted. "By all means." He then turned to address his men. "The rest of you are dismissed. No one leaves the perimeter of this camp except McKirnan." Pointing at Michael's chest, he added, "You've got twenty minutes. If you can't take care of matters in that time, I'll send over someone who can."

"Yes, sir," said Michael automatically. He turned to start walking to the tree line.

Josephine looked at him incredulously.

"Whoa, soldier," said the auctioneer. "Before we head out, you need to give that gun belt to one of your compatriots. We wouldn't anyone to get hurt."

"Of course not," replied Michael, reigning in his sarcasm.

Speak for yourself. He couldn't wait to get his hands around that scrawny lecher's neck. Quelling those thoughts, he unbuckled his belt. His bunkmate was within arm's reach, so he handed the ensemble to him.

"Very well, then. Off we go." With that, the three headed away from the camp. Josephine struggled to get out of the man's grip, throwing every insult at him that she could come up with as they went along. The sun dipped below the horizon. By the time they entered the grove of trees, they were engulfed by darkness.

"Take a spot over there," said the man to Michael, indicating a tall oak tree. He then pushed Josephine in the opposite direction.

She scrambled to keep to her feet. Her eyes narrowed in infuriation.

"Just a minute, I paid for that girl fair and square," said Michael through gritted teeth. "She's mine now."

"You'll have her soon enough, my friend," the man replied as he stepped back to Josephine and latched onto her upper arm with his hand. "As an ethical businessman, I can't in good conscience sell you a product that has not been tested."

Josephine's faced blanched. Obviously realizing the implication of his words, she tried to break free of his grip. "No!"

"Have we not had this conversation before, *ma petite*?" The sound of a switchblade opening cut through the air. The man grabbed the lace collar of Josephine's dress and pulled her next to him. He placed the blade of the knife along her jawline. "You will do as Marcel tells you, or you will pay. If you so much as utter one more word, I will practice my carving art on your sublime canvas." He moved his hand up to caress her cheek.

That was precisely the opportunity that Michael was waiting for. With the blade temporarily away from Josephine's throat, he sprang toward Marcel's side and brought his arm crashing down to separate the two from each other.

Josephine let out a muffled scream and fell backwards to the ground, holding her shoulder.

Throwing his weight into the lighter man, Michael knocked Marcel to the ground. Marcel still clutched the knife, so Michael wrestled to take it from him. What the smaller man lacked in stature, he made up for with speed and agility.

Eventually, Michael was able to constrict the other man's wrist in such a fashion that the knife flew out of his grasp. It landed several feet away from the pair. Without a weapon to defend himself, Marcel disengaged and attempted to back away from his adversary.

With a moment to regroup, Michael glanced at Josephine. He felt like he had taken a blow to the gut. Crimson red stained the bodice of her saffron colored frock. Blood seeped from a shoulder wound. Michael scrambled up and rushed in her direction. "Josephine!"

She looked down at her dress and began to sway on her feet.

Michael lunged toward her.

"Michael, watch out!" she screamed.

He turned to see Marcel sprinting towards him, a knife blade glinting in the moonlight.

In one swift move, Michael ducked and upended the smaller man. When Marcel hit the ground, Michael pounced and pinned him down. The man gripped the switchblade, and they struggled for control of the weapon. The longer they fought, the more it became apparent that Marcel was no match for Michael. Having the advantage, Michael wrestled the knife from his opponent's hand and turned the blade on him.

Marcel laid his head back in resignation and tried to catch his breath. "You know the young lady, eh, my friend?" he panted out. "Here, I thought the daughter of a brigadier general would be unsullied. If only I had known, I would have enjoyed some entertainment with her myself before bringing her to this camp."

Michael's jaw tightened, and he slipped his hand around the man's neck, ready to throttle him.

"Well, aren't we the sensitive one," the man jeered. "Tell me, was she as spirited behind closed doors as she was out here tonight?"

Michael had the urge to wipe the smirk off the man's face with his fist. Before he could pull back his arm to strike him, Josephine called out, "He's got another knife!"

The warning came too late. Michael felt a blade thrust between his ribs. With no time to think, he plunged the knife he held into Marcel's neck.

The man's eyes widened in surprise. "Touché, my friend..." He coughed, and blood speckled his lips. "Good luck handling that little one. She will keep you on your toes, mark my words." Having expended that energy, his head slumped to the side. When his eyes rolled back in his head, Michael knew that he was gone.

Michael backed away from the dead man. His shirt stuck to his skin as the blood soaked through it. Taking a deep breath, he got to his feet and staggered to Josephine. He offered his hand to her, and she fell into his arms.

"I know that you're injured too, but we've got to get out of here. I'll help you onto the horse."

"Wait," said Josephine. She dropped to her knees next to Marcel.

Michael thought it odd that she wanted to pay her last respects to the miscreant, but he didn't stop her. He soon found out that he'd misread her intentions.

The girl was digging through the pockets of the dead man's overcoat. She pulled out the wad of Greenbacks. "If I'm bought and paid for, I may as well get something out of this."

Chapter XLIII

The wind stung Josephine's face as Michael set the horse off at a breakneck pace. Her dress was stiff from the blood that had been spilled upon it. Hopefully that meant the wound had stopped hemorrhaging. She swiveled her head to assess Michael's injuries.

Fresh blood seeped through the sliced fabric of his gray jacket.

"Michael, we need to stop so your wound can be dressed."

"There's no time for that," he yelled over the sound of the pounding hooves. "You heard the officer. If I fail to return to camp after twenty minutes, they're sending someone out after me. We need to put as much space between us and them as we can before the alarm sounds."

Josephine clung to the saddle horn for dear life as the horse kept up its frantic pace. "Put as much space between us and them as you want, but if you drop dead from this ride because of loss of blood, it's not going to do either of us any good, now is it?"

"Trust me," replied Michael. "I've survived worse injuries. I'll make it through this one."

"May I have that in writing?" Josephine shot back.

"I can write or I can man this horse, you choose."

"Fine. Keeping riding."

The throbbing in Josephine's shoulder intensified as they sped along. Michael kicked his heels into the horse's flanks, and the animal accelerated. She began to wonder if either of them would survive the ride.

Eventually Michael eased up on the reins and the horse slowed to a more bearable pace. The sound of the hooves lessened and she was able to finally talk without shouting. "Where are we going?"

"Immaculate Conception Church in Atlanta."

"Immaculate Conception Church? *The* Immaculate Conception Church?"

"The one and only, that I'm aware of," replied Michael. "Do you know the place?"

"Intimately," responded Josephine.

Michael raised his eyebrows. "How would a girl from Washington, D.C., know anything of a little church in the heart of Atlanta?"

"It just so happens that I was just there."

Michael craned his head to peer at her. "That seems highly improbable but do explain."

"After you were bartered away from Gratiot Street Prison, I traveled with Hubert and my friend Bernadette to Atlanta. She was escaping her keeper — the scoundrel whom you most recently dispensed."

"Hmm."

"Anyhow, Miss Bernadette was in trouble."

"Trouble, as in…" Michael shifted the reins to one hand and gestured with the other, rounding it away from his midsection.

"Precisely. Can you believe that man beat her when she didn't dispose of the *problem*? As though it were her fault. Of course, he may have been a bit touchy since he wasn't sure if the child was his or not."

"Have you got a condensed version of this story? We're less than a mile from the city."

While Josephine preferred to tell stories in her own dramatic style, she acquiesced and did it his way. "Fine, if that's how you want it. But I intend to give you the full details later."

"I'll be waiting with bated breath."

"So, in short, Hubert brought us to Atlanta to find refuge. We came across Immaculate Conception Church, where Father O'Reilly was kind enough to help us. He set Bernadette and me up in the convent on the grounds of the church for safekeeping. Hubert returned to Washington, D.C., to unruffle his fiancée's feathers, which is a story in and of itself. Marcel tracked us to the convent and kidnapped me at knifepoint. We left the city and the next thing I knew, we were in the middle of your camp."

She paused to catch her breath. "There. Brief enough for you?"

"You did an admirable job. But I do have one question. Why did you rebuke me in front of my entire company? I was there to help you."

"Acting!" Josephine exclaimed. "I didn't want to let on that we knew each other. That would have foiled my plans."

"Your plans? Am I missing something? I saved you."

Josephine twisted in the saddle to look at Michael. "Saved me? I would have clawed that man's eyeballs out before I let him touch me. Everything would have turned out fine."

"Fine? As it was, he cut a slice into your shoulder."

"That was your fault."

Josephine felt Michael pull back. "My fault?"

"You heard me. I had a script written in my head where I escaped Scot-free" — she glanced up to see Michael's reaction; he appeared skeptical — "until someone had to barge in and disrupt my plan. Thanks to you, I'll never be able to wear an off-the-shoulder gown again."

"I would say that's the least of your problems, young lady."

"That tells you what you know of my life," she sniffed.

Josephine could hear Michael chuckling behind her. *I swear, men will be the death of me yet.*

As they approached the outskirts of the city, Michael slowed the horse and held a finger to his pursed lips, warning her to be quiet. It was a task but, if put to the test, she could do it.

The streets of the city were eerily still. They traveled several blocks when all of a sudden Josephine felt Michael stiffen. He whispered under his breath, "God bless it!"

Alarmed, she glanced back at him and saw him staring straight ahead. Turning her attention to the road, she noticed a group of men on horses coming around the corner a block ahead of them.

"If you truly have thespians skills, now's the time to use them," he whispered in her ear.

Catching his drift, she immediately went limp in his arms.

Michael pulled the horse to a stop in front of the other riders, who were blocking the roadway.

"Who goes there?" shouted a gray-clad soldier on the lead horse.

"First Lieutenant Michael McKirnan, sir."

"What has happened to the woman?" the man asked, peering at Josephine from his perch.

"She was in an altercation with another camp follower," Michael answered. "I'm taking her to a doctor in the city square."

The man drew his horse closer to Michael and Josephine.

"No disrespect to you, sir," said Michael. "But I wouldn't do that if I were you." The man looked at him questioningly. "The girl suffers from gonorrhea as well."

Josephine's eyes rolled under her closed lids.

The soldier nudged his horse, getting it to step back. "As you were, soldier. If anyone else stops you, tell them that Corporal Turner has given you permission to proceed to a medical facility."

"Yes, sir," said Michael. He saluted the commanding officer and turned his horse to get around the other riders. Then he set off at a trot.

"Gonorrhea? Really?" Josephine asked in a pouty voice once they were clear of the men.

"Acting, my dear, acting."

"I'll show you acting."

Chapter XLIV

Please, God, let Father O'Reilly be here, Michael thought as he helped Josephine slide off the horse. He wrapped the arm on his good side around her waist and assisted her up the porch stairs.

"Hold tight for a second," he said.

Josephine nodded mechanically and reached for the wooden rail behind her.

Michael pounded twice on the paneled door and then descended to ground level to hitch the animal to the metal ring on the wooden post in the yard.

Over the course of the trip, the bleeding from the incision subsided. Michael felt exhausted but his breathing wasn't impaired, so, from what he could determine, the blade sliced between his ribs but hadn't inflicted any major damage. *Thank you, guardian angels.*

Looking up at Josephine, her bleeding had miraculously ceased as well. *Praise be to God!* He bounded up the steps, pounded on the door again, and pulled her close to him.

"I be coming," came a voice from inside the building. Hearing the priest's words, a sense of relief washed over Michael. The door was unlatched and swung open, a circle of light illuminating the scene before the priest's eyes.

"Michael? Didn't I just leave ye in the Confederate camp?" the priest said.

"You did, Father, but there's been some trouble."

"I would say." The priest glanced from Michael to Josephine. He hurriedly ushered the two inside, took a brief glimpse of the yard, then shut the door and turned the skeleton key in the lock.

Father O'Reilly visually inspected Josephine closer to

assess her injuries. His brow furrowed. He squinted and took a step in her direction. "Weren't ye the lady on me doorstep last month?"

"Yes, Father."

"Have a seat, lass," said the priest, pulling out a wicker-seat chair that was tucked under a rolltop desk. Michael felt Josephine stagger as he assisted her to her seat.

"I didn't know ye two were acquainted, or... make that related, seeing that ye have no escort," said the priest.

"We're not related yet, but that that could be rectified straight away, Father, if you choose to help us," said Michael. He held his hands protectively on Josephine's shoulders.

She turned and looked at up Michael inquiringly. Josephine then shifted her eyes to the priest.

"I'd be happy to assist ye, son," said the man, with a tone of benevolence in his voice.

"Excuse me, Father. May I talk to Michael for a moment?" With permission granted, she motioned to Michael to help her to her feet.

Once on solid footing, Josephine grabbed his lapel and tugged him to the far side of the room. She seemed to have regained some of her strength, Michael noted with surprise.

"What's going on?" she blurted out.

"I need to ask you a question, Josephine."

Her eyes widened and her jaw dropped. "A question?"

"Yes. But before you answer, I want you to give this some thought. It's been my observation that you make hasty decisions."

"I prefer to say that I'm decisive in nature."

That girl never lacks an answer, Michael thought, trying not to laugh. "Be that as it may," he said, in a serious tone, "I want you to think through the consequences of the choices I am going to lay before you now."

She nodded sincerely.

"We have not known each other long, but I have developed a fondness for you, and I sense that you have developed similar feelings for me as well." He peered at her to gauge her reaction.

"May I interject?" asked Josephine.

"Of course," said Michael, doing his best to stay patient.

"Just to clarify, *Father O'Reilly,*" she said, turning her head toward the priest, "we've known each other since I was thirteen years old. We just recently have become reacquainted."

"Duly noted," said the priest.

"Continue, Michael," Josephine prompted.

"Would you concur with the second part of my statement?"

"The part about the fondness?"

"Yes," answered Michael.

"I would say that you have assessed my feelings towards you properly," she replied, matter-of-factly.

Michael smiled in satisfaction. "Excellent. Now, if we weren't in the middle of a war, I would get permission from your father and court you properly. After having done such a thing for an acceptable length of time, I would ask for your hand in marriage."

Josephine's mouth opened slightly. She nodded her head mechanically.

"Once you agreed," Michael continued, "we would post our nuptial bans. Then you and your mother and the women in the bridal party would take several months to prepare for a wedding befitting royalty. From what I've heard, it's an event that women start dreaming of as little girls."

Josephine nodded again. "Uh-huh."

"Unfortunately, time isn't on our side. We need to get you to a place of safety until the war ends. God only knows how long that will be. As for myself, I would imagine the

Confederate Army is in pursuit of me, considering that they probably found that man's body in the thicket by now."

The priest cleared his throat. Michael could just imagine what the man was thinking.

"Not to worry, Father O'Reilly," Josephine interjected. "It was in self-defense, wasn't it, Michael?"

"Essentially, yes. We'll discuss that in the confessional," he said, directing his words to the priest, who hardly seemed assured.

"To get back to where I was..." The sensation of nervousness was foreign to Michael. He pushed through it and continued. "Josephine, considering your status in society, I'm sure you had a dream courtship and wedding sketched out in your mind years ago. I can't give you that, but I do have something to offer you."

Michael inhaled deeply to steady himself. He reached for Josephine's hands and dropped to one knee.

Josephine's heart caught in her throat. *Was this really happening?* She listened for Michael's next words.

"I may not be able to give you the wedding that you envisioned," he said, gently squeezing her hands, "but, if you agree to marry me, I'll give you my heart. And when this war is over, we will build the life of our dreams together."

Tears sprang to her eyes. She tried to speak but no words came to her lips.

"Josephine Katherine Bigelow, will you marry me?"

"Yes!" she said without hesitation.

"Remember the part about thinking it over?"

Think it over? She'd spent the last two months doing nothing but thinking. Michael had been in her thoughts continually. She had gone over every word, every look, every moment that she could remember sharing with him since their reunion.

He was a man of faith, intelligence and compassion, who was conscientious, industrious, loyal, and so much more. To top it off, he was amazingly handsome, which certainly didn't hurt his cause. In short, he was everything that she could possibly ever want in a man.

Knowing his penchant for getting directly to the point, Josephine replied, her face beaming. "What's to think over? I've been mad about you since the day I first set eyes on you at West Point. This is the moment I've dreamed of for three years."

Michael stood, pulled Josephine into his arms and held her tightly to his chest. "Then we shall get married." He planted a kiss on her forehead. "We may need to postpone the honeymoon, but we are on church property and a priest is at hand, so I suggest we do this now."

"Are you serious?" asked Josephine incredulously. Any thoughts of bridal gowns and bouquets and banquets were discarded. None of that mattered anymore.

"Absolutely," said Michael.

"What happened to the man who doesn't make hurried decisions?" Josephine asked cheekily.

Michael's face took on a serious expression. "That man shall soon be on the run," he said. "If you prefer to wait, I understand. Neither of us knows what the future holds. Father O'Reilly will make sure that you are in good hands after I leave, but my situation is more precarious."

Josephine shook her head. "Michael, I would be willing to stand before the Confederate officials and testify that you took Marcel's life to save mine."

"If only it were that simple. This situation is more complicated than it appears." He turned to the priest. "Father, I need to confess something. Not a formal one, considering that we're in the presence of another person, but I would ask that the Seal of Confession cover this."

"Without a doubt, Michael, whatever ye say here will be between ye, myself and God... and Miss Josephine, of course."

"Well then, here goes. As you can see, I am wearing the uniform of a Confederate soldier. However, in actuality, I am a major serving the Federal Army of the United States of America."

"A major? In the Federal Army?" said Josephine. This was turning into an even more interesting story. There was more to Michael than she realized. She gazed at him in admiration.

"That's why I'm in a predicament. Not only is the Confederate Army pursuing me, there's a good chance that the Union Army is as well."

Josephine's breath caught in her throat. That news was distressing but it would not alter her decision. "With God on our side, we'll get through this, Michael."

Michael squeezed her hands tighter and she responded in kind. "I don't know what has transpired in your life since you enlisted, but I do know one thing. Blue or gray, Union or Confederate, it makes no difference to me what side of the battle you're on. Only, that at this very moment you are *on* my side and *at* my side. I'm prepared to marry you right now. Even one hour as your wife would be better than a lifetime of regret for not taking advantage of this opportunity that we have now at hand."

A smile broke out on Michael's face.

Father O'Reilly smiled as well and then tapped his chin as if formulating a plan. "It may not be ideal... but the clothes ye have on will have te do. I'll rouse the housekeeper so that she can witness the nuptials. After that, I'll make arrangements for yer safekeeping. I shouldn't be away more than a couple hours. I'll have Honora put a wash basin and towels in the spare room so ye can tend to each other's wounds while I'm gone."

Knowing the location of Michael's wound and her own, heat crept from Josephine's toes to the crown of her head. She rubbed her upper arms as goosebumps starting racing up and down them.

Michael pulled her close in a reassuring gesture.

As if oblivious to her sudden moment of discomfort, the priest resumed ticking off his plan for the two of them. "I don't know why ye were being threatened by that man, Josephine, but I suggest ye go te a convent in another city te wait fer Michael. The further from the warfront the better. Out of consideration fer Miss Bernadette's safety, we shall send her along with ye. I be thinking somewhere in Eastern Texas. There be a convent just across the border from

Arkansas. I know the mother superior, so I'll pen a brief introductory letter asking fer yer admittance." He paused a moment to catch his breath.

"As fer Michael, ye can hide right under both armies' noses where they'll never think te search. I'll secure a position for ye working in one of the hospitals. They're in desperate need of help, especially as the warfront comes to the door of our city. You'll wear the uniform of an orderly, so if ye happen to run into someone ye know, regardless of which side, they won't question yer allegiance."

Both Michael and Josephine nodded in agreement. The priest exited the room to get the housekeeper. The two came back shortly, the woman grumbling. "Why on God's green earth would anyone need te be married in the wee hours of the morn?" the lady muttered.

"'Tis none of yer concern," said Father O'Reilly. "Ye're just here as witness. As soon as we have the knot tied, ye may return te yer quarters."

"Fine. But I hope ye don't make a habit of performing God's holy sacraments in the middle of the night. A lass needs her beauty sleep, don't ye ken?"

"Yes, me dear."

The similarity of the voices led Josephine to believe that the priest and woman were related. Once they entered the room, her suspicions were confirmed. They were the spitting image of each other.

"Honora, ye may remember Michael McKirnan. And this is his intended, Miss Josephine Bigelow."

"How do you do?" Josephine said to the lady.

"'Tis nice te meet ye, me dear," said the older woman, turning on her Irish charm. She viewed the couple over and furrowed her brows. "Such a fine evening fer a wedding. I'm honored that ye asked me to be yer witness."

Michael glanced towards Josephine. He raised an eyebrow and his eyes shone with amusement. Turning back to the woman, he replied, "Ma'am, we are honored to have you join us."

"'Tis me pleasure," she answered.

"Enough with the formalities, time be a wastin'," said Father O'Reilly. Proceed te the nave and we'll begin the ceremony."

Honora fell in step behind her brother. Michael grabbed Josephine's hand and they walked into the candlelit sanctuary together.

Josephine was struck by the stillness and sense of peace she felt in the space. The church setting really hadn't been much of a consideration when she and her friends talked of their future weddings.

Their conversations had centered on the handsome men they'd have waiting for them at the end of the aisle, the pomp and circumstance surrounding the big day, and all the other little details that Josephine now realized were inconsequential.

They never focused on what really was the heart of the matter: a man and woman, being joined in holy matrimony, who loved each other unconditionally and would give their lives for each other.

Josephine had found that. While it was true that she and Michael barely knew each other, she was convinced with every ounce of her being that he was the man that God intended her to marry. If it wasn't so, all the stars would not have aligned to make this magical moment happen.

Her younger self would find this hard to believe, but Josephine knew, beyond a doubt, that it didn't matter what she wore for her wedding, who was in attendance, or what time of day the ceremony took place. It only mattered that she and her intended would become one with the blessing of the Church.

Father O'Reilly ushered her and Michael to the interior of

the church. The two of them knelt in front of the candlelit altar and held hands. The wedding ceremony was brief, but Josephine clung to every word in her heart.

The look in Michael's eyes as they repeated their vows was a sight that would be etched in her mind forever. She had never felt so loved, cherished and protected in her entire life.

At the conclusion of the ceremony, Michael and Josephine turned to each other. They were locked in each other's gaze.

After a moment, the priest spoke up. "You may kiss the bride!"

Michael brushed his lips sweetly against Josephine's and then drew her into a loving embrace. Their hearts beat together as one. He held onto her as if he never wanted to let her go.

They finally broke apart when Honora asked to be excused to go back to bed. Permission granted, her footsteps echoed away as she shuffled to the far side of the building. Father O'Reilly had the newlyweds sign a marriage certificate and then walked Michael and Josephine to the spare room adjoining the rectory. He made his leave, saying that he would be back within two hours.

The rectory door was soundly shut behind the departing priest. Michael turned to face Josephine. "Shall we, Mrs. McKirnan?" He scooped her up into his arms to cross the threshold into the sleeping chamber, showing no sign of being hampered by the injury from earlier in the night. A mischievous smile came to his lips. "It be time te tend those wounds, don't ye think, lass?"

Chapter XLVI

Michael had said more goodbyes in his life than he could remember, but saying farewell to Josephine as he left the rectory to accompany Father O'Reilly to the hospital was the most excruciating departure that he had ever experienced.

Like most anybody his age, he'd lost loved ones through the years, including his own mother, who succumbed to consumption while he was a student at West Point. He loved her as any good son would, but it was vastly different than how he felt about Josephine. In the brief time that they had together, the two of them created a bond that would never be broken. Not just physically but on a deeper level. They had to condense months of courting into about an hour, so all pretenses were dropped and they opened their hearts to one another completely.

Thus, when they had to break away from each other, it felt as though a chunk of his heart had been ripped from his chest. To make matters worse, Josephine, ever the stoic one, was uncharacteristically emotional. Tears rolled down her cheeks and dampened his neck as he held her close for one last embrace. He got choked up as well.

No matter what it takes, I am going to survive this war and get back to her. There was no way that God would show him a glimpse of heaven on earth and not let him experience it ever again.

Father O'Reilly found the ideal way to get Michael's mind off of Josephine after their departure. He deposited him at a hospital in town that was in a complete state of disorder. After the initial tour of the facility, Michael began to wonder if *all* the patients left feet first. He was astounded that anyone survived such an unsanitary environment.

When the priest had suggested the hideout for him, Michael assumed it would be a medical facility similar to the one that his uncle owned in Atlanta. Both buildings had been private residences before the war, but Dr. William Burgess' infirmary was run in a relatively clean and orderly fashion.

Granted, Doc's office was in a state of disorder, with stacks of papers, medical volumes and ledgers strewn everywhere, but there was a method to his madness. Given an adequate amount of time, his uncle could locate just about anything.

As far as the surgery and recovery rooms went, Michael's sister, Amara, would stop in every so often and go through the supplies, cut bandages, and reorder whatever was needed. Amara was a stickler for organization, so those tasks were second nature to her. The nurses on staff were in charge of the overall cleaning tasks and performed them quite well. Michael hadn't been there in more than two years so conditions may have changed, but he couldn't imagine things getting to the deplorable state that he saw in this building.

Michael stepped into the surgical area, where a putrid smell hung in the air and flies buzzed and swarmed around six wooden operating tables. When had they last been washed? He stopped mid-step and turned his attention to the dark splotches on the plank flooring at his feet. It appeared as though a blood-letting had taken place there. It must have been the aftermath of the skirmish yesterday. The staff worked through the night patching up men.

Another step forward set his stomach churning. He'd spotted, under the window on the far wall, the source of the smell and the flies. It was a pile of bloody limbs. Ready to gag, Michael bolted from the room.

From that point on, he became a man on a mission. He'd likely be holed up here for a few months as the war continued to drag on. From what he could determine, even with the failed attack on Kennesaw Mountain, the tide was making a definitive turn in favor of the Union. Sherman was carrying out his plan to cut a swath through Georgia from its northern border to the Gulf of Mexico. Whether it was enough to get the Confederate Army to surrender was really anyone's guess.

At this point, he didn't care what side was victorious, he just wanted the war done and over with so he could be with Josephine again.

He thought about her night and day as he went about his duties at the hospital. When he was first introduced to the facility, his officer instincts set in and he started giving orders. The surgeon who ran the infirmary was too tired and overworked to care if someone was trying to usurp his authority. He was more than happy to have a man take over the day-to-day administrative duties.

After some consideration, Michael came up with a plan to turn things around. He wanted to implement systems that would be simple enough for the staff to follow and that would run the hospital more efficiently. Each time a crop of new casualties arrived on their doorstep, everyone would have an assigned task.

Considering that his only business experience had been helping his father run the dry goods store, he impressed even himself by how he was righting this ship. He didn't just give orders, though, he jumped in to help wherever he could. Working to the point of exhaustion every day proved to be just the medicine he needed to keep from pining away over Josephine.

Before long, the hospital was noticeably cleaner. Michael coined the phrase "If you have time to lean, you have time to clean," and he used it judiciously to keep the staff occupied during the slow hours.

Days turned into weeks and weeks turned into months. His heart ached with longing for Josephine but working his fingers to the bone left him too exhausted to expend the energy to worry about her. He prayed nonstop as he worked, asking God to keep her in His care until they could be together again.

Michael followed the news of the war through the men who came to their door for care. He often thought about making his way to his father's store to let him know that he was alive and well, but he never left the grounds of the hospital. The streets of Atlanta teemed with all types of salacious men. If there was a price on his head, he didn't want to compromise the safety of his family by letting them know that he was living in the city. It would be safer if his father, James and Amara believed that he was still missing in action.

General Sherman waged his Atlanta Campaign through the summer and fall of 1864. On the first of September, General John Hood and his Confederate forces pulled out of Atlanta, and the city was surrendered the next day.

On the fifteenth of November, Sherman set off on his infamous March to the Sea. His departing orders were to burn Atlanta's munitions factories, clothing mills and railway yards. The buildings around the square, including the courthouse, churches and hospitals, were spared, thanks to Father O'Reilly. Apparently, he warned Sherman that there would be mutiny in the ranks if he so much as touched one house of worship.

Sixty thousand Federal soldiers marched with Sherman toward Savannah. On the twenty-first of December, Sherman overtook the city and presented it to President Lincoln for a Christmas gift. Upon leaving Savannah in January of 1865, Sherman and his men burned and pillaged their way through North and South Carolina.

Robert E. Lee surrendered to General Grant on the ninth

of April 1865, signaling the end of the Civil War. But it wasn't the end of the war for Michael and the rest of the hospital staff. Even though the battlefields were deserted, they still had plenty of men to take care of. As the camps started to empty, many men were sent to the hospital for treatment of various diseases.

A measles epidemic that started in the beginning of April filled the hospital beds. It seemed to be quite contagious — nearly as infectious as small pox. Michael was grateful that another hospital was treating the men diagnosed with the pox. He didn't know how diseases spread from one person to the next, but with the war over, the last thing he wanted to do was get sick with anything.

By the third week in April, most of the measles patients had been dispatched — either to their hometowns or to the local cemetery. They hadn't had a new case in nearly two weeks. But the round-the-clock care of the men took a toll on Michael. He developed a cough, sore throat and fever.

The timing was less than stellar. He was anxious to be dismissed from his hospital duties and head off in search of Josephine. But, as much as he wanted to get on the road, it didn't make sense to leave the facility until he was on the mend. Two days in, when he anticipated the cold would break, things took a turn for the worse. He continued to work, as miserable as he felt, but when he rolled up his sleeves one morning to scrub the floor of the bunk area, he noticed a red, blotchy rash on his skin.

"God bless it," was the last thing he remembered thinking before blacking out.

Chapter XLVII

Josephine sat in a pew, twisting her rosary in her hands. She had never been known for her patience, and what little she had was being tried unmercifully since she and Michael parted ways on their wedding day. As she had anticipated, no correspondence arrived from him. It would have been reassuring to hear something, but it wasn't worth him putting himself in danger just to appease her.

The only mail she received was from her mother, who was under the impression that Josephine was on an extended adventure with her new friend Bernadette.

It was an adventure all right. Father O'Reilly was able to find safe haven for the two young women at a convent adjacent to Our Lady of Guadalupe Church, located in a settlement just beyond the Arkansas border in Eastern Texas. Once the two of them were settled in, Josephine had written to her parents. While not revealing everything that had happened since they last saw each other, she shared enough so that they could rest assured that she was safe and, for her mother's sake, having a pleasant time.

Someday, she would confide everything to them. But it was best to be as vague as possible now. No need to go into all the unpleasant details.

Before she and Bernadette fled Atlanta, Father O'Reilly had obtained a new frock for each of them. The dress that Josephine wore the night that she and Michael were married was irreparably damaged from the blood spilled on it, and Bernadette's gown was strained to the limits by her rapidly expanding belly.

For their safety, the two young ladies were escorted on

the train ride to Texas by two seminarians from Immaculate Conception Church. While exceedingly polite, the young men seldom interacted with the two females. They were busy studying for their upcoming exams. The Bibles they carried showed signs of wear, as the two constantly paged through them for reference.

After the seminarians escorted the girls to the door of the convent, they made their introductions to the mother superior and then bade them all farewell. Sister Gregory cordially greeted her and Bernadette.

The group of younger sisters crowding behind her viewed the two girls with varying degrees of surprise on their faces. Glancing at Bernadette, who held her back to ease the weight of the baby from her hips, Josephine realized what caused their startled reaction. The two of them wore black habits. It was the only clothing that Father O'Reilly had been able to scrounge up on short notice.

Not that many months ago, Josephine wouldn't have been caught dead wearing black, since it was the color of mourning. But, at this point, what she wore was the least of her concerns.

Once Sister Gregory apprised the other sisters on the situation, they gathered around Bernadette in excitement. Apparently, it was quite the cause for celebration that they would be welcoming a little one into their community not too many months down the road.

From that moment on, Bernadette was treated like royalty by the women in the convent. They didn't want to overtax her, so her only duties around the house were to help with mending and stitching, including creating a wardrobe and necessities for the baby that she carried.

Josephine, on the other hand, was expected to pull her weight for the community. After her experience with Marcel, she was leery of taking on the role of laundress, so she spoke with the mother superior to see what other jobs were available. Thus began her stint as a kitchen maid.

The heated water used to wash dishes was almost as hard on her hands as the laundry water had been. Determined to pass that task along to one of the novices, Josephine volunteered to help with the cooking. The sister in charge of the kitchen took her up on her offer — not knowing that Josephine was sorely lacking in culinary skills.

The sisters were kind enough to refrain from complaining, but they had to suffer through numerous rounds of burned rolls, scalded soup, and rare cuts of meat as Josephine learned to navigate her way through the kitchen. She often heard rumblings about, "offering it up," *whatever that meant*, when the women were served their meals.

But weeks of trial and error paid off and, in time, Josephine became a respectable cook. The sisters at Our Lady of Guadalupe, after enduring countless rounds of her mistrials, considered that a blessing.

Advent started out eventfully for the sisters. Bernadette went into labor and was delivered safely of a little girl the next day. Monica Josephine Taylor was born November 27, 1864, three days after her mother's seventeenth birthday. Josephine was touched that Bernadette honored her with the baby's name and was happy to accept the role of godmother to the little one.

Baby Monica Josephine was never on her own. There was always a sister waiting in the wings to rock her, pray over her or sing her to sleep with hymns.

The new year came and went, yet no ceasefire had been called. Josephine knew that she and Bernadette couldn't take advantage of the graciousness of their hostesses forever. She spent hours on her knees in the convent chapel, asking for God's guidance and the intercession of the Blessed Mother on their behalf.

She considered where she and Bernadette should travel

next. One thing she knew for certain, their next destination must be somewhere that Michael would be able to find her at the conclusion of the war. As spring approached, news from the front came faster and faster each day. Confederate troops were starting to surrender en masse to their Union counterparts. From what they heard, it was just a matter of time before President Jefferson Davis would formally end the foolish endeavor that he had led the last four years.

By chance, the answer to Josephine's prayers came in the form of a letter delivered to the convent one morning. It was from Father O'Reilly. He'd received word from Michael's sister, Amara, that she had moved to Eastern Texas. There was room for her brother to settle on the land adjacent to her husband's ranch, Heavenly Vista. Amara asked the priest to direct Michael to their homestead if he came to the church in search of her.

When Josephine read the letter, she knew it was the answer to her prayers. She would take Bernadette and the baby to Heavenly Vista Ranch. If Michael was welcome there, she couldn't imagine his wife, and a guest or two, wouldn't be welcome as well.

Josephine considered responding to the priest's letter to tell him of her plans, but as slow as the mail was recently, the war would be long over before he received the note.

She was fairly certain that when Michael was discharged from military service, the first place he'd go was Immaculate Conception Church to ask Father O'Reilly of her whereabouts. Our Lady of Guadalupe was on the route to Heavenly Vista Ranch. The sisters would direct him there.

From the convent, it was less than a day's travel by stagecoach to reach the ranch, so they had no time to send a letter to Amara announcing their forthcoming visit. Josephine made up her mind that they were leaving the next day.

The following morning, she and Bernadette waited with

Monica Josephine in the shade of the stagecoach office for the coach to pull in. Josephine couldn't help but laugh when she saw their reflection in the picture window. She was so used to the habit, she'd forgotten that she was wearing it. If her friends could see her now, she'd be the center of gossip in Washington, D.C.

Josephine was past the point of caring what other people thought about her. She remembered the days when her life revolved around her wardrobe, accessories and trying to keep up appearances. For what? All that mattered now was that she, Bernadette and Monica Josephine were safe and that soon she'd be reunited with her husband.

The trip was relatively short, but it seemed never-ending to Josephine. She was beginning to wonder if the driver had some demonic reason for purposely finding every pothole in the state to roll over. Her back was killing her by the time they arrived at Heavenly Vista.

No doubt alerted by the sound of the horses' hooves, several people gathered on the front porch as the stagecoach pulled up. The driver got down from his perch and opened the door on the far side of the coach. He helped the ensemble disembark from the conveyance. As they were escorted around the vehicle to the front porch, seven sets of eyes opened wide.

An older, dark-skinned woman made the Sign of the Cross and whispered, "Ave Maria." The others stood stock still, absorbing the picture in front of them, until a man stepped forward to greet them.

"How do you do, sisters?" he said politely. "I'm Nathan Simmons."

Josephine took a glimpse at her garb and had to refrain from laughing again. *Well, that explained the dumbfounded looks everyone had on their faces.* She smiled and extended her hand to the man.

This man's a match for Michael if I've ever seen one. Not only in size but countenance as well. The thought renewed her longing to be with her husband again.

"Pay no attention to the habit. It's a long story," she said as she shook his hand. "My name is Josephine. It's a pleasure to meet you. And this" — she turned toward the younger girl — "is my friend and traveling companion, Bernadette Taylor."

Shifting the baby to her left hip, Bernadette made a slight curtsey to the group.

Turning to the young lady before her who, she quickly determined, was in the motherly way, she inquired, "Would you by chance be Amara McKirnan?"

"Indeed, I am," she said, stepping off the porch step. "Or should I say, *was*. It's now Amara Simmons." Nathan affectionately put his arm around his wife.

Josephine examined the pair. They made quite the striking couple. "Perfect," she said, as she clasped her hands together in front of her. "Then Father's information was accurate."

Amara looked at her in confusion. "May I ask who your father is?"

"Brigadier General Matthias Bigelow. But that's not the father I was referring to. I was speaking of Father O'Reilly."

Now Amara seemed even more perplexed. "Are you referring to Father Thomas O'Reilly from Immaculate Conception Church in Atlanta?"

"The one and same."

"He sent you to our ranch?"

Josephine gave a nod. "Basically. He told me that I would find Michael McKirnan's sister living here."

"You know Michael?" asked Amara incredulously.

"I would say. He's my husband. My full name is Josephine Bigelow McKirnan."

Tears brimmed in Amara's eyes. She stepped closer to

Josephine and clasped her hands in her own. "Oh, my goodness," was all she could manage to choke out. After a moment, she was able to continue. "Is he safe, then?"

Now Josephine's eyes glistened. "I don't know. I pray to God that he is, but I have not seen or heard from him since our wedding day last July."

Amara let go of Josephine's hands and stepped closer. The two fell into each other's arms and sobbed in earnest. There wasn't a dry eye around them.

When they finally broke apart, Amara pulled herself together and exclaimed, "No matter what happens, you are welcome to stay here. The day you became Michael's wife, you became my sister." The waterworks began again.

Josephine's own parents had never come through when she prayed all those years for a sister, but God answered — in His own time as He was wont to do.

The sound of baby Monica Josephine fussing brought Josephine's thoughts back to center again. Regaining her composure, she stepped forward to greet the rest of those gathered around. The woman who was praying was their housekeeper Maria, next to her was her husband Eduardo, and beside him were the two other ranch hands: Snapping Turtle, who Nathan said was a full-blood Cherokee Indian, and Ol' Joe. Josephine had seen many a free black in Washington, D.C., but had never talked to one before. She was pleasantly surprised at what a well-spoken and cordial fellow he was.

When the introductions were done, the men and Maria returned to their chores. Amara asked Bernadette permission to hold the baby. Once the little one was passed along to her, Monica Josephine settled down almost immediately. Holding the baby securely, Amara gave the women a tour of their dogtrot house, pointing out various features and rooms with her right hand as she snuggled the baby in the crook of her left arm. Within minutes the infant was asleep.

That evening, after enjoying a repast of Mexican food that Maria lovingly prepared — with a little help from Josephine, who wanted to expand her cooking repertoire — the baby was laid in the cradle that Nathan and Amara had prepared for their own child and the adults gathered in the parlor to talk and get to know each other.

In the Bigelow household the hired help was not invited to join in casual conversations. It warmed Josephine's heart to see that Nathan and Amara considered everyone on the ranch to be part of their extended family.

Nathan caught Josephine and Bernadette up on news of the war. Hearing of the burning of Atlanta, she was sick to her stomach. Maybe Michael would have been better off confined at Gratiot Street Prison for the duration of the war. What if he had been injured, or worse, killed during the inferno?

Josephine went to bed that night in a bad humor. She resorted to doing what the sisters always did when they had concerns. She got out her glass-bead rosary and began to pray. Regardless of the day of the week, she was reciting the Joyful Mysteries every day until she was with Michael again. She just prayed that it would be on this side of the heavenly plane and not the other.

Within several days of the women's arrival, news reached the ranch that the war had ended. General Robert E. Lee surrendered the Army of Northern Virginia at the courthouse in Appomattox. Josephine had never heard of that village, but the name would ever be burned into her memory. She prayed that their country would never have to endure such a tragedy again.

From that day on, they waited. Playing with Monica Josephine helped pass the time. It was remarkable watching her grow and develop. Every day she learned a new skill. She was adorable when she cooed. The first time she stuck her baby toes into her mouth while lying on her back, Josephine couldn't help but laugh. Someday she hoped that she and Michael could experience those same things with their own child. *If only he would make it to the ranch!*

As the weeks continued to drag on, Josephine began to worry herself sick. One evening she was so miserable that she excused herself from the dinner table and made her way down the hallway to the bed chamber that was intended for her and Michael to share. *If he ever arrived,* she thought morosely. Not more than twenty minutes later, a commotion outside caught her attention. She made her way to the front of the house to see what was happening.

By the time she got to the door, she could clearly see two men, one wearing a gray uniform and the other in a blue uniform, making their way toward the house. Nathan's dog Checkers was at their heels. She couldn't make out their faces, but a spark of hope flickered in her chest.

As the soldiers drew near, Nathan flew off the porch, broke into a sprint and charged into the man wearing the blue uniform.

Amara picked up her skirts and hustled over to the pair, who were now wrestling on the ground. Josephine watched in disbelief.

"Nathan Michael Edward Simmons, what has gotten into you?" Amara panted out when she reached them. She grabbed the back of her husband's collar. "That is no way to greet a guest." She read Josephine's thoughts exactly.

The two men stopped in mid roll and both fell to their backs, trying to catch their breath while they laughed uproariously. "This isn't a visitor," exclaimed Nathan, punching the man in the shoulder. "It's Dominic, come back from the dead."

If this was the Dominic that Josephine had heard of, it

would be quite remarkable. That was Nathan's business partner and best friend. He had been missing in action for nearly a year.

The men stood and dusted themselves off, still chortling. Dominic wiped his hand on his sleeve and formally offered it to Amara. "Dominic Warner. It's a pleasure to meet you, ma'am."

She accepted his hand and looked at him incredulously. "Dominic?" She threw her arms around him. "The Lord be praised." Wiping her eyes, she loosened her grip on him and turned toward the other soldier.

The man lowered his hand, which he had been using to block the setting sun from his eyes.

She stopped midstride. "Oh my." She inched forward hesitantly. "Can it possibly be you?"

"It is me, sis." The man reached out to embrace her.

Watching the scene play out before her, Josephine stood paralyzed, her hand frozen on the frame of the woven wire door. The pounding in her head made it hard to follow the conversation. She blinked in order to focus on the man's words.

"... Father O'Reilly set me off in the right direction. Along the way, I encountered this fellow who, coincidentally enough, was headed the same way."

Amara held onto her brother's hands as if he might disappear if she let go. She finally released her grip when Nathan stepped up to greet their guest.

"I'm Nathan Simmons, Amara's husband," he said, extending his hand.

"Michael McKirnan," said Michael as he shook Nathan's hand. They sized each other up.

Nathan furrowed his brow as he peered closer at Michael. "Have we met? I have this uncanny feeling I've seen you somewhere before."

Michael scrutinized him. "You do have a striking

resemblance to a Union soldier I encountered in a skirmish once. Strangest story, I had taken a bullet to my leg—"

"And the enemy officer patched you up," interrupted Nathan.

"Yes, as a matter of fact, that is the short version of the story. How did you come to have knowledge of this?" asked Michael with a note of surprise.

"I knew I recognized those blue eyes. They're an exact match to my wife's. You're the man I gave my belt to on the battlefield."

A look of revelation crossed Michael's face. "You're the soldier who saved my life?" He stepped back in astonishment. "I always prayed I would be able to thank that man in person someday."

"One miracle after another," Amara exclaimed. "For both of you to not only survive the war but end up on our doorstep on the same day..." She glanced between the three men, and joy overtook her. "What have I done to deserve this, Lord?" she questioned out loud, turning her face skyward.

"Everything," said Nathan, wrapping her in his arms. "Everything."

Chapter XLVIII

The sound of rusty hinges being forced apart made Michael look toward the house. With the woven wire door wide open, he recognized the figure in the doorway. He broke into a grin and, his heart nearly bursting with joy, he ran to the porch, cleared the steps in one leap, and gathered Josephine into his arms.

They rocked back and forth for a few moments before Michael pulled away to peer at his wife. She was the most beautiful sight he'd ever laid eyes on. That enchanting face had haunted his dreams for months.

"I can't believe we're finally together again." He had to dislodge the coal-sized lump from his throat before he could continue. "I prayed unceasingly for this day since we parted ways."

"And me as well, Michael." Josephine's eyes shimmered with tears. "Praise God you've returned!"

Michael smiled at his wife and then kissed her full on the lips. He had no intention of stopping anytime soon, but a slight movement between them caused him to disengage and take a step back. He inspected Josephine from top to bottom.

His heart skipped a beat. "You're going to have a little one?" he asked incredulously.

"*We're* going to have a little one," said Josephine with a joyous tone.

"When?"

Josephine's face blanched. She lifted her gown a few inches and peeked over her rounded belly towards her feet. A puddle of water was forming around her kid leather boots.

"If I had to guess, I'd say now."

Epilogue

It turned out to be quite the homecoming for Michael as he and Josephine welcomed Bartholomew Michael McKirnan to their family early the next morning. The little fellow had his father's dark hair, his mother's eyes and — as they soon discovered — her penchant for theatrics. If it took more than a few seconds to be positioned to nurse, he wailed as though his little heart was breaking.

A couple days after the baby was born, Dominic hooked two horses to the wagon and left the ranch. Everyone wondered what could possibly entice him to leave Heavenly Vista so shortly after his arrival. "I need to collect something of value in Little Rock, Arkansas," was all he would tell them. He promised to return within four weeks.

True to his word, Dominic was back before a month had passed. The evening he returned, Josephine was in the cane back rocking chair in her bed chamber, nursing Bartholomew. Bernadette was in the next room, getting Monica Josephine ready for bed.

Through the open window, Josephine saw the horses and wagon crest the hill that marked the eastern boundary of Heavenly Vista Ranch. Seated next to Dominic was a young lady. *So that was the treasure the rascal spoke of,* she thought. *It all makes sense now.*

When the wagon came to a halt near the front porch, Dominic jumped down from the bench seat and helped the woman disembark. Snapping Turtle, Ol' Joe and Maria quit their chores and rushed to welcome him back and meet his travel companion. Josephine nearly squealed with glee when she overheard him introduce his *wife* Brigid to the others on the ranch.

Moments later, Nathan and Amara walked out of the house onto the porch. Brigid stepped away from the group, held her hand held up to her eyes to block the glare of the setting sun, and approached the couple. She gasped, covered her mouth with her hand, ran up the porch steps and threw herself into Amara's arms. The two women broke into tears.

Their reaction caught Josephine by surprise. She stopped rocking and scooted forward in the chair so she could hear the conversation.

She couldn't believe her ears. It turned out that Brigid and Amara knew each other. They had been friends at the Lucy Cobb Institute in Georgia.

"We never imagined we'd see each other again," she heard Amara say. The two began crying again and fell back into each other's arms. Nathan suggested that they go into the house to get reacquainted.

The women agreed and walked inside. Even though Bartholomew was done nursing, Josephine continued to cuddle him as she sat in the rocking chair. She imagined that Amara and Brigid wanted to chat for a while after being apart for so long. In due time she would make Brigid's acquaintance.

The ladies hadn't talked for more than a few minutes when Josephine saw them walk back outside hand-in-hand once again. Dominic and Nathan stood talking near the wagon. When the pair reached the men, Brigid put her free hand on Amara's rounded belly. Then Brigid patted her own stomach.

Josephine didn't have to hear every word to figure out the meaning of that gesture. "I think you're going to have another playmate, Bartholomew!" The baby gave her a sweet smile. He seemed to be just as delighted as his mother was.

Dominic's booming voice caused Josephine to glance back

outside. "Truly, I am lucky and blessed beyond measure."

"We *are* lucky and blessed beyond measure," replied Brigid. Josephine strained to hear the softer voice. "This may not be the life that either of us planned for ourselves but a greater power has been at work. We truly are living a life such as heaven intended."

The scene brought tears to Josephine's eyes. They looked so in love, it made her feel badly for Bernadette, who more than likely was watching everything from her bed chamber as well. The girl was a loving and attentive mother, but behind the smiles that she had for her baby, sadness showed in her eyes. Josephine knew that she was pining away for Hubert.

It wasn't often that Josephine was nagged by guilt, but it did bother her that she brought the two together in the first place. Of course, how was she to know that they'd grow sweet on each other?

Josephine hadn't heard anything from Hubert since they parted ways in Atlanta. He never had been one for correspondence, even more so now since it was part of his everyday tasks at work. She did get letters from her mother, but Hubert was only mentioned in passing. The social life in Washington, D.C., was her primary topic.

In all likelihood, Hubert was caught up in government duties as the war machinery ground to a halt. He probably had an ungodly amount of paperwork to do as the hundreds of companies disbanded and men were discharged from active service.

Who knew? Maybe by now, Francine had finally backed him into a corner to pin down a date for their wedding. He may even now be in the midst of preparing for that extravaganza.

Giving a sigh, Josephine held Bartholomew to her shoulder, patted his back for a moment and then walked outside to meet Brigid. The girl was so darned adorable that Josephine could have pinched her cheeks. It was easy to see why Dominic was wrapped around her dainty pinky finger. *And sweet as sugar.* Upon seeing the baby, Brigid immediately asked if she could hold him. *The young lady obviously knew a stellar child when she saw one.*

After she made her acquaintance with Brigid, Josephine left her and Dominic so they could continue their conversation with Amara and Nathan. Seeing the couples together made her want to spend time with Michael, who was out surveying the land beyond the barn.

As she walked through the yard with Bartholomew, Josephine thought back to the week Dominic left. Two nights before his departure for Arkansas, he and Nathan invited Michael to join their partnership in the ranch — with the goal of someday creating a small community on the surrounding land. At the center would stand the Catholic church that Nathan had started building before the other couples arrived.

With the war over, they expected an influx of people in the Western territories. So much of the infrastructure of the South had been destroyed during the hostilities, people would be looking for new opportunities and a fresh start in the untamed West.

The men partitioned off one hundred acres of land with the intent to make parcels available to homesteaders. Dominic and Michael would get first pick so they could build houses for their respective families.

In the quiet of the evening before Dominic's departure, all the occupants of the ranch gathered to brainstorm ideas of what they'd like to see in a community if enough families settled on their land.

Both Amara and Michael envisioned having a small hospital, and they had the experience to run such a facility. A school house would be appreciated by families. In deference to the diversity of their ranch family, the school would be open to all children, regardless of race.

Dominic spoke of building a manufacturing plant so men could earn decent wages to support their families. Josephine insisted that women have employment opportunities as well.

Someday Josephine would like to return to Washington, D.C., to meet with other women from Bernadette's walk of life and offer them the opportunity to move West. There was dignity in honest work, and she wanted to restore that dignity to those disadvantaged souls.

It would be something to bring up with Michael to see if such a plan seemed viable. As she approached him, he was jotting notes into a journal with a stubby pencil. Like usual, he was absorbed in his work. He probably hadn't even heard Dominic and Brigid pull in.

Josephine stopped and admired Michael for a few moments. She couldn't imagine ever growing tired of viewing him — even when the two of them were old and gray.

Michael must have felt her eyes on him; he turned and smiled. Then he set his journal down and held open his arms. Josephine stepped into his embrace, the baby wedged between them. Bartholomew cooed in approval as Michael pulled them close.

In the distance, the sound of a horse galloping from the north came to their ears. *Who could it be now?* Josephine wondered. She hadn't even had a chance to mention Dominic and Brigid's arrival to Michael, and now they had another guest.

Michael tucked the baby into the crook of his arm, grabbed Josephine's hand and strode toward the yard. Josephine endeavored to match his long strides and while they walked, she shared the *abbreviated* — for Michael's sake — story of Dominic and his new wife.

Rounding the corner of the barn, Josephine was glad that she wasn't holding Bartholomew. There was a good chance that she would have dropped him.

"Oh, my goodness!" She picked up her skirts and ran to greet the rider as he dismounted from his lathered horse. It was Hubert! Bernadette obviously saw his arrival as well. She burst through the woven wire door and raced in the same direction, reaching Hubert well ahead of Josephine. Maria rushed through the door on her heels with Monica Josephine held securely in her arms.

If she hadn't just given birth a month earlier, Josephine was sure she could have outrun Bernadette. But, putting her competitive nature aside, she stopped to watch the scene between Hubert and Bernadette unfold.

The look on each of their faces was priceless. Hubert held his arms open to Bernadette and lifted her off her feet when she reached him. Putting her down, he kissed her full on the lips.

Josephine's jaw dropped upon witnessing the act of affection. She could hear Amara and Brigid say, "Aww..." The men surrounding them clapped and nodded in admiration.

"Hubert, I didn't know you had it in you," joked Michael. He stepped forward and shook the man's hand.

Josephine stared at Michael like he was crazy. What kind of thing was that to say? He knew darn well that Hubert was engaged.

"Just because you live with a fellow for four years, doesn't mean you know everything about him, does it?" Hubert shot back with a laugh.

It was time to break up the fraternity party. Josephine approached her brother. "Speaking of knowing things about you, Hubert, has something changed since I saw you last?" she asked. "Aren't you supposed to be in Washington,

D.C.?"

"Actually, Washington, D.C., is the last place I want to be now, sis," said Hubert with a twinkle in his eye. "Francine didn't take it too well when I broke off our engagement. She wants my head on a platter. Now I know how John the Baptist felt." He ran his finger under the collar of his shirt for effect.

Bernadette stood gaping at Hubert. *He couldn't be serious, could he?*

"This seemed to be the ideal time to make a clean getaway... I mean, break," Hubert continued. "So, I packed what I could, loaded my horse, shook the dust of D.C. off my boots and headed West. It's time to plant some new roots."

He then turned to face Bernadette, dropped to one knee and reached for her hand. "I'm here to start a new life and a new family if you will take me to be your husband, Bernadette. Would you do me that honor?"

"Yes, yes, a thousand times yes," said Bernadette as tears trickled down her cheeks. Hubert stood, gave her a hug and then turned to look at the child held in Maria's arms. "Is that our baby?"

Bernadette peered at him questioningly. "That's Monica Josephine."

"May I hold her?" Hubert asked. Bernadette nodded and Maria stepped forward to hand the baby to him.

He looked down at the infant, his face beaming with pride. "The way I see it," he said, glancing up at Bernadette, "you're a package deal. How blessed am I? One day I'm single, and the next day I have a full-fledged family." Bernadette stepped closer to him and he put his arm around her.

There was only a glimmer of light left in the sky, but it was enough to illuminate the couples standing in the yard. Hubert had his bride-to-be and the baby by his side, Nathan had his arm around Amara's shoulder, Dominic stood behind Brigid with his hands wrapped around her waist, and Michael embraced Josephine and Bartholomew.

It was such a beautiful sight. Josephine stood quietly, soaking it all in. A thought came to her, and she addressed the group. "Amara, I've heard you sing the song "Minstrel Boy" numerous times since we first met. There's a line in that song that mentions 'a world such as heaven intended.' I thought of that earlier this evening when Brigid told Dominic that they are living 'a *life* such as heaven intended.'"

Her voice broke as she blinked back tears. "I have my own version of that sentiment." She paused and turned to speak directly to Michael. "God saw fit to bring us together again after all those years apart, and we've survived our share of trials and tribulations over the last few months. We too are lucky and blessed because, like all of our friends gathered here, we have found 'a *love* such as heaven intended.'"

"That we have, my darling," said Michael as he pulled her closer. "That we have."

Acknowledgments

For my husband John Lauer, our children Stephanie, Nicholas, Samantha and Elizabeth, their significant others, our grandchildren, and our entire family for their continued love, support and encouragement.

For our daughter Elizabeth Josephine Lauer, after whom the determined, adventurous, generous and loving Josephine Bigelow is modeled.

For our daughter Stephanie Dokko, the beautiful cover model for this book.

For William "Doc" Syverson and his wife Donna, for sharing memories of Doc's great-great Uncle Ira, whose adventures during the Civil War were the basis for the Heaven Intended trilogy.

For Carol Schubert, mother of two West Point women graduates, Wisconsin District 6 and 8 Congressional District Coordinator for West Point admissions, for her insight into the traditions, history and life at West Point.

For Brad Birkholz, for shooting the photo of our cover model.

For Sue Kiesau, who provided the Civil War gown for our cover model.

For Lois Gegare, hair stylist and makeup artist for our cover model.

For Anna Coltran, Belle Gente Photography, for shooting the picture for the back cover of the book.

For James Hrkach, for creating another outstanding book cover that entices readers to pick up this Civil War romance.

For my publisher Ellen Gable Hrkach, for not only continuing to believe in me and my works, but for all the work she does to promote Theology of the Body works of fiction through her publishing and marketing efforts.

To Full Quiver Publishing for its dedication to bringing books to the public that entertain, enlighten and bring readers closer to Christ.

For all the people who've purchased, downloaded, read, enjoyed, shared and reviewed my books in the Heaven Intended series.

To all the soldiers who fought in the Civil War — all gave some; some gave all.

About the Author

Wisconsin resident Amanda Lauer saw her debut novel published October 29, 2014. *A World Such as Heaven Intended* hit the number one spot in its genre on Amazon two months later and was the 2016 CALA winner (Young Adult). The second book in the trilogy, *A Life Such as Heaven Intended*, was published April 1, 2018. Lauer learned the technical aspects of writing as a proofreader in the insurance, newspaper and collegiate arenas. Over the last eighteen years she has had more than 1,400 articles published in newspapers and magazines throughout the United States. In addition to her proofreading, copy editing and writing career, Lauer is involved in the health and wellness industry. She and her husband John have been married thirty-eight years and have four grown children and five adorable grandchildren.

Published by:

Full Quiver Publishing
PO Box 244
Pakenham ON K0A2X0 Canada
www.fullquiverpublishing.com

Made in the USA
Monee, IL
30 July 2023

40155132R00182